Stone Field,
True Arrow

Stone Field, True Arrow

a novel

KYOKO MORI

Picador USA
METROPOLITAN BOOKS
Henry Holt and Company
New York

The author wishes to thank the Ucross Foundation, where this novel was started, and the following artists whose work has inspired her: John Bjerklie, Diane Fitzgerald, Bethann Handzlik, Chad Alice Hagen, Jim Neilson, Gregor Turk, and Hiro Yokose.

www.picadorusa.com

Picador® is a U.S. registered trademark and is used by Henry Holt and Company under license from Pan Books Limited.

For information on Picador USA Reading Group Guides, as well as ordering, please contact the Trade Marketing department at St. Martin's Press.
Phone: 1-800-221-7945 extension 763
Fax: 212-677-7456
E-mail: trademarketing@stmartins.com

Library of Congress Cataloging-in-Publication Data
Mori, Kyoko.
Stone field, true arrow: a novel / Kyoko Mori.
p. cm.
ISBN 0-312-42042-0
1. Fathers–Death–Psychological aspects–Fiction.
2. Japanese American women–Fiction. 3. Milwaukee (Wis.)–Fiction.
4. Women weavers–Fiction. I. Title.
PS3563.O871627 S76   2000
813'.54–dc21   00-020408
CIP

First published in Canada by Fitzhenry and Whiteside Ltd.

First published in the United States by Henry Holt and Company

First Picador USA Edition: September 2001

10 9 8 7 6 5 4 3 2 1

For John Bjerklie, Jim Neilson,
and little Oscar the Wilde-cat

Stone Field,
True Arrow

As her father stood against the wall, his long black coat made him look like a shadow. Her plane to Minneapolis was leaving in ten minutes. Maya gave her ticket to the man at the gate and watched him tear it along the perforated line. At a birthday party the year before, a magician had reached into a glass bowl full of paper and brought out the letters that spelled out the birthday girl's name. "So this is you," the magician had said, as though the girl had been turned into the paper he held spread out like a fan. As the man at the gate handed back the ticket stub with her seat number, Maya imagined herself becoming the piece of paper in her hand: cut along the line that was always there, though she didn't know it. She had been torn off and let go.

Her father had embraced her and smoothed her long hair, whispering, "I'll miss you. I won't see you again.

"Be good," he now called across the ten steps that separated them. "Your mother is waiting for you."

Maya entered a narrow corridor with gray carpet on the floor. When she glanced back over her shoulder, he was waving. She did not turn around again until the corridor had curved. From there, all she could see behind her was the wall, with a hinge like an accordion. Maya pictured herself running back to the gate. Her father would still be there, looking into the space where she had been. But if she went back, they could only hold each other and repeat their goodbye. Ahead, the silver doorway of the plane looked like a picture frame. She continued walking.

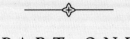

PART ONE

— 1 —

When Maya comes home from work in the late afternoon, the leaf truck is in front of her house, taking away the last of the maple leaves she and her husband have raked. Her engine idling, she waits in the street. Next door, Mrs. Nordstrom is standing behind her living room curtain, her thin, wrinkled face bunched up into a frown. Last year, a heavy downpour started while the truck was in front of Maya and Jeff's house. The men finished their pile, drove away, and did not return to the rest of the block for a month. Maya beeps and waves to her neighbor, wishing there was a universal beep that meant, Don't worry. This year will be different.

The truck lunges forward. Mrs. Nordstrom taps the window. She is smiling. Parking her car in the driveway, Maya gets the mail from the box and sits down on the front steps. She listens to the whine of the machinery turning the leaves to dust.

Near the bottom of the stack, there is a padded envelope sent to Maya in care of her mother, Kay, in her Chicago suburb. Kay has forwarded it to Milwaukee. The envelope has three Japanese stamps: a woman in a red kimono, a white egret soaring across the sky, a child's wooden toy. The return address is written in black ink, the color of the steeply pitched slate roofs of Maya's childhood. Her house in Osaka had a hedge of yews that blocked out the sun, so they had to leave the light on in the kitchen even on sunny days; two small bedrooms; a garage where her father painted. She has never forgotten the address, but the handwriting on the envelope is a painstaking imitation of the Palmer method, with exaggerated loops around the *G*s and *M*s. Her father's handwriting was spiky and slanted to the left, the letters leaning together like people standing shoulder to shoulder.

Maya rips open the envelope and finds another sealed envelope the size of a manila folder, an onionskin sheet folded in two, and a black-and-white photograph from which her father stares straight ahead without a smile. His hair, though gone gray, is parted in the middle and tied back, the way he always wore it. He is dressed in a dark kimono— brown, navy, or gray, it is hard to tell. His face is covered with tiny wrinkles, his mouth grown smaller and more round with age. Still, in his high cheekbones, large wide-apart eyes with long lashes, and dark arched eyebrows, Maya recognizes her own face. His hair was once thick and very black like hers, and his mouth, of which hers is an exact copy, was full, shaped like a small heart. She cradles the photograph in her palm. His eyes look sad, as though he were speaking to her from another world. She does not have to read the letter to understand that he is dead.

The leaf truck is moving down the street as she unfolds the onionskin paper. In his meticulous handwriting, in the formal Japanese Maya struggles to follow, Mr. Kubo, who introduces himself as her father's assistant, gives her the news. Her father died of cancer in the last week of October, leaving the house in Osaka and everything in it to Mr. Kubo and his family. He was sixty and had no relations; his parents and older brother had died years ago. Mr. Kubo says little except that the end was sudden but peaceful. He closes the letter by assuring her that everything is being done to honor her father's spirit. Mr. Kubo and his wife, who have moved into the house with their two daughters, have been burning incense every morning at the Buddhist altar, offering fresh tea and flowers. He is enclosing a copy of the portrait that hangs above the altar, along with an envelope her father had left in his desk.

On the front of the sealed envelope, her father had written her name, Ishida Mayumi, in the four pictorial characters that mean Stone, Field, True, Arrow. The family name leading the given, it is the name Maya lost at ten, when her mother—newly remarried—sent for her. Kay had left Osaka three years earlier to finish her doctorate in the States. In Minneapolis, Kay lopped off the end of her daughter's name just as she had changed her own from Keiko to Kay. She made Maya take her stepfather Bill's last name, Anderson, so that no one who saw her listed on a school roster knew she had grown up in Osaka. Maya changed her last name back to Ishida during her junior year in college, but by then she and her father had lost touch. He had sent back every letter she wrote to him, unopened.

In the planter by her door, the marigolds have withered standing up; they look like seaweed. Maya opens the envelope and takes out a piece of cardboard folded in two. It contains a pencil drawing on white sketching paper. The date in the lower left corner—March 20, 1996—was her thirty-fourth birthday seven months ago. Her father's signature is next to the date: Ishida Minoru, in pictorial characters that mean Stone, Field, Harvest. The sketch is the only thing in the envelope; there is no letter. That does not surprise her. Every morning when she was a child, Maya woke up to find her father sitting at the table in their dark kitchen with the light on, drinking his tea and drawing on a sketch pad. Sometimes the images showed what was on the table—a vase of flowers, a piece of fruit, a leaf—but more often they were pictures of people and landscapes she had never seen, or random lines and shapes, swirls and angles. They came from his dreams. Then there were the things he drew over and over. Trees, because Kay's maiden name, Hayashi, meant *stand of trees*, rice plants growing next to boulders for his own name, and arrows for Maya's. Many of his sketches had a line of arrows drawn across the top. He would point to them and say, "See, I was thinking of you even before you got up." Then he scribbled the date in the lower left corner and got up to fix their breakfast. The sketches were a diary. While other people wrote down words, her father drew pictures to record what was in his head. He had sent her a page from his diary, with the familiar arrow drawn in the top right-hand corner and the numeral 2. *To Mayumi*, he meant.

Maya holds the sketch up to the afternoon light. The left half shows a young girl in a hooded jacket and jeans as she walks through a narrow tunnel. The jacket is the one Maya was wearing on the day she left Osaka. The scene she is walking away from, which occupies the right half, is some kind of hell—jagged flames are leaping everywhere, and several *oni*, the horned demons from Japanese folk tales, are gathered around them. Between the two halves of the sketch, a man in a long black coat, with his hair tied back in a ponytail, stands facing the demons. His back slightly bent, he is cradling an instrument, plucking the strings with his fingers. The man has placed himself at the entrance of the tunnel to keep the demons from pursuing the girl; all he has are his own body and the music he is playing.

Maya goes into the tunnel in her memory and comes out on the other side. She sees the departure gate, the attendant reaching out to take her ticket, her father standing against the wall. But the tunnel goes on past the airport, over the city they crossed on a train that last day, back to the house, where in their last three years alone together Maya spent every evening in the garage, watching him paint. While he worked, he told her stories. One of them was about Orpheus, who traveled to the world of the dead to find his wife, Eurydice. In the palace of the dead, Orpheus played his lute for the king and the queen of hell. The music he had composed in his grief brought tears to the multitude of dead souls and so the king allowed Orpheus to take Eurydice back to the world of the living under one condition. In the long passage between the two worlds, Eurydice was to walk behind him, and Orpheus was forbidden to glance back at her. "Maybe he didn't trust the god of the underworld after all," Maya's father told her, "or maybe he loved her so much that he couldn't wait to see her face. When they were almost back to the world of the living and he saw the distant light ahead, he couldn't resist. He looked back. Her footsteps stopped. The next moment, he was standing alone inside a dark tunnel, and he knew he would never see her again."

In the drawing, her father is Orpheus, but the person he wants to save is Maya and he knows that only one of them can walk away. Don't look back, he is telling her in this small message from the world of the dead. No one can live in two worlds, traveling back and forth through a dark tunnel year after year. He had no choice but to let her go and refuse to read her letters. He must have drawn this picture on her birthday because he thought the picture—and the letting-go it depicted—was the only gift he could offer.

Maya pulls her handwoven shawl tighter around her narrow shoulders and gathers her long hair in her hand, into a ponytail that won't hold together. On the inside collar of the red hooded jacket in the picture, her father had stitched her name in purple embroidery thread. Alone in her room in Minneapolis at night, she used to take out the jacket and trace the letters—Stone, Field, True, Arrow—remembering who she used to be. All that first winter, she could feel the letters touching her nape, each stitch a reminder of the life she'd left behind. For so long, it was impossible to forget him. The last letter she sent him was an invitation to her senior art exhibit at college twelve years ago. It was the only letter he did not send back, but he never responded. Sitting in the empty gallery at dusk after she took down the show, Maya promised herself that she would never again write to him. Late that night, she put his name on a leftover invitation, lit it with a match, and tossed it, flaming, into Lake Michigan while her best friend Yuko watched. "That was my last letter to him," she told Yuko. "You saw it."

Burning the letter had been Yuko's idea. She is a believer in ritual. Though Maya was more skeptical, the ritual has worked. For several years now, she hasn't thought of her father the way she used to. There were days when she didn't think of him at all, and other days when what she missed wasn't him anymore, but the idea of missing him. "I don't feel sad about him anymore," she told Yuko two years ago. "The past seems so far away." Now she wonders why she has always measured the past in distance, as though it were a place she left on the other side of the world instead of a time that has gone by. Looking at her father's sketch now, Maya feels the ground shift under her. The geography of her mind is about to rearrange itself one more time against her will. If he had wanted her to forget and go on, he should have sent nothing, not even a picture.

Maya puts the drawing back into the envelope on which her father had written her name. She slips that envelope back into the large one with her mother's address. Underneath the red x Kay drew, Mr. Kubo's looped handwriting resembles vines climbing up a trellis. The trumpet-shaped flowers of morning glories tremble in the wind, singing out the lies Kay has told. Kay pretended she lost touch with her first husband decades ago. "For all I know," she claimed, even while Maya was in high school, "your father might have remarried and moved away. I'm sure he has by now." Yet his assistant knew her latest address. Kay must have written to Minoru three years ago when she left Minneapolis and moved to Park Ridge to marry her third husband, Nate.

The street in front of Maya's house is quiet. The leaf truck has moved to the end of the block. Maya gets up from the step but doesn't go into the house. Her husband will be home soon. Even if she said nothing about the letter, Jeff would sense she was upset; he would ask her what was wrong. If she answered, "I *am* upset about something, but I don't want to talk about it," there would be a hurt silence between them all night long. At dinner, they would sit across the table from each other and find nothing to say. If she asked him about his day, he would give her short, mumbled answers: "I don't know," "Not really," "Whatever." By the time they'd cleared the table and moved to the living room, each with a book, the silence between them would feel large and complicated as a maze, with every unsaid word adding another narrow pathway to nowhere.

Between the storm door and the front door, the paperboy has placed the evening paper as usual. Maya takes a pen out of her purse and writes across the top of the front page: *I went back to the studio to work. May be late. Sorry. M.* Gathering all the mail except the envelope from Japan, she shoves it behind the paper and closes the storm door. She gets into her car and drives away. All the way down her block, the leaf piles have been cleared. Nothing remains except dried-up fragments.

Maya's weaving studio is upstairs from the boutique where she works during the day. The building is a remodeled barn twenty minutes north of the city, in countryside that's as quiet at night as it must have been a century ago. Alone at the loom by the window overlooking the gravel parking lot and the cornfields beyond it, she will think of her father and wonder how she ended up so far away from him, in a landscape he never saw. The silence in the flat stretch of landscape is full of history, but there is no comfort in it for her.

When the light changes, she veers across two lanes of traffic to turn left, away from the freeway. It's only a few minutes across the bridge to the health food restaurant on the east side where Yuko works.

"Is Yuko around?" Maya asks the girl behind the deli counter.

The girl points to the back door. "She's in the back lot with the produce guy."

Yuko is standing on the flatbed of a farmer's pickup in her jeans and denim jacket, her arms around a cardboard box. Her long hair is tied back under an indigo-colored bandanna. "Hey, Maya, what's up?" she asks, her voice rich and deep. Unable to speak, Maya imagines her own voice, thin and reedy, like a broken plastic toy that won't even squeak. Yuko jumps off the flatbed and drops the box down on the ground. She turns briefly to the man who has been waiting by the truck, holds up her hand, and nods to him with her eyebrows arched. "Are you all right?"

Maya has left the envelope in her car. She'd meant to show it to Yuko, but maybe it doesn't matter. "My father died." Immediately, Yuko steps forward and puts her arms around her. "I got a letter about it, from Osaka. I don't want to talk about it, but I don't want to be alone."

"Oh." Yuko's voice trails down. "Oh, Maya. I'm so sorry." She hugs her hard. Her face pressed against Yuko's denim jacket, which smells faintly of lavender, Maya concentrates on breathing evenly. When they let go, the produce man is gone—he's standing on the far edge of the parking lot, pretending to be interested in whatever is going on across the street.

Maya blinks hard to make sure she won't start crying. "Your produce guy is pretty tactful."

"You can say that again. He's a good guy." Yuko places her hands on Maya's shoulders and holds her at arm's length to peer into her face. Yuko has always been taller than Maya and larger-boned; her arms and shoulders are muscular from working out in the gym. She cocks her head a little, frowning and trying to smile at the same time so that her eyes are squinched together while her mouth curves slightly upward. "Let's get out of here," she says. "I'm taking the afternoon off." She points across the lot toward her ancient white Plymouth Barracuda—"the fish," as she calls her car. "See the fish over there? The door's unlocked. Sit inside and wait for me. I'll be right back." She squeezes Maya's shoulders and runs into the store.

Maya watches her friend push open the door and stride inside, taking big steps in the battered hiking shoes she wears to work. She has left the box on the ground, with the top flap open. Inside are twelve heads of green cabbage, the veins on their leaves like the lines on geological maps. Cut open, each would reveal the parallel lines going around and around to its core. This was one of the things Maya's father had given her to draw when she was seven. He set up a drawing board for Maya next to his own canvas. "The secret," he said, "is not to have too many ideas ahead of time about what everything looks like.

Then you can draw what you see, not what you think you see." He found odd-shaped gourds and vegetables and torn leaves, a knob that had come off its door, a photograph of pipes and hydraulics from an engineering textbook, turned upside down. "I'm trying to trick your mind," he said. "It's okay to be confused."

As she goes to Yuko's car and sits down, Maya pictures the garage where her father painted. In the winter, he sectioned off an area about twelve by fifteen feet with sheets of canvas hung all the way from the ceiling to the floor. Standing in this cocoon of white cloth, with a kerosene heater to take off the chill, he worked for hours while Maya tried her drawings or sat on a stool, listening to his stories. The bright overhead lights made the cloth around them glow like a tent of skin. Maya daydreamed that she and her father were the last two people in a long-lost nomadic tribe in a desert. Using oils and beeswax on the canvases and linens he'd stretched, he painted swirls of white light overlapping with blurred squares of rust and beige, thin strokes of green or plum like mirages in the distance. A child in Osaka, she had never known any climate except the humid, warm summers, the mild winters, and the gradual changes of temperatures and colors in between. All the same, if the past were a place she could go back to, that's where she longs to be: painting with her father in the desert of their imagination, inside the skin of light.

— 2 —

On the loom in Maya's studio, five shades of blue travel across the length of plain warp, growing darker like water leaving the shore. On the finished jacket, the colors will move in slow gradations from left to right, starting with pale blue and ending with petal pink. In between, the shades of blue, violet, purple, lavender, mauve, and rose will shift so gradually that the eye will follow along, scarcely noticing the change. The effect she wants is a small surprise—toward the middle of the jacket, somewhere over the heart, the blue will stop and the pink begin, but no one will be able to pinpoint the exact border between the two. She winds the next shade of blue around her shuttle and weaves another inch before loosening the tension. She will come back after supper to work, stay the night, and continue in the morning before she goes downstairs to open the boutique. It's the last week of November. A month has passed since her father's death.

The skeins for the rest of the jacket are arranged on a table by the wall, each one hand-dyed and spun last winter when business was slow and Maya could do her own work while tending to her customers. The wool is from the white sheep that belongs to her boss, Peg, who lives on the other side of the ten-acre property and keeps two sheep in a toolshed-sized barn her husband, Larry, built from a kit. The corn-fields surrounding the buildings belong to Peg and Larry, but they're city people; they rent out the fields to the farmer down the road. Larry owns a construction company, Peg used to be a nurse. Twelve years ago, Peg quit her job at the hospital and converted the big barn into a boutique with a weaving studio upstairs for herself. But Larry didn't like her driving across their property at night to weave. "Why do you want to get away from me?" he complained. He turned one of the spare bedrooms into a workroom for Peg, leaving the loft empty until three and a half years ago, when Maya was about to move to Jeff's. She'd been living alone in an efficiency on the lower east side, in a room mostly taken up by her loom, spinning wheel, sewing machine, and worktable. She had considered keeping the place for her weaving but couldn't afford to. "You can have the loft for free," Peg said. "Consider it your fringe benefit. I've been thinking I don't pay you enough."

The loft looks exactly like her old efficiency: her loom and spin-ning wheel by the windows to the west; her worktable and sewing machine against one wall; yarn, beads, and other supplies on shelves above the couch against another wall; the kitchen and the bathroom off to the left. It has everything she owns except for her clothes and dresser. She has spare clothes in the closet and the kind of single-person food she used to eat—yogurt, salad, apples—in the dormitory refrigerator. It's as though, when she married, she put half her life inside a tent and moved it to this countryside. Turning off the light and heading down the stairs, she feels like a person making a temporary trip into town.

At the counter in the boutique, Maya picks up the phone and dials her number at home. The machine comes on after one ring. Jeff doesn't answer between five and eight, the hours when telemarketers call. His recorded voice identifies the number and asks the caller to leave a mes-sage. "Hi, it's me," she says. "No need to pick up. I'm on my way. I know it's my turn to cook but I'm late. I still have to stop for groceries."

Outside in the dark, a few flurries are coming down on the highway. When a streak of white flashes across her headlights, she realizes, too late, that an animal has dashed out of the ditch into her path. There's no time to veer. She has never hit anything in her eighteen years of driving. Holding the wheel straight, she slams on the brakes and hears them screech. She stumbles out of the car, not really wanting to see, and finds a white kitten crouched on the asphalt an inch from her front wheel. He is half the size of her shoe.

Far behind her, where the highway crests up a low hill, she can see the headlights of the cars approaching them. They are still a mile away, but Maya has an awful vision of the kitten dashing across the road just as those cars are coming down the hill. She kneels a few steps from him. He raises his head slightly and fixes her with his blue eyes. His fur is completely white; he wears no collar.

"Come on," Maya coaxes. "You can't stay here. Someone else is going to hit you."

The kitten arches his back and stretches; then he saunters over to her, pushes his face hard against her ankle, and begins to rub his forehead back and forth. After ten seconds, he lies down on his back at her feet and rolls to the side, showing her his belly. The skin under the white hair is smooth and pink. She reaches down and picks him up. He is small enough to fit into her hand, but the noise he is making is unmistakable: he is purring. The kitten doesn't flinch when several cars speed by in the left lane, honking. More cars come and swerve around them. Maya has left her dark blue car in the middle of the right lane without the hazard lights. She watches the traffic flow away around her. It's a minor miracle. Any of the cars could have hit the Civic and pushed it forward, rolling its front end over her as she stood holding a stray animal on the highway. No more cars in sight, she walks around to the passenger side and opens the door. She places her shawl on the seat, rolled up into a makeshift nest. Then she puts the kitten in its center, closes the door, and jogs around her car to the driver's side.

The kitten doesn't do what she feared—run around the car in panic, trying to get under the dash. He curls up on her shawl, with his paws tucked under his chin. Halfway into town, she realizes that he is sleeping. Maybe he is too sick to do anything else. But he might be like Yuko, whose response to stress has always been to fall asleep. "Imagine," she says to the sleeping cat. "If you were a person, I'd be spending the next fifteen years waking you up to go take an exam, dress for a date, greet your parents when they visit, even get ready for your own wedding." She pictures Yuko sitting by the sunny window of the upstairs room at the Unitarian Church where she and Dan were married. Yuko kept dozing off while Maya combed and braided her hair, pinning the braids up to form a shiny black crown. "I hope no one cries," Yuko said, waking up with a start. "That would make me feel so weird, to have people crying." Later, at the reception, when her new in-laws tapped their coffee cups with their spoons and the tinkling noise filled the room, Yuko stood up alone and waited till everyone quieted down. Then she motioned for Dan to stand up. Before she kissed him, she cleared her throat and announced in her strong, low voice, "This is the one and only time. After this, no more kisses on demand." Maya smooths the kitten's fur with her fingers. "You'll meet my friend Yuko," she tells him. "I'm going to let her name you."

As she pushes open the front door, holding the kitten, Maya remembers she was supposed to stop for groceries. Jeff is sitting in his armchair by the window in the living room, grading essays. There are folders and books everywhere—stacked up on the coffee table, scattered over the hardwood floor, propped against the window ledge. A high school English teacher with five classes every day, he has a complicated system of keeping things separated. The room is full of breakable objects: the porcelain bud vase on the coffee table, the crystals on the low shelves, the ceramic and tile coasters, none of them hers. The kitten's claws will scratch the hardwood floor Jeff sanded and refinished all by himself. He lived here for eleven years, the first nine with his former wife, before Yuko's husband, Dan, introduced him to Maya. All the knickknacks are his. Unless the cat is sick, it won't be long before he starts knocking them down. Just last week, Peg's cat Caliban swiped five coffee mugs off the counter and shattered them in the middle of the night. Peg and Larry laughed about it, but Jeff won't find much humor in broken cups. He is staring at her, his gray eyes squinted behind his new reading glasses.

"I found a cat on the highway." Maya tilts her arm so Jeff can get a better look from across the room. Wide awake now, the kitten sits up in the crook of her elbow. She cups her hand around his head and feels his throat vibrate. "I'll still go grocery shopping, but I'd better get him settled first."

"Maya, I don't know." Jeff hasn't moved from the armchair. She stops in the middle of the room.

"I almost killed him with my car. My front tire was an inch from his head. I couldn't just walk away. I'm going to keep him. I'll be responsible so you won't have to do anything. As far as you're concerned, it'll be like we don't even have him."

He sighs, gets up, and walks toward her. "You can keep him overnight. After supper, we should talk about what to do. I'm not sure about keeping him, but we don't have to decide now."

"I'm not taking him to the humane shelter." Maya feels her voice rise. "They euthanize a dozen kittens every week." She's about to explain how Yuko's mother volunteered at the shelter in Minneapolis once and had to quit because it was too depressing. But she doesn't get to talk anymore. When Jeff is two steps away, the kitten wriggles out of her arm and leaps into the air. Jeff puts his hand out and the kitten lands on his wrist, wraps his legs around his forearm, and bites down.

"Jesus Christ!" Jeff yells. He shakes his arm, but the cat clings on, his little legs curled tight as he hangs upside down.

"Hey, take it easy," Maya cautions. "You'll hurt him."

"He's hurting *me*." The next moment, Jeff is throwing the kitten across the room. The kitten lands on the floor by the couch; it's not a myth that they always land on their feet. As soon as Maya kneels down next to him, he jumps up on her shoulder and clings to her, pushing his face into her neck as if he wanted to burrow under her skin. She is sure the guttural noise coming from his throat is vibrating in her own. He's hissing, spitting, and growling, but not at her.

"Jesus." Jeff groans. "We can't have that thing in the house. He's a wild animal."

"He's not." Maya stands up with the kitten on her shoulder, where he perches like a bird and continues to hiss and growl at Jeff. "You scared him. No wonder he bit you."

Jeff holds his arm out toward her. "Look at this and tell me who scared who." There are red marks several inches long and blood is coming out, but the cuts don't look too deep. "How do you know he's not rabid?"

"A cat this young isn't going to have rabies and live long enough to pass it on." She doesn't know this for a fact, but it sounds good—like it might be true. The kitten stops hissing and taps her face with his paw; with his claws retracted, the bottom of his paw is soft and cool. He rubs his head against her cheek. "If you don't want to share *your* house with a cat who has nowhere to go," she says to Jeff, "that's your problem. But he's mine. I don't care what you think." Lifting the kitten off her shoulder and cradling him in her arm, she runs out the door to her car.

She's left her shawl on the passenger seat. The kitten lies on his side, his legs pumping. He's biting the fringes and scratching the fabric, his mouth open as if in a big grin. He's not sick at all, he's having a good time.

"You're trouble," Maya says, as she backs her car out of the driveway. "You're lucky I'm a weaver. I didn't buy that shawl, and I can make another one if I want to." She's going to have to cat-proof her loft, because that's where he's going to have to live. Peg can show her what to do to protect her loom.

At Peg and Larry's house, Maya leaves the kitten in the car and knocks on the door. She steps inside the kitchen, where Larry is doing the supper dishes. Their three cats are sitting under the table. Peg comes downstairs, dressed in a blue sweatshirt and jeans, her long silver hair braided down her back. Tall and straight-backed, she is a strong-looking woman with a kindly face. "Have a seat," she says.

"Thanks, but I can't stay. I have a bit of an emergency."

"What's that?"

"I found a kitten on the highway. He's out in the car now. I don't think he's hurt or sick, but he bit Jeff and drew blood. So he's not going to be allowed to live at our house."

Larry is drying his hands on a dish towel. There's a tattoo of a plant that starts near his wrist and winds up his arm, disappearing under his T-shirt, but it's faded. Maya has never been able to figure out if it's a grapevine or a marijuana plant. He got it when he was a young man, decades before it was fashionable to have tattoos. "When we went to get Ms. Bronze at the breeder's," he says, indicating their Siamese cat by jutting his chin toward her, "her mother bit my ankle and wouldn't let go. She was worse than a snapping turtle. I was bleeding through my sock. But Ms. Bronze turned out all right. She's more docile than Caliban or Pip."

"I'm sure this kitten will turn out fine too, but he needs a place to live. I came to ask you if I could keep him in the loft. I'll make sure he doesn't come down and attack the customers."

"Of course," Peg says. "Maybe he'll mellow out in a few weeks, and then he can come down to the store. A store mascot is just what we need. Are you going to take him to the loft now?"

"Yeah."

"Did you feed him?"

"No. He's so small. Would he eat cat food?"

"He has teeth, right?" Peg asks.

"Yeah. Pretty good ones. I saw them in action."

Peg laughs. "I'll get you cat food and a litter box. In the morning, you ought to take him to the vet to make sure everything's all right.

They'll give you some special food for kittens. But what I've got is good enough for tonight."

When they go out to the car, the kitten is sitting on Maya's shawl. As soon as Peg leans down to look at him through the passenger window, he rears up on his hind legs, puts his paws on the upholstery, and opens his mouth. His hair puffed up, he's hissing at Peg through the glass.

"I'm sorry," Maya says. "He's an embarrassment."

"He's a spunky guy. What are you going to name him?"

"I don't know. I'm going to ask Yuko to name him."

"Why?"

"I named all her pets when we were kids. My mother wouldn't let me have a dog or a cat because she and my stepfather were too busy working. Yuko and her brothers had a dog, a parakeet, an iguana, and a bunch of rats and guinea pigs, and she didn't complain when I named the rats after my favorite candy bars. Snickers, Carmello, Hershey, and most ridiculous of all, Kit Kat."

Peg laughs. "You and Yuko go back a long way."

"Fourth grade. Her dad and my mother taught at the same college, and the Nakashimas lived two blocks away from us. Yuko and I went to the same grade school." Maya remembers walking into Miss Larson's fourth-grade class in the middle of the semester and seeing Yuko raise her hand. "That girl's my cousin from Japan. I'm going to sit next to her." Yuko's mother had told her to be on the lookout for Maya and be friendly toward her, though perhaps this wasn't exactly what Mrs. Nakashima had in mind. Maya sat down next to this tall girl with her big frank smile and knew they would be friends for life. "It was the friendship version of love at first sight," they always tell people. "There couldn't be any other best friend."

Peg puts the cat food and the litter box in the trunk. "Good luck. Let me know if you need anything else."

Maya thanks her and drives down the dirt road that leads through the cornfields toward the barn.

—————

The kitten eats the food Maya has put in a bowl, drinks some water, and jumps on the couch. Curled up on the blanket, he closes his eyes and falls asleep as if he has always lived in this loft. Maya goes downstairs and calls Jeff.

"How's your arm?" she asks him. "I'm sorry if I sounded indifferent about it."

"My arm's all right," he answers. "I'm not going to need stitches or anything. Maybe I overreacted a little."

"The kitten drank water, so he must not have rabies."

"Oh, I never really thought he was rabid."

"I was afraid you were going to have his head cut off."

"I would never do that."

"I'm going to keep him here at the loft. It's all right with Peg and Larry. I don't know why I didn't think of that in the first place."

Jeff sighs. "If you really want to bring him home, we can talk about it." His voice sounds tired and resigned. If she insisted, he might give in. But Maya thinks of the day she found out about her father's death. She and Yuko drove to the lake and sat on the bluff to watch the hawks migrating south on the stiff north wind; then they stopped for coffee, for dinner, for some mindless movie in a multiplex on the north side of town. It didn't matter what they did. They didn't talk about her father's death after the first half hour, but Yuko was there with her and that was what counted. Maya couldn't imagine wanting to be with anyone else that evening. When she came home at eleven, she felt calm enough. "I found out that my father died," she told Jeff. "But it's all right. He's been gone a long time anyway." "Look," Jeff said before they went to bed. "If you ever want to talk about it, you can, with me. If something comes to your mind in the middle of the night, you can wake me up and tell me." He put his arms around her and hugged her. Maya tried to see herself waking up in the middle of the night with a perfect sentence in her head—all her feelings summed up in a few concise words she could hand over to Jeff. She knew it would never happen.

"Don't worry about the kitten," Maya tells him now. "He'll be just fine here."

"Okay. Let me know if you change your mind."

"Thanks, but I won't. I'm going to do some work now and stay over. I'll see you tomorrow evening. I'm sorry we missed dinner."

"You don't have to apologize. Something came up that you weren't expecting. That happens to anyone."

"Have a good night."

"You too."

Maya weaves for an hour and then lies down on the couch. The kitten settles in the crook of her neck. Listening to his purring, she closes her eyes. In a weaving cottage near the Japan Sea with her father, Maya once saw a black cat sitting in the window, eating fish from a bowl. It was the summer Kay left. Her father was delivering designs he had drawn for the weavers, an old married couple who owned eight semi-mechanized looms in a ramshackle building next to their house.

Seven of the looms were working, the heddles moving up and down and going *shuck, shuck, shuck.* The cloth being formed on the loom near Maya had interlocking patterns of gold fans against a bright red background. Behind that loom, in the light from the window, the cat looked glossy and sleek. When he raised his face out of the bowl, his long whiskers glittered with fish scales like sequins. The woman turned to Maya and smiled. "You have such a lovely daughter," she said to Maya's father, who nodded and smiled too.

Her father took pictures of the looms. One of them had the cat in it: he was on the window ledge, his back rounded, his face leaning down into the bowl. If her father had kept the negative, the colors would be in reverse so the cat would appear pure white instead of pure black. The white kitten continues to purr. Maya draws him closer.

On the way home from the weaving cottage, the blue of the sea filled the bottom half of the train window. Her father told her a story about a fisherman who found a beautiful garment caught in the branches of a pine tree along the seacoast. As the fisherman reached out and took down the garment, a woman appeared, dressed in a dazzling white kimono. She was a *tennyo*, an inhabitant of heaven, and the garment was her *hagoromo*, a jacket of feathers. The *tennyo* asked the fisherman for her *hagoromo*, but he refused to give it back. He had fallen in love with her. If she couldn't fly back to heaven in her *hagoromo*, he thought, she would stay on earth and marry him. She begged him for a long time, but he would not change his mind. Finally, with a sigh, she said, "Very well. Perhaps it was some fate from another life that has brought us together. I will stay here and become your wife, but you must grant me one wish. My friends in heaven will be sad to part with me. If you will let me have my *hagoromo* for a while, I will perform one final dance to bid them farewell. After that, I will become your wife." Moved by her melancholy smile, the fisherman handed her the *hagoromo*. The *tennyo* put it on and floated up into the air. When she had risen above the treetops, she began to dance. The fisherman watched mesmerized for hours, never noticing that she was soaring higher into the sky over the sea. Finally, she disappeared beyond the horizon, leaving him with the afterglow of the sunset. Her dance had not been for the other inhabitants of heaven. All along, she was dancing her farewell to him.

Across the room, the cloth on the loom has begun its transformation from blue to purple. The colors move in fine increments, each bar the width of a piano key. If the shades could make music as they moved toward pink, they would sound like the waves of the sea. The notes would glide across the blue silence, one wave overlapping the next until they reached the shore and found the pale pink of seashells. Maya pictures the finished jacket, its sleeves spread out. The jacket is already flying in her mind. In time, her fingers will set it free into the sky over the sea.

— 3 —

Yuko is waiting outside her house on the lower east side. It's the house Maya lived in for two years after college, she and her boyfriend Scott helping Yuko and Dan with the repairs and the mortgage, but the neighborhood has changed. "Our area is the new yuppie frontier," Yuko tells Dan whenever she sees a FOR SALE sign in Maya's neighborhood across the river. "We should move to where Maya lives, a neighborhood that has old people and people of color." Dan counters, "You can't choose a house according to your political convictions," though Yuko suspects that he's just too lazy to move. "Change scares him," she says. "It's too big a drain on his energies." As if to prove her wrong, Dan painted the siding a bright green instead of white. Even after six months, Maya still feels as though she's come to the wrong house.

Yuko takes off her jean jacket and throws it on the backseat. Crumpled up, it looks like a compact sculpture on top of Maya's hand-woven coat, which lies flat, its teal-colored threads glossy and smooth as calm water. Yuko is wearing jeans and a black turtleneck; Maya has chosen a lavender dress she sewed. They never dressed alike even as teenagers.

"So where's Jeff?" Yuko asks, as they start driving toward the freeway. He was supposed to come with them to the opening of Maya's weaving show.

Maya shrugs.

"I knew he'd leak out on us." Yuko blows air through her lips, making a *whoosh* sound like a tire suddenly going flat.

"When I got home from work to pick him up, he was sitting around in his T-shirt and sweat pants. But he insisted he would come if I wanted him to. 'It's up to you,' he kept saying."

Yuko rolls her eyes. "That is so lame."

"Actually, I'm glad it's just you and me. If he came, he'd stand around looking bored. I wouldn't know what to do with him. He doesn't care about my weaving. He hasn't even been to my studio lately."

"Dan hasn't heard me play, either." Yuko sighs. "For all I know, he still envisions me singing 'I'm Looking Over a Four-Leaf Clover' in that crummy variety band from ten years ago. I hated when he sat alone in the corner, staring at me. He'd order some wimpy cocktail and sip it through a straw. He'd come up and request all the songs I sang lead for. I was mortified. I wanted to go back to playing in the loudest garage band in town so he wouldn't come any more. But now I'd be glad for some attention."

"Yeah, but attention can be such a burden. You were there when Scott used to explain my paintings to me. He had his own interpretation for every painting in my senior show. I felt like I could hardly breathe. I'd rather be with someone who leaves me alone."

"Why does it have to be one extreme or the other?" Yuko asks.

"I don't know, but it always is."

"When we go to my parents' next week," Yuko asks, "can we take your car?"

"Sure." Maya accelerates into a less crowded lane. They are south of the airport, headed toward the Illinois border. This time of the evening, traffic moves as much sideways as forward. "Is there supposed to be a blizzard next week?" She is the designated driver in bad weather. Yuko and Dan have both slid off the freeway into the ditch; their Barracuda bears the battle scars.

"No, Dan needs the fish. He's staying home."

"Why?"

"He's got a big job lined up, installing cabinets in a mansion on Lake Drive. He has to start right after Christmas, that's when these people are going on vacation. They want the work done while they're away."

"We can come back earlier than usual. I don't mind."

"Forget that. Dan can fend for himself. I want to stay longer. We're supposed to go to a New Year's Eve party at Annie Weakland's, and you want to spend time with Bill."

"That's true." When Kay left him three years ago, Maya's stepfather stayed in Minneapolis alone. Now Maya only sees him once or twice a year during her trips with Yuko and Dan. Bill sold their old house and moved to a much smaller one; his hair has turned white. "I was thinking about him this morning because Jeff was listening to a talk show. Remember when Bill used to pick me up after my track practice? My mother was teaching, so it was his job to give me a ride?"

"Yeah."

"I never told you this, but one of those times, I found him slumped over the steering wheel. He barely looked up when I got in. He was listening to a call-in show, and the voice on the radio sounded familiar. It was my mother. The topic was the stress of being married and working full-time. The show had been on earlier in the day, and the evening broadcast was a rerun. When I got in the car, she was saying that she and her husband weren't fifty-fifty in sharing the household chores. 'Even though we're both college professors and work the same hours, I end up doing most of the housework,' she said. 'I don't mind that so much. Only he's a typical Minnesota man who doesn't know how to say thank you. I feel very unappreciated.' I *knew* it was my mother. I whispered to Bill, 'Um, is this, you know?' and he said, 'Fucking-A, it is. She actually called me and told me to listen to this shit.' He turned the radio off and started driving. We didn't say another word all the way home."

"That's awful. How come you never said anything?"

"I was too embarrassed, but I felt worse for Bill. Some of his friends probably heard the show."

"Poor Bill. Your mother really did a number on him."

"I'm not looking forward to seeing her tonight. Now I know she'd been in touch with my father the whole time and she knows I know. But I can't figure out how to talk to her about it."

"Maybe you don't have to say anything today. If she's been lying to you all these years, you can't make her honest by having one talk. You have the rest of your life to confront her. It's okay to procrastinate. Why do something today that you can put off till tomorrow? That's my motto." Yuko grins. "I should write it down and hang it on the wall. It's good advice."

In spite of herself, Maya laughs. "Right. You always used to say that the world's problems would go away if people had a good lunch and took a nap every afternoon."

"I still believe that." Yuko pats Maya's shoulder. "Don't worry," she says, "your opening's going to be great. You'll know what to say to your mother when the time comes."

When they get out of the car in Evanston, a sickle moon hangs low in the sky. Lillian's store is on a busy street near the El station. In the window, there is a neon sign shaped like a red lizard. The name of the store, SALAMANDER, is on the tip of its tongue.

Lillian is standing near a table of food and drinks. All around the room, Maya's jackets, vests, shawls, dresses, and scarves are hanging, some from the ceiling on piano wires and others on racks. A few women are walking around, stopping now and then to examine the garments; there's classical music on the stereo. The poster for the show, displayed on the door, has a picture of the last jacket Maya made and the title HEAVENLY GARMENTS: HANDWOVEN CLOTHES BY MAYA ISHIDA. The jacket is hanging from the ceiling, its hem at the height of people's shoulders. The colors have completed their journey from blue to pink.

Lillian steps forward and hugs first Maya, then Yuko. Lillian used to own a boutique near Peg's, but she got divorced and moved down to Evanston two years ago. Dressed in black with her hair put up in a bun, she looks like a ballet instructor. "Someone already put one of the shawls on hold," she tells Maya. "She wants to show her husband."

"She needs his permission?" Yuko frowns.

"She's one of my regular customers," Lillian explains. "About once a month, I let her take clothes home so she can try them on in front of her husband for his approval. The guy's loaded. He seldom says no. I don't know if the private showing is his idea or hers. It's sick, but it's none of my business."

"We see all kinds of strange things," Maya says to Yuko.

Only last week, a woman came into the boutique with her husband, who stood looking out the window. The man didn't glance away from the window when his wife stepped out of the fitting room, wearing an elegant rose-colored dress. Standing in front of the mirror, clear across the room from him, the woman whispered to Maya, "My husband couldn't care less about the dress or me, but I know a man who'd love to see me in this." Her customers often confide in her. Maya learned long ago to suspend her judgment. As she walks around the exhibit and waits for her mother's arrival, she remembers the moments when she felt compassion for these women. If she could pretend that her mother was a customer, maybe she could find the right things to say.

When Kay and Nate come in, the gallery is already crowded. Peg and Larry have driven down with one of their neighbors. They are talking in the corner with Yuko. Among the many women and the few men who fill the room, Maya can spot Kay and Nate right away: Kay in a conservative beige suit, her gray hair cut short in the style Yuko calls "the helmet"; Nate in blue jeans and a brown wool *haori* jacket he bought in Japan Town in San Francisco, his limp hair tied back in a ponytail. He is a washed-out blond version of her father: the dark jacket and blue jeans, the ponytail. At forty-three—fifteen years younger than Kay—he belongs to that in-between generation: too young to have been a full-fledged hippie, too old for much else. Nate is a travel agent and a Japonophile. He and Kay met four years ago on the afternoon Nate went to see an exhibit of Japanese foldout screens at the Art Institute. He stopped at the bookstore near the Water Tower, where Kay was browsing; she was in town to attend a political science convention. Within a year, Kay resigned from her teaching job in Minneapolis and moved to Park Ridge to marry him.

After a lifetime of studying and teaching the politics of the Soviet Union and the Eastern bloc, Kay works part-time as a consultant to Japanese companies in Chicago. The house she shares with Nate is full of memorabilia from Nate's high school year in Nagoya and subsequent trips to Japan. Perhaps Kay is trying to regain her heritage, the way people in their old age often embrace the religious faith of their childhood. She has a long journey ahead. She has spent the last twenty-four years telling Maya how much she despises Japan. Asked where she is from, she always replies, "I spent most of my childhood and adolescence in Canada. My father was a diplomat," conveniently overlooking her childhood in Tokyo, her first marriage in Osaka. To Kay, the past is a story on a cassette tape. She can rewind it and hear only the portions she wants to, skipping through the rest. The tape screeches forward before anyone has time to ask questions.

Kay and Nate are making their way through to the back wall, where Maya is talking with a man who works in the textiles collection at the Art Institute. "I live a mile from here," he says. "I came because I saw the poster. From your name, I figured you were Japanese. My specialty is Japanese weaving and dye techniques."

"I don't know much about them. You can see that." She waves her arm toward the jackets hanging from the ceiling, the scarves and shawls displayed against the walls. The only Japanese techniques she tried were indigo dying and ikat weaving, both of which she gave up after a short time. The somber blue and brown fabrics they produced depressed her.

The man squints behind his rimless glasses. He must be in his thirties, her age. His hair is parted on the side; his eyes are pale blue. He looks mild-mannered and studious—Yuko would say nerdy—like many of the people who want to talk to Maya because she is Japanese. She pictures him walking down the narrow streets of a Japanese city, trying to blend into the crowd even though his reddish hair would never allow him to. "Your colors," he says. "Have you considered experimenting with more Japanese color juxtapositions?"

"I don't know. What are they?"

Her mother is at her side, with Nate hanging back a little. "My daughter grew up in Minneapolis," Kay chimes in, fixing the textile specialist with her direct gaze. "She's been bilingual from birth. She lives in Milwaukee now. Why should she care about Japanese colors?"

The man blinks a few times.

"This is my mother, Kay Hayashi Mueller." Maya gestures toward Nate with her hand, "And her husband, Nate Mueller. And you are—?"

"Jim Paine," the man says. "I'm a Japanese textile specialist."

"It's not fair to assume that my daughter would know all about Japanese textiles just because she has a Japanese name, is it?" Kay asks him.

"No, I suppose not." Jim Paine shrugs. "So who are your influences?" he asks Maya. "You learned to weave at a craft school in the States?"

"I didn't go to a craft school. I studied art at college. One of my professors taught me to weave."

"Who were your favorite artists?"

"It's hard to say. The later Impressionists. The Blue Riders. Rothko and Pollock and Frankenthaler. Diebenkorn. You know, the usual." As she rattles off this list, she glimpses the slivers and blocks of blues, lavenders, pinks, and greens in the garments against the wall. They are the colors of the landscapes by Pierre Bonnard or Gabrielle Munter—the paintings she saw with her father long ago in the museums in Kyoto. "My father was a Japanese painter," she offers, "but he was trained in Western-style art. He studied in Philadelphia. I suppose his influences are mine." She looks away from Jim Paine and meets her mother's eyes. Kay's jaw tightens, and the lines around her eyes deepen. The next moment, Nate is taking Kay by the hand and leading her across the room.

"Excuse me," Maya says to Jim Paine, who is still leaning toward her, expecting further explanations. "I'm glad you came to the show. Thank you."

Several people stop her to chat. When she catches up to Kay and Nate, they are standing by the drink table with plastic cups of mineral water. Kay looks away pointedly, but Nate shakes his finger at her.

"You were rude, Maya. Your mother was trying to defend you from that dumb guy and you just went on talking to him like she wasn't even there."

"Yeah, I'm sorry." Mentioning her father is the same thing as ignoring her mother. Her parents might as well be the sun and the moon; only one of them is supposed to be visible, but most of her life has been like the sunny days when a three-quarters moon appears in the low sky, pale and lopsided as a lemon slice cut too thin. "I didn't mean to offend you," Maya mumbles.

Kay holds her drink to her lips and takes a sip, peering at Maya from behind her bifocals. Her eyes, unlike Maya's, are narrow and slanted. Her nose is thin and delicate, her mouth tiny and button-shaped; as a young woman, she resembled the beauties in the *ukiyo-e*. When Maya left Minneapolis to go to college in Milwaukee with Yuko, Kay was an inch taller than her daughter. Now they stand eye to eye.

"I hope you'll forgive me and stick around for a while," she says, to both Kay and Nate.

Before they can answer, Yuko is at their side. "Hi, Mrs. Mueller." She sticks her hand out for a handshake. "It's nice to see you. How've you been?" Sometime in the last ten years, Maya started calling Yuko's parents by their first names, but Yuko doesn't see Kay often enough to be so informal with her. When Kay got married the third time, Yuko practiced saying "Mrs. Mueller" so she wouldn't call her Mrs. Anderson by mistake. "You look really well," Yuko says, still offering her hand. "Are you enjoying the show?"

"Hello, Yuko," Kay finally responds, taking Yuko's hand and shaking it.

"Lillian wants to talk to you," Yuko says to Maya, as she lets go of Kay's hand. "You should go see her. That'll give me a chance to visit with your mom."

"Okay. I'll be right back," Maya says. Yuko turns away from Kay a moment to wink at Maya, letting her know she is making this up to bail her out.

As Maya turns to go, she hears Yuko say to Kay, "My parents will be happy that I saw you. My father misses working with you." Maya can't help smiling. For someone who's usually so honest, Yuko can tell the glibbest lies with the straightest face. "It's the way I was raised," she always says. "*Thou shalt be nice* was the first commandment in our family. Even though we went to a Congregational church, our real religion was the Dogma of Politeness."

At ten, people are beginning to leave. Kay and Nate are talking to a woman Nate knows from work.

"I just know what my mother's going to say about the show," Maya whispers to Yuko. "She won't talk about my work at all. Instead, she'll complain that I spent the whole evening avoiding her. I should ask her and Nate to go out for a drink with us. She'll still complain then, but maybe not as much."

"That sounds like a good idea, but I'd better grab a ride with Peg and Larry."

"I don't have to go with them if you can't."

"No, you should go ahead. You don't want to hear your mother complaining for months. But I have to go home. Dan and I," she blurts out, "we had a big fight. We have some things we need to straighten out."

Although they are surrounded by the bustle of people getting ready to leave, Maya feels the background noise recede. "What's wrong?"

Yuko turns down the corners of her mouth. "I'll tell you another time. Listen, I'm so proud of you. I don't want to spoil the evening by going on about myself. I'll tell you next week on the way to Minneapolis."

"If you want to talk before that, you know where I am."

"Yeah, I'll come pound on your door if I have to."

When they hug, Maya's long hair swings forward and touches Yuko's. The strands are almost the same color and texture. If they were woven together, no one would be able to tell the difference.

After Nate drives home alone, Kay suggests a restaurant halfway between Evanston and Park Ridge. "You won't have to drive too far out of your way to drop me off later," she explains. In the car, she sits with her right shoulder pressed against the passenger window, her neck held straight and stiff-looking. She doesn't talk except to give directions. When Maya was studying photography, she could never get the right focal distance for objects in landscape—trees, rocks, ruined houses. If she stood too far, they receded into the background; if she was too close, they loomed too large and turned into shapes that made no sense. With her mother, too, there is no good place to stand.

There is a thin covering of snow on the lawns in residential areas. The sickle moon has disappeared. "I'm glad I did that show," Maya says, to break the silence. "The opening was nice. Lillian put a lot of work into it."

"Maya," Kay says with a sigh, "you can do so much better than this."

"What do you mean?" Maya asks, even though she knows exactly what her mother's answer will be.

"You're making artsy clothing for idle suburban women. Even with your art degree, you could have done better. It still isn't too late to go into graphic design or museum work. You can do something more professional."

"But I don't want to do those things." On the cabbage her father cut open, the green lines circled toward the center like a road map. If he had answered her letters, she might have followed that map back to her childhood. She could have become a painter like him. "I'm happy doing what I do," she insists. "I wish you wouldn't talk about it anymore."

They pull into the parking lot of an Italian restaurant. In silence, they walk through the heavy oak doors. The hostess seats them right away and hands them menus, but no one comes to take their order.

"I just want a glass of wine," Kay says loudly. "I don't know why the service is so bad everywhere I go."

"They'll come and wait on us soon enough, I'm sure," Maya whispers. "We should be patient."

Kay gets up from the table and goes to the hostess stand to complain. In a few minutes, when a young girl comes to the table, Kay orders a glass of Merlot; Maya asks for the same. The waitress shrugs and raises one eyebrow. "I waited on this bossy woman who was in a big hurry and all she wanted was a glass of wine," Maya imagines her telling her friends later. "She was with this other woman who was really mousy. Maybe it was her daughter. She looked like she wanted to disappear into a hole in the ground."

The waitress returns right away. The wine trembles inside the glass when she sets it down. *The wine-dark sea*, Maya's father used to say when he told her about Odysseus' adventures. The miniature red horizon inside her glass is almost still now. "I wanted to ask about that envelope you forwarded to me," Maya says to her mother.

"What about it?" Kay says, taking a sip of her wine.

"I didn't realize you'd been in touch with my father all these years."

Kay tilts her head to the side and squints. "I wasn't, really."

"How can you say that? He knew that you lived here, not in Minnesota. His assistant had your address."

"It depends on what you mean by being in touch." She sets her glass down.

"That's nonsense." Maya tries to keep her voice down. "Either you were in touch or you weren't."

"I wrote him just once. I sent him my new address when I moved, so when he died someone would notify me. That's all." Deliberately, Kay picks up her glass and takes another sip. "Now I can forget about him. I suggest you do the same."

Maya glances away from her mother's glass to her own. The candle on the table is reflected in a convex shape. If she stared long enough, she might be able to find her own reflection there, distorted and shrunk. Her mother is smiling and nodding a little.

"You can't dwell on the past, Maya," Kay says. "You should just let it go." As Kay lifts the glass to her lips, Maya feels as though her mother were toasting her father's death. If she picked up her own glass and drank from it, she would be joining that toast.

"Excuse me." She pushes her chair back and stands up. "My head is killing me." As soon as she says it, she knows it's true. She's getting a migraine. Her medicine is in the glove compartment of her car. Walking across the restaurant toward the oak door and then pushing it open, she is not sure what explanation she has given her mother. She might have said, "I'd better go get my medicine," or she might only have thought it. Though the light in the parking lot comes from white fluorescent lamps overhead, her vision turns into a narrow tunnel with yellow flames burning on its edge. In the halo of her migraine, she struggles to find her car.

Maya closes the car door, takes the medicine out, and swallows the bitter pill. Slumped over the steering wheel, the way Bill was the afternoon Kay broadcast her unhappiness on the radio, Maya sees yellow and purple disks colliding like angry coins. She thinks of Kay lifting her glass and drinking wine, waiting for her to join, her lips stained red. When Hades, king of the underworld, offered the pomegranate to Persephone, he might have looked like that. Persephone held the cracked fruit in her palm, picked three seeds, and ate them. Each seed meant a month in hell.

Opening her eyes and leaning back in the driver's seat, Maya feels the yellow and purple flickers receding. She turns the car key in the ignition and backs out of the parking space. As she rounds the corner of her row, the other parked cars look like shipwrecks preserved underwater. She keeps going past the next row, then the next, until she is at the exit. It's late at night; there is no parking charge. The orange arm goes up, allowing her out on the street.

In ten minutes, she is driving up the ramp onto the freeway, her car pointed north toward Wisconsin. Soon Kay will realize that her daughter is not coming back to the table. She will have to decide whether to get up and look for her or to go on as though nothing were amiss, pay the bill, and call Nate. Maya has no idea which her mother will choose. She has never walked out on her before. In Minneapolis, Kay screamed at her, shook her by the shoulders, dragged her down the stairs, and locked her up in a storage room in the basement, only to let her out in tears to deliver a long lecture. Maya watched her mother's mouth open and close, open and close, the words darkening the air between them as though they were the black locusts in her father's stories about famine. If she concentrated, she could make those words go silent. She put up with the scoldings for eight years until she was able to move away; she has kept at least a layer of civility between them on their short visits since.

Now she keeps driving past one exit after another, thinking she should get off the freeway and turn around; at the very least she should find a gas station and call Nate so he can meet Kay at the restaurant. But it's as though the car were driving her. She can't even slow down.

— 4 —

The storm that was predicted for two days has finally arrived. Carried by the wind, snow slants over the freeway in white shafts of light. Jeff stares straight ahead as he drives past trucks that look like ice floes.

"I know your mother means well, but I wish she'd leave me alone about being a vegetarian," Maya says, when they are halfway home.

Jeff sighs and does not reply.

"If I had lunch with someone who was allergic to wheat," Maya continues, "and if we had soup, I would never say, 'Some crackers would be so nice with this soup. I always have crackers with my soup.' I wouldn't go on about all the wonderful bread I could get at the neighborhood bakery and then mutter, 'Oh, but of course, you don't care about that. I'm sorry I mentioned it.'"

"My mother is seventy-five. She's spent her whole life on the south side. You're the only vegetarian she's ever met."

"That's no excuse for treating me like a freak." A couple of years ago, her comment about the crackers might have made him laugh. "Your mother's the only person I know who has macramé owls on her living room wall, but I don't comment on them. I never say, 'Macramé, how interesting. When did you learn to tie knots?'"

"You don't have to make fun of my mother," Jeff hisses.

Maya doesn't know anyone who doesn't say occasional mean things about their in-laws. She left her own mother stranded at a restaurant the week before Christmas and didn't call to apologize for ten days, but she never told Jeff. For the rest of the ride home, she watches the snow fall.

After the station wagon pulls into the driveway, Maya moves her car off the street. Jeff waits for her—his right hand holding the front door open, his left arm loaded with the Christmas presents his parents gave her. She can smell the raspberry-scented soaps and peach-scented candles his mother had put inside gold and silver boxes, wrapped in glossy red paper, and tied with green ribbons curled with scissors. The gifts under the tree—all Maya's because the family had exchanged theirs a month ago—looked like a flower arrangement. Maya has always spent Christmas and Thanksgiving with Yuko's family instead of Jeff's, but he has never complained. Standing in the doorway, she leans up and kisses his cheek.

"I'm sorry. Your mother doesn't treat me like a freak. I shouldn't have said that."

As they step into the foyer, he puts his arm around her shoulder. "It's all right. My mother *is* weird about the food. I know it bothers you." He lets go and closes the door behind them.

The phone rings while they are watching a movie. It's ten o'clock. Jeff puts the movie on pause while Maya goes to the kitchen to answer the phone.

"Maya, can you come over?" Yuko asks. "Dan split. We're finished."

Maya is standing next to the cabinets Dan built for Jeff. They have handles carved from dark walnut, solid doors made of cherry.

"When I got home from work this afternoon, he was waiting for me. His stuff was all in boxes and moved to the basement. He had a couple of backpacks he was going to take with him. They were in the foyer, in plain view, just in case I might not get the point." Yuko sniffles. "He said leaving me was the only honest thing he could do. He couldn't be with me when he was so completely in love with someone else. I was forcing him to lead a double life."

"He said that?"

"He went on and on about how much he loves this other woman and can't stay away from her."

"I'll be over in ten minutes," Maya says. "You just hang in there."

"I'll try."

In the living room, Jeff has fallen asleep on the couch. The movie has restarted without him. Maya pushes the PAUSE button on the VCR again before shaking him. He sits up and puts his arms around her. "Maybe we should forget the movie and go to bed," he says, his hand caressing her back. His fingers cupped behind her neck, he pulls her closer and presses his lips against hers.

Maya pulls back. "I need to be with Yuko. I'll probably stay over." She edges farther away. "Dan just moved out. She didn't say where he went, but I assume he went to his girlfriend's."

Jeff drops his arms. "He must have."

When Maya returned from Minneapolis a week after New Year's, she and Jeff agreed not to discuss the trouble between Yuko and Dan. Jeff had talked to Dan and heard his side of the story. "We should let them be," he said. "I'm sure they don't want us, or anyone, talking about them and taking sides."

"Did Dan tell you what he was going to do?" Maya asks him. "He promised Yuko he'd stop seeing the other woman while he and Yuko got some counseling. He lied. He must have been in touch with her all along. Did you know that?"

"It's not fair to ask me. You and I agreed not to talk about this."

"That's a yes, I think."

"Not necessarily."

"You didn't want to talk because you were keeping a secret for Dan."

"What if I was? If he confided in me, that's none of your business."

There's a click from the VCR, and the movie restarts. Maya gets up from the couch. "I'd better go. I'll see you tomorrow after work." She walks to the foyer without looking back, puts on her coat and boots, and steps outside. There's already a layer of snow on her windshield. Sweeping the car with her brush, she watches the flakes swirl up into the air and mingle with the snow coming down.

Yuko has left the door ajar, so Maya goes in without knocking.

"I'm in here," Yuko calls from the kitchen.

She is sitting at the table Dan built the year they were married. There's a bottle of wine on the table and two empty glasses. Yuko is wearing a sweatshirt and blue jeans, and her hair makes a blunt, slightly crooked line across her nape. She doesn't get up from the chair. Maya kneels down on the floor and takes her hand.

"I cut my hair," Yuko says, pressing her other hand into her eyes. "I braided it, chopped it off, and stuck it inside a big envelope addressed to Dan at his girlfriend's house. I walked through the snow to drop it off in the mailbox."

Maya puts her arms around her friend and hugs her for a long time. Then she walks around the table and sits down.

"Standing by the mailbox, I thought, Maybe this isn't so bad," Yuko says. "I heard the envelope hit the bottom of the box. Then I slammed the lid shut. I listened to my boots crunching the snow. Everything made a nice clean sound. But by the time I got home, I felt stupid. What was I thinking? I cut my hair and made myself look ugly because Dan hurt me. That's sick."

"No, it's not. Besides, you could never look ugly."

"I must have acted ugly," Yuko insists. "Otherwise, Dan wouldn't have fallen in love with someone else."

"It doesn't work like that. You can't blame yourself for the wrong things he did."

"You think it was wrong for him to fall in love? Dan talked about his affair like it was the bravest thing he's ever done. 'For once in my life,' he said, 'I'm not afraid to accept that someone really loves me. I don't have to run away.' Can you believe that? He's making himself out to be a hero."

"Regardless of what he says, what he did was wrong."

"Because he was married?"

Maya shakes her head. "No, because he was married to *you*. How could he be married to you and not see how lucky he was?"

"He said he never loved me, not like he loves this woman—Meredith. He didn't know what love was till he met her. The moment he saw her, he had this incredible feeling he'd never known with me."

They met in September when Dan went to buy two tickets for a play he had meant to see with Yuko. Meredith was working at the ticket office. He called her the next day and asked her out to lunch. By the time he told Yuko in early December, they had been lovers for two months and already talked about getting married as soon as he was divorced.

"Tonight, he confessed," Yuko continues, "that he'd only agreed to see the marriage counselor so he could leave me with a clear conscience. 'I didn't want to rush things with you and start my life with Meredith on the wrong foot, but I can't wait anymore,' he told me. Then he had the nerve to cry about how much he cared about me and didn't mean to hurt me. He'd spent the whole day packing his stuff. He must have been planning his getaway for some time. But he wouldn't shut up and go away. I had to ask him to leave. I wish he'd taken off before I got home."

"Yes, that would have been better," Maya agrees. Her mother had simply loaded her clothes and books in her car and driven to Park Ridge when she left Bill. She'd stopped in Milwaukee at midnight to tell Maya. Until then, Maya had had no idea, and from what she gathered from

Bill, it was a complete surprise to him too. Kay had done the same thing when she left Osaka. She'd pretended she was going to the States to finish her doctorate and would be back in two years. She was gone a year before she wrote to Maya's father and asked for a divorce. She had made a clean getaway, which at least allowed everyone else to hold on to a sense of dignity, while Dan had lingered and talked, making things worse. Perhaps there is no connection between people's intentions— kindly or selfish—and their ability to hurt others.

Yuko pours the wine into the two glasses. "When I chopped off my hair, I meant it to be a ritual. Remember when we read *Genji* in college? Women were always getting their heads shorn when their husbands left them or died. They were going to renounce the world and join a nunnery, which I'm not, but it doesn't matter where they were going. They were trying to move on, and so am I. Cutting their hair meant wanting to be free."

"All right." Maya picks up her glass and touches it to Yuko's. "To your freedom, then."

"And to us. You're still with me. You'll never lie to me and take off."

"Of course not." They clink their glasses and take a sip. Outside, the snow continues to fall.

The room where Maya goes to sleep is the same one she lived in twelve years ago with Scott. Yuko has converted it into her music room, but the green wallpaper—patterns of men in red coats on horseback, chasing foxes—is the same. Maya turns off the light and lies down on the futon couch. She can still see the red riders in the light from the windows.

She closes her eyes but can't sleep. Yuko would never have met Dan if it hadn't been for her. During their sophomore year, Maya told her mother she was living in the dorm with Yuko, but she had moved in with Scott. They lived in a dilapidated three-bedroom house on the lower east side with Dan and another roommate, Peter. Yuko was at the house almost every day.

Dan had a girlfriend then, a theater student named Judy. At a party in March, a friend of Judy's told her that someone in their English class had a crush on her. "The guy thinks you're gorgeous," she said. "Who is it?" Judy jumped up and shrieked, clapping her hand to her mouth, and the two girls began to whisper even though Dan was standing next to them. "Let's go out for a smoke," Maya said to Dan and Scott. Judy came to the porch after a while, hooked her arm through Dan's, and reached for his cigarette. Taking a long drag, she smiled sweetly at him. The next morning, she was sitting in the kitchen, wearing one of Dan's flannel shirts, while Dan cooked some eggs and bacon at the stove.

At the beginning of the summer vacation, Maya and Yuko were walking back to Scott's house from a grocery store when Yuko stopped abruptly on the sidewalk and cleared her throat.

"I want to tell you something," she said. "It's about Dan."

"What about him?"

"I'm in love with him."

"You're what?"

"I've had the biggest crush on him since the first day I met him." Yuko blushed.

"That was nine months ago."

"I don't give up easily. I'm pretty persistent." With her white sneakers, she kicked a broken branch lying on the sidewalk.

"But you never let him know how you feel. Persistent means keeping at something for a long time. You haven't started."

"What am I supposed to say? Long-suffering? That makes me sound like a martyr."

They walked on in silence.

"He wouldn't notice if I disappeared tomorrow," Yuko said. "I know that. I think about him every minute, and he never thinks about me."

"But he should notice you. We'll make him."

Yuko cocked her head slightly. "Of course, he has a girlfriend. That's a hitch."

"Judy treats him badly. We shouldn't feel guilty if he broke up with her and went out with you."

Yuko shifted the bag of groceries in her arms. "You know that ritual group I go to?" She belonged to a women's group at the Unitarian church that met once a month. "Next week is the summer solstice. We're going to do a love ritual because solstice is the time of high female power. Everyone's going to bring a love charm: a piece of their hair and a piece of their lover's hair, braided together into a knot. We'll throw the hair into a fire pit and say words of empowerment. It won't make Dan fall in love with me, I know, but it might give me courage when I'm around him. Right now, I can't carry on a decent conversation with him because I feel light-headed and woozy the moment he comes into the room. The ritual can change that."

"How are you going to get his hair?" Maya asked.

"I need to ask you a big favor. It's something only you can do, because you live with him."

"You want me to bring you a piece of his hair?"

Yuko nodded.

"Just a few strands from his brush?"

"No. It has to be long enough to braid. I'll cut my hair so you can see."

"Oh, Yuko."

"I thought of staying at your place and tiptoeing into his room at night with the scissors. But I can't. What if he wakes up and sees me?"

"He might wake up if I do it, too."

"But if he sees you, you can tell him you need his hair for an art project. You can say you were too shy to ask. You'll have a perfect excuse."

When they got to the house, Yuko took the scissors from Maya's sewing basket and cut her hair from the back. The piece she cut off looked like a kitten's tail. "Here, you keep this for me. And use the same scissors for his."

Maya wrapped the hair in tissue paper and put it in the box under Scott's bed where she kept her clothes. As she pushed the box back under the bed, she remembered a braided cord her father had made from the first cutting of her baby hair. He kept it in a blue porcelain box in his drawer, along with the other things he treasured: a framed photograph from his wedding, the green agate cuff links Kay had given him on their first anniversary, a postcard announcing his thesis exhibit in Philadelphia, the amethyst prayer beads that once belonged to his mother, who had died when he was eighteen, two months before he left to study in America. Her father used to take the things out of the drawer and tell Maya a story about each one. Maya loved to hear about what a colicky baby she used to be—she had howled in the middle of the night, so loud her father was afraid the whole neighborhood could hear her. Listening to his voice, she would touch the black braid with her fingertips in wonderment, as though it were a part of an animal she used to be but wasn't anymore. "You are such a quiet girl," her teachers said to her. They had no idea that she used to cry all night, announcing her unhappiness with earsplitting wails.

Every night when Maya walked into Dan's room with her sewing scissors, something went wrong. The floor creaked when she took the last step and she lost her nerve. Or she found him sleeping on his back so she would have to lift his head and slide the scissors between his neck and his pillow. She might nick his scalp or earlobe. Dan would wake up swearing in pain, and in spite of the lie Yuko had concocted, he would sense that something suspicious was going on.

Earlier that year, when Dan's old girlfriend, Sheila, came to visit, the two of them spent every afternoon listening to their favorite albums from high school—R.E.O. Speedwagon, Foreigner, Clash— smoking cigarettes and nodding in silence. At night, Dan gave up his bed to her and slept in the living room. "Sheila and me, we're just good friends now," he said. Scott snickered. "They're so mellow it's sick." Dan liked Judy because he mistook her indifference for independence. If he ever found out that Yuko was trying to work a love charm on him, he would move to another country just to get away from her.

Maya's high school home ec teacher used to say that good cooks can make a substitution in any recipe, using honey for sugar or an extra egg when caught short of baking powder. A love charm wasn't much different from a special dinner. If the hair was a stand-in for Dan's heart, then something else could be a stand-in for the hair. Dan had a Brewers cap he wore every day. It would have to substitute for his hair.

Yuko's ritual was scheduled for Friday. On Thursday morning at two, Maya entered Dan's room and snatched the cap from the closet door. Sitting at the table where she worked on her art projects, she cut a piece of the blue fabric from the back of the cap. Then she put half of Yuko's hair, coiled tight and knotted, into the folded cloth and made a small heart-shaped amulet. She undid the necklace Scott had given her on Valentine's Day and sorted out all the red glass beads that looked like seeds. Embellished with the beads, the heart resembled a ripe fruit. Maya cut another square from the cap and sewed a second amulet exactly like the first, so Yuko would have one to burn and one to keep. By the time she was done, it was six, already light out.

Maya hid the cap at the bottom of her box of art supplies. She got dressed and walked the couple of miles to the dorm. Yuko came to the door in her green terry-cloth bathrobe, rubbing her eyes. Maya took the two amulets out of her pocket and handed them to her.

"I couldn't cut his hair, so I sewed yours inside the cloth from his favorite cap," she said. "I made two, one to use in the ritual, one to remind yourself of the courage you're supposed to get."

Yuko threw her arms around Maya and hugged her tight. She was holding the amulets in her right hand, making a soft fist around them with her fingers curled loosely. Maya remembered that gesture: it was the same one Miss Larson, their fourth-grade teacher, had made to show how big each human heart was.

The next evening, the sun was just setting as Maya and Yuko stood holding hands with eleven other women around the fire pit. One by one, the women went up to cast their love spell. Yuko declared in her strong voice, "I, Lucy Yuko Nakashima, want Daniel Johnson to fall in love with me and love me for the rest of our lives." She dropped one of the amulets into the fire and stepped back into the circle.

After the sun disappeared, the clouds continued to smolder in the low sky. Maya was the only one who had come without a spell to cast. A woman in her mid-forties said, "I want my husband to be passionate toward me. I want him to fall in love with me again."

As the woman rejoined the circle and the next went forward to say that she wanted one of her coworkers to take notice of her, Maya thought about Scott. If he hadn't noticed her, she would have gone out with someone else or been happy alone. If they broke up, she would move back to the dorm to live with Yuko. She wouldn't keep talking about him for weeks and months, and she would hope he'd get over her too. When Maya imagined her future, she didn't picture Scott in it. He wanted to move to northern Wisconsin after graduation and teach at a country school; she would never go with him. They had met because he was taking a class called Art for Elementary School Teachers, which was held the hour before her drawing class in the same room. The day he got his clay camel back from the kiln, he stopped her in the hallway and asked, "Excuse me, you're an art major, aren't you? Do you think this looks like a camel?" She examined the clay model the size of a football with a long fragile neck. "No. A camel has ears. Your animal looks more like a dinosaur. You're lucky the neck didn't break in the kiln." He joked about how his camel-a-saurus had brought them together. She liked him when he told that story, but not when they were alone and he suddenly looked at her as though he could see nothing else in the whole room. "I love you," he whispered. "You are so beautiful." Maya stiffened and pulled away. "Don't be so melodramatic," she told him. "Talk to me like a friend."

The women kept stepping forward with their wishes for love. They stood tall and determined, but their heads were bowed with sadness. Their voices cracked because they wanted something they might never have. The burning sage, oak, and hair filled the air with a sharp scent that was both sweet and acrid. Even Yuko seemed far away, her eyes to the sky, dreaming about love. Maya tightened her grip on Yuko's large square hand, calloused from years of guitar-playing. There were plenty of boys who saw Yuko performing with a garage band and went crazy over her, a tall Japanese girl in blue jeans and a plain white T-shirt strumming the bass next to the boys in leather jackets. She could have had all kinds of boyfriends, and yet she had to fall for someone who paid no attention, who made her nervous and quiet instead of her usual talkative self. Maya imagined Yuko rising up to the sky like a balloon filled with hot air. If she didn't hold on, Yuko would fly away, leaving Maya alone on the ground.

Scott worked the graveyard shift at a factory for the summer, so he slept all afternoon and was gone at night. Peter had moved most of his things to his girlfriend's house. It was easy for Maya to invite Yuko and throw her together with Dan. But the love spell seemed to be having the opposite effect from what Yuko had intended. She was more nervous than ever—too chatty one day, too silent the next. Something had to happen soon, before Dan began to think of Yuko as high-strung and moody.

In July, Maya asked Yuko and Dan to see a movie at a nearby theater. She made dinner beforehand, and just as they were clearing the dishes she said she didn't feel well.

"I have a headache. I have to lie down. You guys go to the movie."

"No," Dan protested. "We can't go without you. Seeing the movie was your idea."

"But you can't help me by staying. I'd feel better if you were gone."

In the end, Yuko was the one who insisted on going. She knew Maya hated to be fussed over when she was sick.

"Let's get going," Yuko said to Dan. "We'll be late."

"See you guys later," Maya said, walking toward the bedroom. "I'll be okay."

After the movie, Yuko and Dan called from a diner.

"Maya." Yuko spoke first. "We stopped for some coffee. Do you feel better? Why don't you walk over and meet us?"

"We're at that Greek diner next to the theater," Dan added.

Maya pictured the two of them standing in the dimly lit corner, leaning toward the receiver to hear her answer, their hair touching. The love charm was beginning to work. In a few weeks, Yuko would start visiting the house for Dan instead of for Maya. Maybe she would stop spending time with anyone except him. In ninth grade, when Doris Sugiyama stood them up because a boy had asked her out that afternoon, Maya and Yuko had promised that they would never do that to each other, but Yuko might have forgotten. When Maya spoke, her voice came out shaky as though she were really sick.

"I'd better go back to bed."

"Do you want us to come back?" Dan asked.

"No. Don't come back. I'll be sleeping."

Yuko was saying something, but Maya hung up without hearing her.

Yuko and Dan talked for hours at the diner and went for a walk in the park, where they stole three lemon lilies planted by the pavilion. They came into Maya's room at one, with the lilies in a glass jar.

"Go back to sleep," Yuko said, putting the lilies on the nightstand. Dan was standing in the doorway.

Maya turned over and closed her eyes. After Yuko and Dan were gone, she lay awake, looking at the stolen flowers. She didn't hear him come back.

The lilies lasted a week. Before the yellow petals shriveled and shed like dropped feathers, Maya saw Judy storm out, carrying a box of clothes and kitchen utensils. On the sidewalk, she glared at Maya and quickened her steps. By the end of the summer, Yuko had moved in, Peter had gone to live with his girlfriend, and they were a household: two young couples living together. When Yuko and Dan got married after graduation and moved into another house nearby, Maya and Scott went with them. She was convinced by then that Yuko's marriage didn't diminish their friendship. There are things between friends even a husband can't replace.

When Maya wakes up in the middle of the night, she can't remember where she is until she is sitting up, looking across the room at Yuko's stand-up bass propped against the wall. The white T-shirt Yuko gave her to sleep in is tangled around her legs. The blankets and sheets are falling off the bed. Outside the door, the stairway light is on.

Almost nightly, when she lived here, Maya dreamed about her mother chasing her through their house in Minnesota with a huge knitting needle, a baseball bat, a metal ruler—always something hard and grim. Maya would escape through a long stairway, only to find herself back in the house in Osaka, where the garage was on fire. Her father would be painting inside his cocoon of canvas, utterly unaware of his own clothes and hair catching fire; all Maya could do was watch as he and his painting turned into columns of bright orange flames. No matter where she was in these dreams, there were always secret passageways that led her, against her will, back to the houses of her past. The dreams went on even after she moved to the efficiency. Sitting up in Yuko's futon bed, Maya hopes they won't follow her back to the places where she sleeps now—Jeff's house with white daisies on the blue wallpaper, her loft above the boutique.

Outside, the wind is whipping the bare trees in the backyard, and snow is blowing around, hitting the windows with a dry, tinny sound. Maya goes out to the hallway between the two bedrooms. Yuko's door is open and the light is on, but her bed is empty. The furnace starts up, sounding like a labored sigh. Maya runs down the stairs. Yuko's not in the living room or the kitchen, but the light is on over the stairway to the basement.

Her bare feet make almost no sound on the wooden steps. Yuko is seated in an old rocking chair next to the laundry machines. She's wearing a T-shirt like the one she gave Maya, only gray instead of white. Reaching up to the ashtray on top of the washer, she flicks the ashes from her cigarette.

Maya stops under the bare bulb that hangs from the ceiling. "You scared me," she says. "I thought maybe you went outside in this weather."

"I'm sorry." Yuko stands up and shakes her pack of Marlboros. Maya accepts the cigarette even though she quit smoking soon after college. Taking the Bic lighter Yuko hands her, she lights the cigarette and inhales the smoke. In silence, they tap the cigarettes against the blue ashtray Maya made in her ceramics class at college. The indentations around the rim were made with peach pits. She can remember the feel of their hard dry skin against her fingers.

The basement is still crowded with Dan's woodworking machines and tools. The boxes he packed are against the wall on the other side of the laundry machines. From the pipes overhead hang the five model planes he made. They're fighter jets—three B52s and two Japanese Zero's—strung on a fishing line. Each plane tilts forward, looking like it's ready to go into a tailspin.

Yuko points her cigarette at the planes. "Dan made those when he was really depressed. He forgot to take them down when he packed his stuff. Or maybe he didn't want to be reminded of that time. It was a couple of springs ago. He had to go build basements because no one was ordering furniture."

"I remember. He was on a construction crew."

"Every night, he ate supper without a word and holed up down here, working on his models. He took to calling in sick and building planes instead. I asked him what was wrong, but he wouldn't tell me. 'Don't pressure me when I'm already feeling bad,' he said. He'd be down here till two or three in the morning. If I came down, he'd just continue painting and pasting those little parts together, like I wasn't even there. After about a month, I couldn't take it anymore. I told him I was sick of his tight-lipped misery." She stubs out her cigarette, which has burned down to the filter. There is a deep crease between her dark eyebrows. "I said some harsh things to him."

"You were angry because you were worried about him. He can't hold that against you. Anyone would be upset if her husband missed work to build planes and refused to talk."

Yuko shakes her head. "You wouldn't. You'd never scream at Jeff the way I did at Dan, even if Jeff was doing something you didn't understand. You'd leave him alone and let him figure things out on his own."

For the last two years, Jeff has been sitting in his armchair night after night, grading stacks of papers with the TV on, while Maya drives back to the loft to weave. Maya and Jeff had never confided in each other much, but they had more things to talk about once—anecdotes about their days at work, a piece of gossip about people they knew, the books they were reading. They used to make each other laugh. Nowadays, when she thinks of their time together, it's like a silent movie.

"Maybe you're right," Maya says to Yuko. "I'd leave Jeff alone no matter what he was doing, but that's because I don't know how to talk to him. Leaving people alone isn't always a sign of love or generosity."

"You don't think so?"

Maya shakes her head.

Yuko lights another cigarette. "One afternoon that same spring, at a grocery store, I was shoving my cart toward the dairy case to get some milk. I almost bumped into this guy. We'd gotten there exactly at the same time, reaching for the same carton of milk. He put the milk in my cart and got another one for himself. He smiled and walked away before I could thank him. I stood there wanting to cry all of a sudden. I was floored by the kind gesture because I'd been so unhappy. When I got home, though, I was madder than ever at Dan. Even a stranger was kinder to me than he was, I thought, but that was the wrong way to look at the situation. Instead of yelling at him, I should have told him I knew how he felt. I was unhappy, too; he wasn't alone."

"Don't be so hard on yourself. How could you tell him you felt lonely when he wasn't talking to you?"

"I should have tried. Maybe that's when Dan and I started drifting apart. If I hadn't said all the wrong things then, we'd still be together now."

Maya pictures Yuko pushing her cart down the cold aisle by the dairy case, stunned by her loneliness, while Dan was probably in this basement, gluing tiny propellers and wing decals. For Maya, loneliness like that is as permanent as a piece of metal some people have, fusing their broken bones. Even in their first months together, she never expected that Jeff or anyone else could take away that feeling.

"I want to give you something." Yuko holds her left hand out to Maya. She opens her fingers. On her palm is the charm Maya made fourteen years ago. It's smaller than she remembered, the size of her thumbnail. The red beads and stitches are still bright against the navy blue. "I want you to keep this for me. I have the cap somewhere, too. Remember? You gave it to me the night before my wedding?"

Maya takes the charm from Yuko. It's surprisingly soft, with the hair coiled inside.

"I woke up wondering what Dan was doing. Maybe he's curled in bed with the ticket girl, crying about how bad he feels for me and being consoled by her for being such a sensitive guy. The thought drove me nuts. I came down here to burn this charm. I remembered the time you torched your last letter to your father."

"Do you want me to burn it?"

"No, I changed my mind while I was sitting here. Who am I kidding? I'm not going to feel better even if I burn down my whole house. There's no instant cure for heartbreak and misery. You know how they say a cold will go away in seven days if you take really good care of yourself and in a week if you don't? Heartbreak is a massive, psychic head cold. I have to feel bad until I don't feel bad anymore. I want you to hold on to the charm and promise you'll see me through this."

Closing her hand around the old charm, Maya steps forward and embraces Yuko. "I'm going to be with you always," she tells her. "You know that." She can see the crooked line Yuko's hair makes across her neck. Yuko was like a person whose long hair has gotten caught in a machine. The original spell had turned against her and was now churning around, trying to eat her alive. Taking the scissors to her hair was the only way she could get free.

— 5 —

From the rooftop of Yuko's new apartment, Maya can spot the comet to the northwest. Low in the sky among the constellations she remembers from grade school—the upside-down question mark of the Big Dipper, the tilted **W** of Cassiopeia, and the North Star—the comet blurs white, larger than any star. When Maya raises her binoculars to her eyes, the lenses isolate the hazy light and rearrange it into a cone fanning out to the upper right, its center resembling a silver disk. No longer stationary, the comet is plunging toward the horizon, trailing a path of light; but as soon as she puts down the binoculars, it turns back into a large star going nowhere.

Her breath rises into the dark, a scattering of white puffs. There may not be another comet in her lifetime. A week ago on the spring equinox, her thirty-fifth birthday, she imagined herself walking around the elliptical circle her teachers drew to demonstrate the movement of the earth around the sun. She had reached the midpoint of her circle, but while the earth moved toward longer days this year, she would travel in the opposite direction, toward longer nights. Training the lenses again on the white tail of the comet, Maya notes its exact shape, its cold silver light, wanting to memorize every detail as if she were bearing witness or saying good-bye. Finally, she walks back to the square opening on the roof where a ladder goes down to Yuko's back porch on the fourth floor.

Her steps clonk against the metal rungs. The door opens into the kitchen, the linoleum floor covered with the cardboard boxes they moved this afternoon. Down the narrow hallway is the only bedroom, which Yuko has set up as her music room: a piano by the window, two acoustic guitars and an electric bass in the middle of the room, a stand-up bass by the door. Last Sunday, Yuko's four brothers drove down from Minneapolis to help her move her instruments. Though the rest of the apartment is crowded with boxes, her music room is ready for tomorrow morning's practice. For the last year, Yuko has been playing with an all-female, all-Asian-American rock band called the Demographics. The band is booked to play in Chicago, Minneapolis, Asheville, and Seattle this summer. Yuko's desk is scattered with the notes for the songs she's been writing.

Maya walks to the living room, where Yuko is kneeling on the beige-carpeted floor among the boxes, taking the books out a handful at a time and stacking them up. The ceiling has no overhead light; the inverted clay bowl that covers the old fixture looks like the breast on a cheap statue. Yuko has plugged in her two floor lamps and four reading lamps and placed them around herself. Bathed in this circle of white and orange light, wearing a black T-shirt and black jeans, she looks like a character from a one-act play—the kind of experimental theater they used to see in college. Behind her in the corner is the futon she has put on the floor, neatly made up with pale blue sheets, a navy blue blanket, a flat thin pillow.

Maya stops in the doorway and surveys the room in which her friend plans to sleep, read, and eat, dedicating her one bedroom to her music. "I don't need a special room to sleep in," Yuko said, when she decided to leave the house to Dan and his girlfriend and move into an old apartment building a mile north of Maya's house. "I can sleep anywhere."

Maya sits down, facing Yuko across the pile of books and boxes. It's surprisingly warm in the light. She takes off her sweater and puts it on the floor next to the binoculars.

"I found the comet. Do you want to see it?"

"I don't know. This place is a disaster area. I can't decide where to start." Yuko runs her hand through her hair, which has been cut in a trendy asymmetrical style: one side flush with her earlobe and the other side cropped close to her temple, the bangs trimmed over her eyebrows. The morning after Yuko chopped off her braid, Maya drove her to a hairdresser. "We had too much to drink last night," Maya told the hairdresser. "At the time, it seemed like a good idea to cut her hair. As you can see, I made a big mess." She felt pathetic, as though she had really given her best friend a botched haircut. The blizzard of the night before had coated the freeway signs with a thick layer of snow. On the drive back, Maya missed the North Avenue exit, though she has lived within three miles of it for the last seventeen years. Yuko had fallen asleep in the car. She didn't wake up until Maya parked on the driveway and shook her shoulder.

"Where are your tapes and CDs?" Maya asks. The stereo is against one of the walls in the living room. "We should play some music while we unpack."

"I have no idea where anything is. I did such a lame job of marking my boxes. I can't remember what I meant by the abbreviations I made up. All I understand is LV for living room."

"Maybe we should first sort through the boxes then—just open the top and see what's inside each."

"You know what we should really do?" Yuko looks at her wristwatch. "We should quit. It's eight o'clock on a Friday night. We should order a pizza."

"Are you sure? I don't want you to unpack by yourself. I have to work tomorrow."

"Don't worry about it. I'm exhausted anyway. It'll be better to start out fresh tomorrow morning. I'm going to be living here a long time. I don't have to unpack right away."

"Where's the phone? I'll call Pizza Man. *Pizza Man Delivers.*" Maya holds up her right hand, palm up, and turns her face to the side, imitating the man on the restaurant's logo, but Yuko doesn't laugh. She just points to the wall behind Maya. The phone is on top of a makeshift bookcase: four long pine boards supported by cinder blocks. They haven't had shelves like these since college.

"I might have to put my clothes on some of those shelves," Yuko says. "My desk's blocking the bedroom closet because my brothers and I couldn't figure out where else to put it, and the only drawers are in the kitchen pantry. I don't have a place for my sweaters or coats unless I take down the shower curtain and hang them over the tub. Maybe I'll just forget about the shower and take baths."

"You don't have to do that. I have plenty of room in my closet at the loft. You can store your winter clothes there."

"Thanks." Yuko stands up. "Let's grab a beer, okay?"

"I'll call for the pizza first. We can drink our beer on the roof while we wait. You really have to see the comet."

"If you say so."

"It's the brightest one we're likely to see in our lifetime. I've been reading up on it. *Time* magazine says the comet isn't really a falling star but a burning dust ball hurtling through space. This one looks very similar to the one in the Bayeux tapestry. People used to think comets were messages from God, a warning about the end of the world."

"Oh, Maya," Yuko says, smiling faintly. "Only you can get so excited about a dust ball in outer space."

"Give it a chance," Maya coaxes. "This particular dust ball is spectacular."

Jeff has left the porch light on for her. Maya parks her Civic in the driveway behind his station wagon. The bike rack on the roof is beginning to rust, but her car, at one hundred seventy-five thousand miles, is still running fine. If she had to leave her marriage, she would at least have a vehicle that works. Yuko turned down everything Dan said she could have: the house, the furniture he'd made, even the dishes her parents had given them. She gave him the Barracuda and bought an old Ford Escort for two hundred dollars. "I need to start from scratch," she said. "How else can I find out who I am without him?" Yuko has been with Dan almost as long as she had lived with her parents before college, longer than she was with her youngest brothers. It wouldn't be the same for Maya. There is a clear line that slices through her life with Jeff, distinguishing what is hers from what is his, who she is from who he is. She was thirty and he was thirty-five when they met. They'd already lived a whole lifetime without each other.

The house is dark except for the night-light in the upstairs hallway. Jeff is asleep beneath the quilt his mother made. Maya walks quietly to her dresser by the window. A pale white light comes through the blinds from the aquarium lamp their new neighbor leaves on every night. In January, Mrs. Nordstrom's son came up from Kentucky to move his mother to a nursing home in Lexington. The new owner of the house, a young woman with a child, leaves their aquarium light on all night, and Jeff worries about the fish, who must be going blind. Unlike mammals, fish have no eyelids—their eyes burn out if the light never goes off. "Maybe we should tell her," Maya suggested. "No," Jeff said. "She'd feel funny about us if we did." Maya joked about sending an anonymous note. Just the picture of a lightbulb next to a fish with dark glasses and a white cane, and the woman would get the idea. Jeff frowned and shook his head. "Everything is a joke to you," he said. "You're so quiet most of the time, but in your head you're always making fun of people. You should have a little more compassion."

Maya puts the binoculars on top of her dresser and takes off her sweater. As she pulls out the drawer, the fragrance of the cypress wood rises in the dark, mixed with the rich wool smell of her hand-knit sweaters and woven scarves. Her great-grandmother, for whom the dresser was made, would have kept her heavy silk kimonos in these drawers. The dresser was the only thing Kay asked to have sent to her when she told Maya's father that she wasn't coming back. On the day the movers came, Minoru continued to paint in the garage with the door thrown open—it was August, at the height of summer heat. The rest of that summer, Maya was afraid to sleep in the dark, and the brown moths that came through the holes in the screen bumped into the bare bulb above her futon, singeing their wings and falling down on the white sheets all night long. For years in Minneapolis, Maya couldn't look at this dresser in Kay and Bill's bedroom without being reminded of that time, but when Kay left the second time, forsaking the dresser and leaving it to Maya by default, it became a piece of her childhood home she could finally reclaim. She brought it from Bill's house and put her handmade sweaters and scarves inside, along with the clothes she had saved: the red hooded jacket she was wearing on the day she left Osaka, the dresses and sweaters her father had packed in her suitcase. Yuko burned sage and scattered dried chrysanthemum petals. She made up a musical mantra for the dresser's new life and played it on her guitar while Maya scratched her name in Japanese inside the bottom drawer.

"Maya," Jeff says. "You're back." He's half lying down, half sitting up, rubbing his eyes.

"Sorry I'm so late. I should have called."

"Did everything go okay?"

"Fine. I told you her brothers moved most of the heavy stuff last weekend. The two of us just had the boxes."

"You could have called me if you needed extra hands."

"I know, but we didn't have to."

Jeff hasn't sat up because he is planning to go back to sleep. It's one-thirty in the morning.

"I want to ask you something," Maya says.

"What's that?"

"Do you think I can put my sweaters in the linen closet for a while?"

"Why would you want to do that?"

"I want Yuko to have this dresser." She puts her hand on top of the dresser as if she needed to show him which one she meant. Hers is the only one nearby; his is clear on the other side of the room.

"Yuko asked to borrow your dresser?"

"No, she didn't say anything about it."

Jeff sits up and sighs, his silence saying, So what's the point?

"I want to help her out. I can take my sweaters to the loft, if you'd rather. I'll need to borrow your station wagon, that's all."

Several seconds pass after she's finished, before he says, "Why do you always come up with these big projects in the middle of the night? Do you know what time it is?"

"I'm not asking you to do anything right now."

He scoots back toward the headboard. Pulling the pillows from behind his back, he tugs at them hard and plonks them back down.

"Don't be angry."

"I'm not angry."

"Yes, you are, but you shouldn't be. Moving a dresser ten blocks isn't a big project."

"Why don't you come to bed?" he says, in such a begrudging voice that it's scarcely an invitation. "We can talk about this in the morning. We don't have to decide in the middle of the night."

"No. I don't want to come to bed. There's nothing to *decide* or talk about."

"So what are you going to do? Sleep standing up?"

"Yeah, like a horse."

He shakes his head and they start laughing.

"Okay," he says. "I lose. We'll move your dresser in the morning. Now I want to go back to sleep."

"Fine, go ahead and sleep away." She waves her hand as though the bad feeling in the room could be cleared up by a joke.

Jeff makes a neighing noise and then plops back down under the covers.

Maya brushes her hair in the harsh yellow light from the bulbs that frame the bathroom mirror. If this were really her house, she would have taken out the bulbs and put in an overhead light. But it isn't her house; it never will be. When Maya moved here a week before the wedding, Yuko was worried. "People leave their energy behind long after they're gone," she said. "I'm worried about you living in the place where Jeff and his first wife must have felt a lot of anger between them. The fallout from their fights might be floating around in there. If we live near big power lines, we're more prone to getting cancer or leukemia. Anger is worse than a power line. I don't want you to get sick."

Maya pictured anger like electric currents surging through big steel towers, but she wasn't worried then. Not everyone is capable of rage that leaves a mark on the universe, strong enough to make people sick. Her mother was about the only person who had anger like that. Jeff and his first wife, Nancy, must have bickered in the same half-hearted way that Maya did with Jeff, letting their arguments peter out in lame apologies and silent resentments until something else stirred them up again. They couldn't have had terrible fights that left psychic marks on the house even if such a thing were possible: it takes two to fight like that. If Nancy had yelled at him, Jeff would have stayed quiet.

Nancy had been a social worker at the high school where Jeff still teaches. She and Jeff grew up together on the south side and got married at eighteen. Sixteen years later, she divorced him and moved to Colorado with a man she met at a rock-climbers' convention. That's all Maya knows about her. She'd been gone a year before Dan introduced Jeff and Maya. Jeff has said little about his marriage, and Maya hasn't asked. Someone else's past is like a box of newspaper clippings from a faraway city. The details would not make sense even if he told her. Nancy is living hundreds of miles away, married to someone else. If she was the one who chose the couch in the living room or the wallpaper in the kitchen, these things are no different from the traces left by numerous other owners. The house is seventy years old. People have come and gone. The only person who can make her feel slighted is Jeff, who is still here.

In the bedroom, Jeff is snoring softly and hugging the pillow. Maya gets a shawl from her dresser and wraps it around her shoulders. Downstairs in the kitchen, she opens a drawer, the top one to the farthest left, where she keeps everything from a ball of twine to bills, scraps of yarn, beads that fell out of old necklaces. Jeff gave her this drawer when she moved in. "Everyone needs one private drawer," he said, pulling his papers and bills and old letters out of it. Maya thought it was a generous gesture then, but now the drawer looks merely cluttered.

The padded envelope Maya received in November is at the bottom, along with the letter on onionskin paper. The photograph of her father and the picture he drew are at her loft, but for months she moved the envelope and the letter between the house and the loft, trying to find a moment when she could be alone and concentrate on a reply. Around the end of February, she gave up. Even when she lived alone, she seldom found inspiration to do something she didn't want to do in the first place. Now, her mind feels like a chalkboard that hasn't been cleaned completely. The minor irritation from her talk with Jeff is like the lesson from a previous class—too faint to make sense but legible enough to be a distraction.

Sitting at the kitchen table, Maya rereads the letter. Like the business letters they studied in her advanced Japanese class at college, this one is full of elaborate greetings and formalities. It's hard to separate them from the actual content. After reading it over three more times, Maya still finds no information about how long her father had been ill, what kind of cancer he had, what his last months were like, whether he was at home or at the hospital, if he left any last words.

Maya tries to picture Mr. Kubo, a man with a wife and two daughters. He must be thirty-five or forty, Maya's own age. She wants to imagine him as someone she might have gone to college with, but instead, she is thinking about the Japanese businessmen she met during her freshman year when she worked as an interpreter. Always dressed in black as though they were attending a funeral, they whispered to each other and never gave straight answers. While the American businessmen asked her what she was studying at college or where she grew up, the Japanese men never looked her in the eye. Her mother had been right: her Japanese wasn't good enough, and Japanese businessmen treated her as though she were nothing more than a machine—a special tape recorder that repeated everything in two languages.

"The Japanese are such hypocrites," Kay used to say before she was married to Nate. Even though she said the same things at least once a month, her voice always cracked with bitterness as if she had just discovered something new to be angry about. "If you want someone from Japan, especially a man, to do you a favor, you have to pretend that it's not important. Otherwise, they won't say yes and they won't say no. But if you pretend to be dumb, they'll let their guard down and you'll get what you want. I had to leave the country because I was too honest to play that stupid game."

Since Maya left Kay at the restaurant, they have only talked on the phone once or twice a month, and every time Kay mentions how she sat alone for an hour, worried and then upset, before she gave up on Maya and called her husband. "I waited," she said, "because I couldn't imagine you'd leave me. Why did you do that to me?" Maya wonders how many times she'll be forced to go over what happened that night. In the previous years, she visited her mother in January after spending Christmas with Yuko's family, but this year she sent her gifts and didn't offer any excuses.

Maya writes down a few sentences, thanking Mr. Kubo for sending her the news. She comments on the weather. There is still half a page left blank. Trying not to sound too blunt, she asks him to give her more details concerning her father's death. In particular, she would like to know if her father said anything about her in his last days. Even if it was the smallest remark, she would like to hear it. She repeats the polite formalities as best she can and closes the letter.

Her handwriting looks like a child's. The letter sounds alternately insincere and diffident, but it's the best she can do. Sealing the envelope, Maya slips it inside her coat pocket on her way upstairs.

Her back toward Jeff, she curls up tight under the covers, but she can't stop shaking. Jeff puts his arms around her. His breath is warm against her back.

"Hey," he whispers. "Are you all right?"

"I couldn't sleep."

He hugs her tighter. "Was it because I acted like a jerk about your dresser?"

She shakes her head. Her ear scratches against his jaw and makes a muffled noise.

"No, I wasn't a jerk or no, that wasn't the problem?"

"I don't know."

"Go back to sleep. You'll feel better in the morning."

"It *is* morning. I don't feel better."

Pulling herself out of his arms, Maya sits up. Jeff turns on his side and leans on his elbow. Compared to everything that happened in her past, their fight—their whole marriage, really—is minuscule, nothing Maya would lose sleep over. But that isn't the right thing to tell him. *I am upset about something else. I wasn't even thinking about you.*

"Listen," he says. "I know you've been upset about Dan and Yuko. You've known both of them a long time. I should have been more sensitive. I'm sorry." He sits up and moves closer.

Leaning toward him, she lets her shoulder touch his. "I'm sorry too. I haven't been myself because I was so upset about them."

"I understand. I'd be mad at Dan too, if Yuko were my best friend. You're irritable with me because I'm guilty by association. I shouldn't have made such a big deal about moving a piece of furniture."

She doesn't move away when he takes her hand into his, but she can hardly look at his face. When they were first married, Maya believed that their silence about the past was a sign of trust. Jeff didn't ask her about her childhood and accuse her of being cold when she refused to talk about it. He didn't use what little he knew about her history against her; he would never say, as Scott did, "You're afraid to love me because of what happened in your family." He asked no questions and assumed the best about her. Comfortable silence seemed like the closest she could come to love. If it had been up to her, they would have gone on seeing each other indefinitely without getting married. But Jeff promised that nothing would change between them if they married. Now she is sure they are separated forever by everything she's kept from telling him.

"I didn't mean to hurt your feelings," Jeff says, pulling her close.

Maya puts her arms around him and buries her face in his chest. His T-shirt is warm and soft, with the familiar scent of his soap and laundry detergent. She is overcome by terrible, sudden fondness, like regret, as though they were already parting. "I know. I'm sorry too," she murmurs. Across the few feet of darkness on the other side of their window, her neighbor's fish circle the aquarium, their bodies glittering like a handful of small coins.

— 6 —

On the hardwood floor of the boutique, three dead mice are lined up, their heads pointed toward the cash register. Their legs are bent at odd angles. Maya picks them up by the tails as her cat comes bouncing down the stairs.

"Thanks, Casper." She pats him on the head and goes back outside to throw the mice in the trash. When she comes back in, Casper flops down at her feet. He's grown tall and lanky, with a long tail that has a crook at the end. Maya closes the door and kneels down to scratch his stomach. Purring loudly, he jumps on her left shoulder and perches there while she rearranges the chairs and the tables for the party Peg is throwing to celebrate her sheep's birthday. The caterer should be here any minute. Peg has hired a string quartet to play Mozart. As Maya goes about her work, Casper keeps his paws on her shoulder and leans into her as if they were dancing cheek-to-cheek.

Casper hissed at Yuko the afternoon she named him. "Casper the Ghost," she said to him, backing away a little. "Don't tell me you don't like the name." He has settled down since then. Shy with everyone but Maya, he runs up the stairs to the loft as soon as customers come in. The mice who used to nest in the drawers have no chance. Every week,

Maya finds several dead ones on the floor, lined up in a neat row. Casper is paying her back for saving his life. Like her friends at college who picked up squashed birds from the roadside to put into collages and stuck their dead tropical fish in the freezer so they could cast them in plaster, Casper arranges the mice with meticulous care, sometimes surrounding them with rubber bands and twisty-ties he's been stashing somewhere, as if he were making a series of small installations on the theme of mice.

Jennifer, the caterer's new help, stands in the doorway with her hands full, her mouth open. "Oh, that's not a real person," she says, in a surprised voice.

"No, that's just Wilbur." The life-sized doll Peg made is seated at the table. Jennifer approaches gingerly and lowers the punch bowl, careful to keep a couple of empty chairs between herself and Wilbur. Casper scampered upstairs as soon as Jennifer opened the door.

"So what's with the doll?" Jennifer asks, when she's finished setting up. Maya can divide the people who come into the store into two groups. Some are drawn immediately to Wilbur, tugging at his stuffed arms inside the surgeon's coat, tousling his mop of hair, and pulling at the stethoscope around his neck. Once, three elderly women unzipped his pants and marveled at what Peg had accomplished with the fleece of her black sheep, Baba, and flesh-colored pantyhose stuffed with cotton. "My boss says it's practically the best sewing she's done," Maya told them. The women squealed with laughter and promised to sign up if Peg offered a class in doll making. But most people are like this girl—they give Wilbur a wide berth.

"Peg made Wilbur in a class in Wyoming," Maya explains. "She wanted to make a nurse doll, but she couldn't get the face to look like a woman's. So she made a man and dressed him like a doctor."

"Huh. That's pretty far out." Jennifer stares at Wilbur without another word.

Maya is witnessing the wordless bovine quality Jeff laments in his students. "You'll show them the most amazing things," he often complains, "and they'll stare and say nothing. I wish they would talk." Last night, he and Maya quarreled after coming home from a dinner with Dan and Meredith. "You scarcely said a word to that poor girl," Jeff said. "You kept talking to Dan about when the two of you were in college. It was so obvious; you brought up the past to exclude Meredith. I was ashamed to be with you." Maya's face burned when she remembered her own thin voice rehashing the past, her hands fluttering over the plates. Dan had sat with one arm around Meredith. Now and then, he drew her closer and kissed her. As they walked back to the car, Dan slowed down, matching his steps with Meredith's. He used to stride on ahead while Yuko stopped to look at something or to talk to an acquaintance at shopping malls. It was three, four minutes before he'd notice she was no longer at his side. Yuko thought Dan was absent-minded; now, watching him with Meredith, Maya saw the truth. "It wasn't my idea to go out with them," she told Jeff. "I acted like that because I was hurt." When she started crying, Jeff shook his head and left the room. He was reading the paper in the living room this morning. She walked past his chair on her way out of the house and didn't even say good-bye.

"I'd better go," Jennifer says. "Sylvia is coming to the party with a date. She's sending *me* back here at eight to clean up." Sylvia, the caterer, runs her business out of a farmhouse down the road.

"You can come back earlier and be a guest too."

"I'll try, but I have to study for a test. I'm still in school." Before Maya can ask her where she goes to school, Jennifer is gone.

Peg drives over in her blue vest-and-skirt outfit with crazy-quilt designs. On the rare occasions when Maya sees Peg and Kay at the same place, she can't help noticing that the two women are complete opposites. Kay wears the most conservative styles and colors—meticulously tailored suits in beige, taupe, ecru—and claims to be shocked by Peg's clothes. "How can that woman wear artsy-fartsy clothes like that?" she once said. "She's only a few years younger than I am." But Kay's stuffy old lady clothes didn't prevent her from getting a divorce at fifty-five to marry a younger man. Maya wishes she had grown up with a mother who dressed wildly but acted with solid good sense.

"The display looks excellent." Peg nods at the handwoven jackets and vests Maya has hung from the ceiling.

"Cheers for Baba and Molly." Maya pours the punch into two glasses and holds hers in the general direction of the sheep barn. The sheep are ten years old this spring. Maya has celebrated their birthday with Peg every year.

"Let me see that necklace," Peg says, as they sit down at the table. Maya takes off the necklace she is wearing with her black dress and hands it to Peg. Made as a collage of flower forms assembled from glass beads, it feels solid and heavy.

"You are so talented," Peg says, as she examines the necklace and hands it back. The beads make a faint clinking noise between their two palms.

"Sylvia sent her new help. She was a little leery of Wilbur."

"Good ol' Wilbur. He doesn't mean any harm." Peg pats the doll's fat stuffed hand.

Peg had made Wilbur for her brother, who was dying from kidney disease in Boston. She'd sent the doll to him with a message: *Sorry I can't be with you, but this guy will take care of you.* Wilbur had come back to the store in January after Peg's brother's funeral. She'd canceled her return plane ticket and driven back with the doll in a rented car.

"I could have shipped Wilbur," she told Maya, "but I'm glad I drove. At all the rest stops along the turnpike, I found people looking into the car, staring at Wilbur in the passenger seat with the seat belt on. It made me laugh. The trip was a pilgrimage."

Remembering what she said makes Maya want to hug her. Instead, she smiles and refills their glasses with punch. Last week, when Maya and Jeff brought the dresser to her new apartment, Yuko put her arms around Maya and cried. Maya patted her shoulder and said nothing.

Words would only remind Yuko of the sadness she would rather forget. All Maya could do was be quiet and hope that her presence was a comfort.

The customers arrive soon after. Maya shows them the racks of hand-woven garments, beaded jewelry, and the ready-mades Peg orders in the Southwestern style. Most of the customers are suburban women in their forties and older. Tired of dressing for other people in stern business suits and nice-housewife jumpers, they want something pretty and comfortable but aren't sure what to choose. They trust Maya, who has a good eye for matching each woman's build, coloring, and personality with the various fabrics and styles.

The string quartet begins to play. Across the room, Peg is talking and laughing with the customers' husbands. Maya hands one of her customers—Mrs. Gordon—a turquoise and lavender vest. Once she tries it on, Mrs. Gordon will see how the vest brings out the blue of her eyes and complements her red-going-silver hair. She will know she is still a striking woman at fifty. With the clothes flying overhead and the women standing before the mirrors in their new outfits, the barn feels like a cocoon of beauty. If butterflies could dream or remember the past—Maya imagines—they would see the particles of light that transformed them, every time they looked inside a flower with their faceted eyes. The splash of purple inside a lily, the dusting of yellow pollen inside a daisy, the soft brown cushion at the center of a sunflower—all would remind them of the mystery of their birth.

All afternoon, Maya shows the new spring clothes while Peg entertains the women with talk. By eight, the customers are gone and those who are left are friends and neighbors: women who own other boutiques and cafés nearby, some with their husbands; the musicians in the string quartet; Lillian, who has come up from Evanston; Sylvia—the caterer—and her date. Their town has become a popular tourist stop in the last ten years, and all the women who own businesses know one another. They attend openings and parties at each other's stores year after year and take buying trips together during the off season. When couples get divorced, it's usually the husbands who leave. The few exceptions, like Lillian, sell their businesses to close friends whom they come back to visit. The women joke about someday ending up in the same nursing home and running a catalog business from there.

At the sheep barn, Peg gives Molly and Baba each an oatmeal cookie and everyone sings happy birthday. Jennifer, the caterer's help, stands next to Maya as they belt out the familiar words. Molly and Baba chomp down the cookies and regard the crowd with their minus-sign pupils.

"Is Sylvia going to help you clean up?" Maya asks Jennifer, when they are leaving the barn.

"Are you kidding? She's not going to help me do something she's paying me to do. She's probably mad that I didn't start right away, but I wanted to see the sheep." Her voice trails off, sounding plaintive and young. Not too long ago, she was a child visiting petting zoos with her parents.

"I'll help you. We can wash the dishes in the sink upstairs so you don't have to do them later. Then we'll load your car and go to Peg's house for the rest of the party."

At the house, people are gathered in the kitchen. Maya makes herself a sandwich, takes one of the few soft drinks, and sits down in the living room. Larry has put on a U2 disk and several guests are dancing. Peg and Larry are the only people Maya knows in their fifties who listen to U2, Counting Crows, Bodeans, the Violent Femmes. That's as adventurous as they get, which is all right with the crowd at this party. Most of the guests are in their thirties and forties. They are at an age where people go to record stores and don't know what to buy unless they see a new album by a musician from their youth.

The cellist from the quartet asks Maya to dance.

"Maybe in a while." She waves what's left of her sandwich as though that was the reason. She is relieved when he asks Jennifer, and the two of them join the group on the floor. On their third date five years ago, Maya and Jeff went to the end-of-the-school-year party for his high school, held in the basement of a restaurant on the south side. The music was too loud, there were no windows, and the heat lamps over the buffet were turning the fried chicken and barbecued ribs into sinewy carcasses. Jeff introduced her to some women whose names she immediately forgot and went to talk to someone else. Maya had seldom attended a party where she didn't know anyone. Even among people she'd known for years, she listened mostly, asking questions when the conversation lagged so other people would keep talking. Jeff was clear on the other side of the room. The women he'd introduced her to started talking and laughing together. Maya slipped out and went to sit in her car in the parking lot. She was surprised when he came to look for her and apologized for leaving her alone. "I don't like parties either," he said. "I do a better job of hiding it, but you're more honest." They sat in the car and listened to her Suzanne Vega tape, returning just in time for the announcements of the awards. Jeff had been chosen teacher of the year. As she hugged him and congratulated him, she thought she had never been so proud of anyone except Yuko.

The guests have moved from the kitchen to the living room. Maya goes upstairs to Peg's daughter's old room and closes the door behind her. Peg's cats are on the bed, all three of them sleeping on the pillows; they don't move when Maya sits down on the edge. She picks up the telephone from the nightstand and dials the number at home. Jeff answers just as the machine comes on.

"Hi, Jeff, it's me."

"Hi, you. How's the party?"

"All right. We're at Peg's house now. People are dancing downstairs. They're having a good time."

"How about you? Are you having a good time?"

"I guess. You know how I am at these things." She wants to talk about that party five years ago and tell him she'd appreciated his coming to look for her in the parking lot, then apologize for the way she acted last night. But there is no good reason to mention these things. "So what are you doing?" she asks instead. "Are you having a good evening?"

"I'm just watching the basketball game."

She doesn't know college basketball from professional and can't remember which team is in what city. All the same, she asks him who's playing, how the game is. He answers cheerfully and describes the major plays. After five minutes, he says, "You didn't call me to ask about the game, did you? Is there something you need?"

"Oh, no. I just wanted to see if you were having a good evening."

"That's nice," he says. "Thanks."

She's trying to think of something else to say, when he adds, "Dan called a couple of hours ago. He asked if I could help him move some of Meredith's things to his house tomorrow morning. Do you want to come along? We can all go out for brunch afterward."

"I don't know." At the restaurant, Meredith didn't like the food she'd ordered. She and Dan whispered for a few seconds before he switched their plates and she began to eat his order instead. "Maybe my seeing them isn't such a good idea. You were right. I acted horribly last night."

"You have to get used to seeing them. You've known Dan for sixteen years. Yuko's not going to be upset if you stay friends with him, is she?"

"Of course not. She would never pressure me to take sides."

"So what's the problem? Why were you so unfriendly?"

"It isn't just Meredith. Dan makes me mad, all on his own. He called me at the store the other day to talk. He used to be so concerned about Yuko, but now he says bad things about her. He went on about how she upset him and Meredith by sending her hair. He said she always made him feel bad about himself. He was making it sound like it was all Yuko's fault that he fell in love with someone else. I didn't want to hear that stuff, so I said, 'You know, when things go wrong, we tend to blame other people, but we all have to take responsibility for our own actions.' I meant that he should take responsibility for his. I didn't say *you* because that's rude. You know what he said to me? He didn't get it that I was talking about him. He said, 'Gee, Maya, that's such a mature way to look at things. Did you say that to Yuko?'"

Jeff bursts out laughing. She can hear him gasping for breath.

"Why is that so funny?"

He's still laughing. "It's classic Maya-talking-to-Dan. It's hilarious. You're always trying to be subtle and he's always missing it."

"Maybe you're right."

"I think Dan would appreciate it if you came with me tomorrow. Do it for me, if not for him."

"Okay. What time?"

"I told him I'd be over at Meredith's apartment at ten-thirty."

"I'll be ready then."

"Are you going to stay out late tonight?"

"Not if I can help it. Why?"

"No reason," he says. "I haven't seen much of you lately. You're so busy working and helping Yuko." He pauses. "I miss you," he adds, his voice low and quiet.

Maya pictures his gray eyes peering at her from behind his glasses. She remembers the loneliness Yuko talked about on the night Dan left. "Don't be silly," she says, trying to lighten the tone. "How can you miss me? I live with you. We're still together."

"I know, but I'd like to see more of you."

"I'll try to be home in a couple of hours. I'll see you then."

As soon as Maya steps out of the bedroom, the music comes blaring up from the living room. At the bottom of the steps, Sylvia is standing with her date, her back to Maya. Sylvia jumps as Maya goes around her, but she and the man keep on talking. Maya can't hear a thing they're saying.

The man is leaning toward Sylvia, waving his hands. Though he must be Maya's age, he has boyish good looks—a thin straight nose, large brown eyes, light brown hair cut above his shoulders and parted in the middle—but his lips are twisted and he's frowning. Sylvia is leaning slightly backward; her pale-faced smile looks more like a grimace. She shrugs her shoulders and gives her head an emphatic shake. The light over the stairway gleams on the creamy skin of her neck and chest outlined by her low-cut maroon dress. Her dark curly hair frames her beautiful face and clear blue eyes, but hers isn't a kind face. She reminds Maya of Dan's old girlfriend Judy: elegant and haughty, mean in a quiet and picturesque way. "A psychoterrorist," Yuko used to call Judy, after she was with Dan and Judy kept calling them in the middle of the night. Maya wishes she could reach out and put her hand, solid and comforting, on the man's back. Wherever he is headed in his pursuit of this woman, it's not a happy place.

From the kitchen, she goes out to the back porch. Lillian and her friend Beth are looking at the comet. Every night, it has moved a few degrees to the west.

"I didn't make up my mind about coming till last night," Lillian tells Maya. "If I'd planned better, I could have brought back your pieces from the show."

Maya hadn't picked up her woven garments since the show closed in February. She doesn't want to have to visit her mother, but Lillian doesn't know that.

"I'll come down in the next couple of weeks. I'll call you."

"Bring some of your beadwork." Lillian points to Maya's necklace.

The white tail of the comet looks less crisp than a week ago.

When they go back to the living room, Sylvia is dancing with someone's husband. Her date is sitting in the kitchen alone. Lillian makes a face.

"Sylvia," Beth says, as if her name explained it all.

Maya looks from one woman to the other, and all three of them shrug.

The party breaks up at midnight. Natalie, who owns a greenhouse, brings down Sylvia's black cape and holds it out to her. Sylvia flings back her head, exposing her pale throat. She looks like a vampire.

"Come on, Sylvia," Natalie says firmly. "Put on your coat. Mark and I are taking you home."

Sylvia is drunk; anyone can tell. Natalie manages to wrap the cape around her even though Sylvia twists like an obstinate ivy that refuses to wind around a florist's wire. Everyone starts going out the door. Jennifer trudges to her car, hunched against the cold, looking forlorn. Maya closes the door and begins to clean up.

At one, Peg walks Maya to the door. They're laughing about the cellist's curly red hair, which has grown down to his shoulders since the last time they saw him.

"He's so serious. His hair and his personality don't go together," Maya says. "He looks like an acid dream of Jesus."

"Oh, Maya, that's so mean!" Peg wheezes. "He'd be crushed to hear you say that."

"You'll never tell him, though."

Maya opens the door. Outside, Sylvia's date is sitting on the steps with a glass full of ice and pale liquid. He hasn't brought a jacket and is wearing only his jeans and a corduroy shirt. Maya can't remember his name. They had talked a little at the store; he said he was teaching part-time in the art department at the university. More customers showed up before she could tell him that she used to be a student there. He wouldn't remember their conversation anyway. He's blinking at her in the vacant way people do when they're very drunk.

"Aren't you cold?" she asks.

He shakes his head and gives her a big innocent smile. His teeth are slightly crooked, the front teeth overlapping a little. He must not have had braces when he was growing up. Maya smiles back uncertainly. Raising his glass, he nods to her and takes a drink.

Out in the front yard, in the grassy part where everyone parks, Maya sees Larry's truck, Peg's Saturn, her own Civic, and a small green car.

"I don't think he should drive," Peg whispers, pointing to the unfamiliar car.

"Don't worry," Maya whispers back. "I'll take him back to his house."

"You know where he lives?"

"No. I never saw him before. I can't even remember his name."

Peg shakes her head. The man smiles again at them.

"At least he's a happy drunk," Maya says to Peg. "It'll be okay. He can't live that far."

Draining his glass and putting it down, the man struggles to his feet and stands on the bottom step, one hand on the railing.

Maya walks up to him and holds out her hand. "Hi, I'm Maya Ishida. Let me drive you home."

"You're the woman on the stairway," he says, as he takes her hand and holds on. "I knew you were sent to save me."

She leads him to the Civic. He gets in without any protest about being sober enough to drive. Maybe he doesn't remember coming here in the first place. Maya closes the door, locking it, and walks around to her side.

"Tell me your name," she asks, as she starts the engine.

"Eric," he says, "with a *c*."

"Okay, Eric. You need to show me where you live."

Ten minutes later, they pull into the driveway of a duplex in a northern suburb, halfway between Peg's house and Maya's. Just as Maya turns off the ignition, a light comes on in one of the windows. The house was completely dark till now.

"I didn't know you lived with someone," she says.

"I don't," Eric answers, staring at the house through the windshield. She waits for him to explain.

"This isn't where I live."

"Pardon me?"

"I thought it was. But apparently it's not."

The window is on the side of the house, where a bedroom would be. Whoever is in there must be fumbling for his glasses or shoes. He will come down the hallway to the front door, look out, and find a strange car parked in his driveway. Maya turns the car back on, yanks the gear into reverse, and peels out of the driveway. She drives several blocks before pulling over to the curb. Eric is laughing as though she had planned a stunt for his entertainment.

"So where do you really live?" she asks.

He peers at the darkness outside the car. "I don't know where I am," he says.

"Somewhere in Fox Point. Which suburb do you live in?"

"Shorewood. But I don't know how to get there from here because I don't know where *here* is."

"We're not far. Shorewood is about fifteen blocks south. Can you remember your address?"

"I hope so." He sounds doubtful.

"If you can, I'll be able to find your house. I've lived around here a long time. Besides, I have a map." Opening her glove compartment, she pulls out a city map and switches on her dome light.

After five minutes, she slows down in front of another duplex but doesn't pull into the driveway. The lights are off. She parks on the street.

"So you think this is the right house?"

"Positive." He pushes the door handle but the door won't open.

"I locked the door."

"You did?"

"I didn't want you to fall out of my car on the freeway."

He stumbles when he gets out. Maya walks around to his side. He's leaning forward, his hand on the hood.

"Do you want me to help you to the door?" He nods. She puts her left arm around his waist and holds out her right hand. "Give me your key."

He pulls a key ring out of his jeans pocket and hands it over. They proceed up the driveway, Eric leaning on her like someone with a broken leg. The second key she tries fits. Maya walks into the living room and lets him go. There's enough light to see by from the street.

"Will you be all right?" she asks.

"I don't know." He looks down at his feet as though he has never seen the shoes he's wearing.

"Maybe you should sit down."

She takes him by the hand. He lets go, only to reach and put his arm around her shoulder. He has to struggle to keep standing. "You're very kind," he says. Even drunk, he has a gentle, soft voice.

As they begin to walk unsteadily together, Maya remembers the weekends in college. Every Friday or Saturday night, she helped Yuko, Dan, Scott, and various other friends—coaxing them to stop drinking and leave the bar or the party, walking them home, getting them to sit down and drink some water. Always the designated sober person, she thought of herself as boring and timid, but it's oddly comforting to help this stranger. When they get to the couch, she lets go and he sinks down on the seat. He leans forward with his elbows on his knees, his hands pressed against his temples.

"I'm going to look for some aspirin."

She returns with a glass of water from the kitchen and the aspirin she found in the medicine cabinet. Sitting down next to him, she holds out the two pills. "Here, take these."

"Thanks." He swallows them with a mouthful of water.

"You should drink all of it." She sets the glass on the coffee table and stands up.

He looks up at her and smiles weakly. "I knew you'd save me," he says. "Thank you." He reaches up and takes her hand. She steps back until he lets go. Looking down at his own hand, he shakes his head. "Good-bye," she says. "I hope you won't feel too bad in the morning." He is still sitting on the couch when she leaves.

Driving on a residential street near her home, Maya pictures Jeff sleeping in their bed under his mother's quilt, the neighbor's aquarium shining through the blinds. It's almost two o'clock in the morning. The satisfaction she felt about helping Eric is gone. Instead, she's thinking about the years in high school when she was afraid to go home. At ten or eleven, she would be riding with a carload of girls, all of them laughing and talking. As the car rounded the corner onto her street, she knew her mother would be waiting up at the kitchen table, claiming to have been worried to death. Kay would tell her to sit down across the table and recount everything she'd done that night, and even after Maya did, she would accuse her of lying. When the car stopped in front of her house, Maya said good night to her friends without letting on how she felt, but it was as though they were abandoning her. Their car was a ship dropping her off on a desert island. Until the last semester of her senior year, Kay expected her to go on to a private college in the Twin Cities and live at home. Maya had to almost flunk out of school and run away from home before Kay gave up in disgust and allowed her to go to Milwaukee with Yuko. Now, the old feeling of despair has found her again. All night, she and Jeff will lie back to back in the same bed like two swimmers lost at sea. If two people were drowning, it wouldn't help them to be only a few inches apart.

Maya stares ahead into the arc of her headlights, trying to chase away the image that keeps coming back to her. Her father is standing alone in a dark, desolate place, his right arm extended in a wave. The brown kimono he is wearing makes him look like a tree, his arm a bare branch in winter. Though he keeps waving, Maya can only guess what he is trying to tell her. *Good-bye*, he must be saying. *I'll never see you again.*

— 7 —

From the path that winds through the bluff above Lake Michigan, Maya watches the sun weaving its way up and around the low clouds on the horizon. White-throated sparrows dart over the brown grass, their black-and-white striped heads like tiny race helmets. A few begin to sing their tremulous four-note phrase from the trees. The binoculars intensify the definition of their white throat patches, the bright yellow dot between the eye and the bill.

All along the path, Maya sees nothing surprising: the robins and the redwing blackbirds who have been back since March, the mourning doves and the starlings who have never left, a flock of blue jays with their wings like thunderbolts of black and blue. Far over the water, herring gulls are circling. The older birds are pure white except for the pale gray mantle of their wings, tipped in black, while last year's young wear their sooty costumes of brown-black. It will take them two winters to slough off this dingy color, first from the head and the underparts, then from the tail. Maya's father once drew a picture of a white bird encased in a block of ice and told her the story of the ugly duckling. In winter, when all the birds flew south, the ugly duckling was alone on a frozen pond. Maya pitied the young bird trapped inside solid ice, but when spring came he turned into a swan and was reunited with the other swans. Most people's lives are like a gull's—struggling year after year to slough off the sooty marks of childhood.

Maya trains her binoculars over the water. Ready for something or nothing, she examines the pure transparent air between shore and sky. The gulls wheel in and out of her field of vision—suddenly, one plunges headfirst into the water. She follows the steep angle of the bird's descent. He crashes into the waves and soars up with something in his beak. He is not a gull but a tern with a bright orange bill, a black cap marking his head. Transformed back into himself by the dip into the cold water, he flies away as the gulls form a tight squadron to give chase. Too late, they congregate to dive-bomb this stranger among them, their anxious cries spreading over the water.

Jeff is reading the Sunday paper at the kitchen table. In his clean long-sleeved T-shirt and jeans, he looks ready to start the day. He doesn't say anything when she comes in.

When they were first married, he tiptoed out of bed and made coffee before waking her up to read the Sunday paper with him. They took their second cups and went back upstairs just as the sun was coming through the large windows, turning the bed into an island of light. Sitting on the bed, he talked about his students; she described her eccentric customers to make him laugh. When their cups were empty, they made love, dozing off for a few minutes afterward. By the time they got up again, it was past noon.

One Sunday a year after they were married, Maya woke up before dawn and did not go back to sleep. She dressed in the dark and rode off on her bicycle, the wind zinging around her. In the deserted park, she stood alone in the near dark before sunrise. The silence was broken only by the sparrows beginning to chirp in the bushes, a single robin trilling among the high branches. She had been away for so long: for a whole year, she had slept through the gray hours of the morning and gotten up to a routine of coffee and small talk. She felt like a person who had woken up from a dream—a dream that was an endless repetition of everyday actions that made no sense.

When birds leave their wintering grounds to fly north, they are not following the trail of food or better weather. There is plenty of food where they are, and the weather is more clement. No one knows what makes them flock up and start their journey or how they navigate the thousands of miles back to the place where they were born. Maya never spent another Sunday morning with Jeff while flocks of grosbeaks and warblers traveled through the sky above her, each bird bearing a mark that distinguished it from all the others. Week after week, she returned to the park alone.

That was more than two years ago. If Jeff minded her going off without him, he hasn't said anything. He has seemed as content as she with the space between them, with lives that resemble parallel lines moving in the same direction. The happily married couples Maya knows—Peg and Larry, Yuko's parents, or Yuko and Dan, she used to think—can keep a steady small distance between them. More like old friends than lovers, they don't cling to each other. Maya hoped she and Jeff would be like them—not like her mother and Bill before Kay found Nate and moved away. At least once a week when Maya lived with them, Kay had screamed at Bill and stormed out, only to come back in a couple of hours to kiss him in tears; every fight ended with them staggering upstairs with their arms around each other.

As she stands in the kitchen, looking at Jeff hunched over the paper, she has a sinking feeling that they made a mistake in marrying each other, that the end is as inevitable as the approach of spring. The temperature fluctuates wildly this time of the year, one day like spring, the next like winter, but after March and April everyone knows where the weather is headed. Change is predestined.

Maya pours herself some coffee and sits down across the table from him, careful not to scrape the chair legs against the tiled floor. Maybe he feels the same doomed way about them that she does. In silence, he hands her the sections of the paper he has finished. After half an hour, she pushes back her chair quietly, gets up, and walks to the counter. "More coffee?" she asks. It's the first thing she's said to him since the phone call last night.

"No, thanks. You should get ready."

Maya glances at her wristwatch. It's nine-thirty. "I was wondering if I could meet you somewhere a little later, instead of going to Meredith's apartment."

"What are you talking about?"

"I have to do something first. I'll be done in an hour."

Jeff puts down the paper and takes off his reading glasses. "Last night you promised you'd come with me."

"I know, but something came up. You don't need my help moving things. I can meet you afterward."

"That's not the point. You made a promise. Why do you always do exactly what you want without any consideration for me? If that's how it's going to be, I don't want any part of this anymore. You should just go and be by yourself."

"What do you mean by that? You sound like you're telling me to move out."

"I don't know," he says darkly. "Maybe we need to talk about it."

Maya walks back to the table, but just as she reaches for her chair, Jeff pushes back his and stands up. They face each other across the table. She puts her hand on the back of the chair even though she doesn't sit down. She imagines a long cord stretched thin. On one side is this house, on the other the tiny efficiency where she used to live. The two begin to spin, but it's the house at the center, flinging the efficiency about, trying to pitch it off.

"So when are we going to talk?" she asks.

"Not now." He steps back from the table. "Don't bother to meet us anywhere. Do whatever you want all day long."

"Fine." Her voice comes out flat and cold. "I could easily have come over later, but that's your choice. You'd as soon make a big deal out of nothing." Slowly but deliberately, she walks out of the kitchen and up the stairs before he has a chance to leave first. While she is in the closet getting her clothes, he goes out to the driveway, moves her car to the street, and gets into his. Then he starts the engine and drives away.

Eric comes to the door in jeans and a sweatshirt, his eyes red and his cheeks pale. His hair, just washed and combed, sticks to his forehead. Maya can almost picture how he might have looked as a young boy.

"I stopped by to see how you were," Maya says.

Smiling, he steps back to let her in. "It's nice to see you. Come in."

"I was on my way up to the store," she explains. "I can give you a ride back to Peg's."

"That'll be great. Thanks."

The living room has only a couch and a coffee table. Just like Yuko, he doesn't have pictures, a TV, or bookcases.

"Come into the kitchen." He leads the way. The kitchen is as bare but at least sunny. "Please have a seat." He points to a round table and two chairs. "Can I make you some tea? I don't have any coffee. I gave it up a year ago because it made me nervous."

"You don't have to make me anything," she says, sitting down.

"Why? Are you in a hurry?"

"No, not at all."

He turns on the burner before filling the kettle and putting it on. "Herb tea or black tea?"

"Black. Are you feeling all right?"

"Never better." He smiles, showing his crooked teeth. "I know I don't look it."

"I didn't say you looked bad."

"You don't have to tell me. You're thinking it." When the kettle whistles, he pours the hot water into two cups with tea bags and brings them to the table with a bowl of sugar. "I don't have any cream," he says.

"That's all right."

They let the tea steep for a while before they begin to drink. Maya feels awkward; it's odd to be having tea in the kitchen with someone she doesn't know.

"You haven't lived here very long."

He puts down his cup and arches his eyebrows. "You would hope not, right? Otherwise, I'd be an idiot to direct you to the wrong house."

"That's not what I meant. I wasn't trying to remind you about last night." The cup clatters when she puts it down.

"It's all right. I'm the one who should be embarrassed."

"No, you shouldn't. Everyone gets drunk sometimes," she says. "It's just that I helped my best friend move a week ago. She doesn't have a lot of furniture because she's starting her life over, and her place looks a little unsettled—"

"And it's the same thing here," he finishes for her.

"Yes. Did that sound rude?"

He reaches across the table and touches her wrist. His fingertips are warm from the teacup. "No, not at all. I can't imagine you ever being rude."

Maya looks away from his eyes, her heart beating so hard she is sure he can hear it from across the table. She is blabbing like an idiot, making a stupid comment and then calling attention to it. She shouldn't have stopped here in the first place; he must have plenty of friends he can call to get a ride.

Eric withdraws his hand. "I moved back to Wisconsin last September from Vermont. My parents live in the countryside near Manitowoc, about an hour north of here. I came back because they're getting old, but I don't know how long I'll be staying." By the way he picks up his cup and looks into his tea, Maya knows his move was motivated by a sense of obligation—if he had his wish, he would be far away from here and much happier.

"Your parents must appreciate your being near them."

He shrugs. "My mother lives alone in a trailer, a few miles from the farm where I grew up. My parents sold the farm to a neighbor some years ago. My father is in a nursing home in Green Bay."

"I'm sorry to hear that."

"How about you?" he asks. "Do you have family nearby?"

"Not really. My mother lives near Chicago with her third husband, but I don't see her often. We don't get along. The last time I saw her, I left her at a restaurant on the north side of Chicago and drove away. She didn't even have a car there."

"Oh, no." He laughs. "It must have been pretty bad."

"It was the same old thing, my mother nagging me and me getting defensive, but I just snapped this time. She and I have talked on the phone since, but neither of us has mentioned getting together again. I think we're both afraid of having another blowup. She's the only family I have. My father—her first husband—lived in Japan, but he died recently, and I don't have any brothers or sisters." Maya tries to laugh as if to say her life isn't as sad as it sounds.

"You've been through a lot."

The kindness in his voice almost brings tears to her eyes. Closing her eyes, she pictures her father from twenty-five years ago, standing at the airport in his black coat. He would have been thirty-five, her age now. How could he say good-bye to her, knowing they would never meet again? When she opens her eyes, Eric is looking into her face. His brown eyes have a faint tint of green around the pupils. "It's nothing," she says, picking up her cup to finish her tea.

Because she was too nervous to stir the tea, all the sugar has stayed near the bottom of the cup. Each sip she takes is sweeter than the one before, and toward the end, the sweetness is overpowering. The summer Kay left for California, Maya and her father fed sugar water to the butterflies they caught. Inside a cage made of green netting, the butterflies drank sugar from white cotton balls; their delicate legs looked like embroidery thread. It was only a few hours before her father told her it was time to let them go.

The sky is overcast and flurries are coming down. It's still early enough for one last snowstorm.

"When we were at the store yesterday," Maya says to Eric on the freeway, "you said you taught at the university."

"Yes. I started looking for jobs in this area two years ago when my father went into the nursing home. Finally, the university offered me a couple of drawing courses, and it looked like I could supplement my income by doing some odd jobs, so I came back. It's basically what I was doing in Vermont—piecing together a living with teaching, carpentry work, all kinds of odd jobs in order to be able to paint."

"My father was a painter." Maya takes her eyes off the road and glances at Eric, who is sitting sideways in the passenger seat. He nods as if to say, *Go on, tell me more.* With the wind blowing and the flurries coming down, the road ahead of them looks like the tunnel in the drawing her father sent—except, in the drawing, all the bad things were behind her in the hell she was leaving. Now she seems to be heading into them. "My father died in October. I left him twenty-five years ago to live with my mother in Minneapolis and never saw him again." She shouldn't have brought up the subject. "I became an art major in college because I wanted to be like him. I ended up not pursuing it, but I went to the university and took classes with some of the people you must work with." She mentions the professors she had back then.

"So you're a weaver now, right?" He is looking at the rose-colored shawl she's wearing. "You made that, and some of the jackets at the store."

"Yes."

"I wanted you to show me which ones were yours, but we got interrupted by your customers. I was sorry we didn't get a chance to talk more."

"I didn't think you would remember talking to me."

"I do. It's what I remember most about yesterday."

She can feel his eyes on her face. "I learned to weave from one of my professors. I was her intern the first semester of my senior year, helping her with a big installation she was putting together. We made bags sewn from handwoven materials. They were supposed to look like rocks in a Zen garden."

Maya can still picture that installation from thirteen years ago. The bags were meant to evoke peacefulness, but they reminded her of bodies. The material was a mix of silk and linen, flecked with gold, yellow, and ocher. It was somber but beautiful on the loom. But once they cut and sewed it, the colors seemed unforgiving. Scattered among the sewn forms her professor, Ruth, placed silk cocoons in small wooden crates. To Maya, the cocoons looked like tiny eggs that would never hatch. The installation made her think of grief without an end. She imagined her father alone in his garage, painting those desert colors and swirls of white light. Day after day, he was still out there, trying to capture his sadness through the shapes on his canvas. No matter how many paintings he finished, his loneliness would never go away, and yet he kept painting. Maya didn't have that courage.

She could tell which of her friends then would become artists. One of them took pictures of himself and superimposed them over the sky-line of Chicago. The expression on his face and the altered sizes of things left no doubt about his feelings. He glared down on the John Hancock Building, where his father lived with his new wife. His foot hovered over the Lincoln Park Zoo, where children were playing. He was a giant of rage; he wasn't afraid to show that. Maya had been painting meticulously executed landscapes, detailed studies of plants, still lifes with wrinkled cloths blooming with blue shadows. Her work didn't show how she felt about anything.

The students who were going to be artists didn't flinch from the things that scared them. If they weren't painting, they stayed up all night talking about nightmares or death or the end of the world or all the ways in which their parents had let them down. When they turned to Maya, she made a lame joke and waited for someone else to speak. She was thankful to come home to Yuko, Dan, and Scott, who were playing cards, watching TV, and laughing about something. If Yuko talked about the end of the world, it was to crack jokes about what canned fruits she would have in her fallout shelter, which Rolling Stones albums and Jane Austen novels she would add to her doomsday library. She amused her friends with wicked impersonations of the musicians in her garage band. "Those guys are all jerks," she'd say, "but I don't care, just so we have a drummer who can keep time." In the house they shared, even the unexpected disasters were minor and comical, like the time Dan came home drunk and stuck his foot in the rotting step on the porch and it took Maya and Yuko half an hour to get him out.

Soon after she finished working with Ruth, Maya quit spending time with the art students. Then she stopped painting. She already had enough work for her senior show. Although her paintings—a series of small oil landscapes showing unplanted fields, many of them with rocks that rose up to the surface year after year—were voted the second-best student work, she never painted again. With her graduation money from Kay and Bill, she bought a floor loom and a new sewing machine. The jackets, shawls, and vests she made were inspired by the same sadness she saw in her father's work. Dedicating herself to their modest beauty seemed like the only tribute she could pay him from far away.

Halfway to Peg's house, Maya is still talking. Eric listens quietly. Even Yuko doesn't know all the reasons Maya stopped painting and became a weaver. Maya is not sure what she wants from this sudden disclosure to a near stranger, except a form of forgiveness. Her father told her the story of Mary and Martha. When Jesus came to their house, Mary listened quietly to his words while her sister, Martha, bustled about, distracted by a hundred trivial chores. Maya wishes she had remembered that story in her senior year. Becoming a weaver was to be like Martha, who chose busywork over truth: she'd settled for second best when the most important thing was within reach.

"I wish we had met earlier," Eric says. "You're the most thoughtful person I've met in a long time."

"That can't be true. If I were really thoughtful, I wouldn't have given up so easily. I would have tried to paint like the other students who weren't afraid to show pain or ugliness. My work was pretty without any depth."

"Maybe the others were self-indulgent. Being obsessed with pain isn't the same as being brave."

"I was running away from the things in my head that scared me. I acted like a coward." I betrayed my father, Maya thinks. Her father had the courage to take up his pencil every morning and draw pictures of his thoughts. If she had learned to do that too, it would have been like stepping back into the tunnel and meeting him there. At least in her work, she would have found him waiting for her after all those years. Instead, she has chosen the comfort of weaving, the obvious beauty of fabric and beadwork. The garments she makes cover up the sadness he laid bare in his drawings and paintings. Instead of being a tribute to him, her weaving denies the things he valued most. When he showed her his favorite paintings and sculptures in the museums they visited together, he pointed to the subtle shade of blue in the background of a painting or the simple shape of the pedestal at the base of a sculpture. "That's a brilliant solution because it's not an easy answer," he said. Her life without him has been a series of easy answers. Even when she walked out on Kay, she was only making an empty gesture. If she'd cared about the truth, she would have gone back inside the restaurant and confronted her mother.

"You're not a coward," Eric says, laying his hand on her arm. "But I know about running away. I'm tired of it too. I'm so glad we met." She keeps her eyes on the road ahead. None of the snow seems to be sticking, but in the gray light she is not certain.

Eric's is the only car in front of Peg and Larry's house. Maya parks next to it on the grass. "Will you know how to get back? It's only a couple of turns to the freeway."

"Yes. I was paying attention this time. I'm going to drive up to see my mother." He takes his car keys out of his pocket but does not get out. "I want to take you out to dinner for all the trouble. Are you listed in the phone book?"

"Yes, but not under my name."

"Why? You have a pseudonym?"

"The phone number is listed under Jeff Schiller."

"Who's that?"

"My husband." Blood rushes to Maya's face. "I guess I forgot to mention him when you asked if I had family nearby."

They are silent for a few seconds.

"I'm not *related* to him like I'm related to my mother."

Eric starts laughing.

"No matter how many times I leave my mother at a restaurant, she won't stop being my mother. She and I are related whether we like each other or not. That's not how marriage works." Maya looks down at her hand. Eric is looking too. "I lost my wedding ring. Maybe I set it somewhere while I was weaving and my cat knocked it down. I decided not to get another one. I don't need a ring to remind myself that I'm married. My husband and I have our ups and downs like any other couple, but we get along for the most part."'

"You don't have to explain. I was married once to a woman I grew up with; we sat next to each other in kindergarten and her dad was my dentist. We got married right after college and moved to Vermont together, and as soon as we were settled there our marriage imploded." He shakes his head. "She lives with her parents, not far from my mother's trailer, but I haven't seen her in years. We said all the things people say about wanting to stay friends. I guess it seldom works out that way. Now I just date women who treat me badly."

"Sylvia is bad news."

"I know. I'm not stupid. We only went out twice, counting last night. Someone set us up a couple of months ago, but neither of us got in touch afterward. Then she called me at the last minute to invite me to the party."

"I thought you were desperately in love with her. She's so beautiful."

Eric shrugs. "She made me feel terrible. While I was watching her flirt with everyone else, I started thinking about all the things that are wrong with my life. I hated moving back here last fall. I'm sick of teaching kids who couldn't care less about art. I haven't been able to paint, and my father doesn't recognize me anymore. Last month, he called me Spotty—that's the name of our dog from twenty years ago, one he ended up having to shoot because he got distemper—and I had to laugh, but cry too. Now I've turned into the kind of man bad women choose to pick on. That depressed me no end. So I started drinking and couldn't remember where I lived." He stops, his face flushed. "You probably think I'm really messed up."

Maya puts her hand on the small of his back. "I don't think that at all," she says.

They sit without moving. Her gesture seems momentous—till he moves closer and puts his arms around her. It's an awkward hug, in a small car with the gear shift between them. A head taller than she is, he has to hunch down to reach her. Maya doesn't pull away. Her cheek pressed against his chest, she can hear a heartbeat and is not sure whether it's his or her own. He sighs and holds her tighter.

Finally, they pull back. "I'd better leave," Maya says. "I'm going to drive over to the store. I work in the studio upstairs. That's where I spend most of my free time."

"Can I come and see you there sometime?" he asks.

"Yes, of course." He still does not move. "Drive carefully," she says. "Don't get lost."

"I won't. I'll call."

She watches as he walks to his car, waits to hear the engine start. As she drives toward the store, she can see his car in her rearview mirror, getting smaller and disappearing.

Casper sleeps on her lap while Maya works on a beaded necklace. Every ten or fifteen minutes, she finds herself looking out the window at nothing. She hasn't called her mother in three weeks now. Kay will never telephone her. Once Maya left home for college, Kay didn't visit so they only saw each other when Maya came home. Maya couldn't stay for more than a few days at a time because Kay criticized everything she did. Months would go by before they met again, but nothing ever changed. After five minutes in the same room, they would be saying all the wrong things—the same wrong things they'd already said a thousand times. The only way they can be at peace might be not to see or talk to each other ever again.

When she finishes for the day, it's already dark. Peg and Larry are still out, so Maya has nowhere to go but home. Driving back the same way she came this morning, past endless strings of stubble fields and strip malls, she thinks everything she told Eric was absurd. She shouldn't have talked so much about the choices she made in college. When people dwell on the past, it's a sign that something is wrong right now. The regrets she feels about her father, about not becoming an artist, even about having introduced Yuko and Dan, must be distractions from the real problem she hasn't wanted to face. She and Jeff are stuck in a bad place, unable to move forward or backward, beginning to act like two animals trapped together.

Maya's downstairs neighbor at the efficiency had two cats who'd grown up together. They'd gotten along fine until a stray cat began to prowl the neighborhood and they could see him lurking beyond the screen doors. The house cats started fighting every day, scratching and biting, pulling out huge clumps of fur from each other's necks and backs. One stopped eating and chewed up his own feet, leaving bloody footprints all over the apartment. After the humane society came and trapped the stray cat, everything went back to normal for the house cats. "My husband and me," their owner told Maya one night in the laundry room they shared, "we were just like those poor cats. We hated our jobs, neither of us could stand our own parents, not to mention the other person's, and life was stressful all around. Instead of sticking together, we started tearing each other into pieces. It was ugly and sad, what we did."

Maya pictures a wild beast lurking in the dark. That's what her marriage has turned into. She and Jeff will go on hurting each other until they can get away from it and be alone. She parks her car on the street and marches into the house. Jeff is sitting in the armchair in the living room with a book. She takes her seat in the straight-backed chair near the door.

"Hi," she says. "I hope you're ready for that talk you mentioned this morning."

He puts down the book and glances up, his eyes without his reading glasses round and tired-looking. They are the eyes of someone who is easily hurt.

"I've been thinking about it all afternoon," he says quietly. "I guess I'm as ready as I'm ever going to be."

Maya grips the arms of the chair, suddenly feeling as though she were about to fall into a big black hole. She imagines herself catapulting over a large dark space. "So tell me what you thought about," she manages to ask.

"I don't know. Maybe you should go first."

The only light in the room comes from the lamp above Jeff's chair. The light angles down toward his face but leaves her in the dark. He might be too scared to talk, or he might be too angry.

"We haven't been getting along for quite a while," Maya says. "We can't go on like this."

"I agree."

"So what do you want to do about it?" she asks.

"You tell me. Do you want to do anything about it at all?" he asks back.

"I don't know." Her voice sounds frightened and unsure. This is nothing like how she planned to talk. "I don't know why I have to be the one to decide. You told me this morning that I should go and be by myself. Do you still feel that way?"

"Of course not," Jeff replies. "I spent the afternoon thinking of how much I wanted us to get along. But you apparently don't feel the same."

"I never said I didn't want to work things out."

"Listen to that double negative." He clicks his tongue. "You sound like my students when they don't want to commit to any position."

Maya takes a deep breath. The room doesn't seem to be spinning anymore. "I want us to get along too," she says.

"How do I know you really mean it?"

"You'll have to take my word for it."

Jeff begins to list all the things they could do better. They should be more considerate but give each other space, they should do more things they enjoy together, take some trips or at least plan special evenings every month.

"I think we've gotten to a really stale stage of our marriage," he concludes. "We need to pay more *attention*. We can't take each other for granted the way we've been doing."

"You think we can be happy if we do all these things?" she asks.

"It's worth a try. I was in a bad marriage before. Nancy and I brought out the worst in each other. We couldn't stop hurting each other, no matter how we tried. You and I are different. We can get along." He shrugs and doesn't elaborate.

"I have nothing to compare this to. I was never married before." I know all about bad marriages too, she wants to say. My mother had two of them while I was growing up. But the thought of her mother gives her pause. After months of avoiding Kay, Maya always visits her again, wanting to get the better of her or wanting to make amends or both, even though neither is ever likely to happen. Her marriage isn't like that at all. Jeff has never said anything to belittle her the way her mother does. He knows how to compromise and forgive.

They sit leaning back in their separate chairs. Finally, Maya says, "You're right. I should have been more considerate. I'm sorry about this morning."

"That's all right," Jeff replies. "I shouldn't have driven away in a huff."

"You don't have to apologize. I made you angry." Maya stands up and grabs her keys. "I should move my car off the street. I'll be right back."

Taking the small binoculars she keeps inside the car, Maya walks to a park down the street and stands on a low hill above the playground. In the western sky, the comet is much hazier than it used to be. Her father might have gone out to see the same comet in Japan if he'd lived. They once climbed to the roof of their house to watch a total eclipse of the moon. Through his binoculars, the disappearing moon looked like a pearl dropped into blue ink. Overhead, the sky is quiet. It's too early in the year for bats and nighthawks.

When she comes back, Jeff is already upstairs. His footsteps move from the bathroom to their bedroom and stop there. It's only nine o'clock. She fills a glass with ice cubes.

As she closes the freezer, she remembers the last fight she had with Scott, on the afternoon she'd gone to sign her lease at the efficiency. The week before, he had asked her to marry him, though for two years she'd told him she wasn't ready. "I don't want to move up north anymore," he said. "I don't want to live without you. We can get our own place in the city." She came home that afternoon and told him she planned to move. "I don't want to be the reason for you to give up your plans," she said. "You shouldn't change your life for me. I wouldn't change mine for you." Scott stood in front of the refrigerator in the kitchen, talking about how he could make her happy if she would only give him a chance. "But I'm already happy alone," she said. She was standing under the kitchen light. She felt dizzy; they hadn't eaten since breakfast. When he stopped talking for a moment, she politely asked him to step aside. "We can't go on talking like this," she said. "I'll fix something to eat." He walked away from the fridge, only to march out of the house, slamming the door behind him. Later, he said this was the moment in which he realized the hopelessness of his situation. "You have a heart of ice," he said. The calm manner in which she offered him food was more upsetting to him than anything else. He would have felt better if she had yelled at him and cried.

Maya goes to the sink and holds the glass under the faucet. The ice cubes float slowly to the top, the air bubbles inside them like the faint scars that fossils leave inside rocks. Turning off the faucet, she takes the glass and sits down at the kitchen table. Jeff must be waiting for her. If she went up now and sat next to him on the bed, she might say something she's never said before. *I married you because you knew how to leave me alone. I trusted your silence, but I don't know about love. If you want to stay with me, help me to change.* But she imagines the awkward way they might kiss and say nothing, as if they could change the years of silence by one gesture. She lifts the glass to her lips and takes a sip. The ice cubes collide against each other like planets destined for extinction.

PART TWO

— 8 —

Several miles north of the city, Maya is caught in a long line of cars creeping along the freeway. The right lane is closed, with a policeman waving everyone to the left. Behind him, a helicopter is waiting, its propellers slicing the air. The red letters on its side spell out FLIGHT FOR LIFE. The air vibrates with a low-pitched winnowing noise.

Two paramedics climb out of the ditch with someone on an orange stretcher, covered under a green army blanket. Maya holds her wheel straight and closes her eyes. When she opens them, she has only advanced a few yards. Her front bumper grazes the back bumper of the car ahead of her, but the driver is looking sideways, his head turned toward the accident. Policemen and rescue workers are gathered around a red car turned over in the ditch. Maya closes her eyes again.

Ten minutes later, the traffic is back to normal. Everyone's driving too fast, trying to make up for lost time. Inside her car, the air feels thick. Maya imagines the helicopter staggering up to the sky, the noise of the propellers drowning out anything the injured person might say.

Her father must have been alone in his last moments, surrounded only by strangers, unable to speak. Mr. Kubo, who has not answered

Maya's letter, could not have been a very close friend. "There's no real friendship in Japan," Kay used to complain. "People don't talk about their feelings. Japan is the loneliest place on earth." Kay has always been the kind of person who says the right things for the wrong reasons. With no friends or family to confide in, Minoru must have felt like that person carried up into the sky, unsteadily and noisily in an awkward machine. The people around him were of no more help than the onlookers driving by. Any thought he had about Maya would have been as fleeting as an image glimpsed behind a car window.

Jeff is waiting in the living room, dressed to play tennis.

"Sorry I'm late," Maya apologizes. "There was a lot of traffic on the freeway."

Right now, the helicopter might be approaching the rooftop of a hospital, its landing gear tilted precariously above the skyline. From its window, the buildings below would look oddly fragile. Maya has a feeling that she is looking at Jeff through a hazy screen that consists of all the things she hasn't told him. The unspoken words multiply like cobwebs in the air.

In the park down the street, no one is on the tennis courts. Maya and Jeff take the farthest one from the street and hit the ball back and forth without keeping score. It hasn't been warm enough to play since last October, but she is hitting better than usual. Even her backhand goes straight over the net. The ball makes a crisp sound on the sweet spot of her racket.

"Good job," Jeff says, when she returns his serve. Her shot, picking up the force of his, goes hard and flat over the net and reaches the baseline. "You're getting good. No surprise, of course." He is smiling. She tries to picture the tennis balls hitting the cobwebs between them, breaking and scattering them.

Maya had never played tennis before they met. "Pretend you're shaking hands with the racket," Jeff told her on the first day. "Your arm should move like a gate. It should only swing back and forth, not sideways." He pointed out two or three things she could improve rather than overwhelming her with a series of hopeless tasks. They had agreed to exchange lessons: he would teach her to play tennis and she would show him how to drive standard shift. They drove her Civic in a deserted parking lot late at night; he circled around in second gear, afraid to shift, while she laughed and laughed, giddy and a little scared. She didn't let him drive alone until he could park halfway down the steepest hill by the lake, restart the car, and drive backward up the incline without stalling. "You're a perfectionist," he said with a grin.

She watches him covering his side of the court in smooth, gliding steps, swinging the racket hard. Her daily life with him obscures the good things about him. His high school is in the poorest section of town. Every morning, all the teachers and students walk through metal detectors to enter the school building. Kids drop out and get into trouble—several of his former students have been murdered and many are in jail. Almost all the teachers he started out with have transferred to safer schools, but Jeff is determined to stay. For the last two years, he hasn't been sleeping well. He tosses and turns, pushing the pillows and the blankets aside as if they were something alive that is trying to suffocate him. When he is moving around the court, the gloom he carries with him is lifted. Maya wishes she could have given him more afternoons like this. They played tennis every week the first year of their marriage, but after that they only got out a few times each summer.

Jeff runs into the next court after the ball she hit out. He lobs it easily back to where she is standing. "People can't play by the same rules when their abilities are different," he often says about his students. "I can't expect everyone in my class to write perfect English. For some of them, I have to change the rules and not think of it as lowering my standards." He goes after her bad serves and accepts his students' mistakes because he doesn't distinguish between fairness and generosity; for him, the two are the same. "You have to forgive Dan," he told her. "You can't always explain why someone falls in love. It just happens. Dan and Meredith can't help how they feel."

Maya is not sure if she can be so kind. Like Dan, her mother claimed to be in love for the first time when she met Nate. "When I'm with him," she gushed, "I feel like we are the only people in the world. Nothing else matters." A month after Kay left, Maya visited Bill, who looked ten years older, his eyes sunk in their sockets, his hair gone gray. If this is what love does to other people, Maya thought then, love should be outlawed. She felt the same outrage when she walked into Yuko's house and saw the jagged line of black hair across her nape.

Standing behind the baseline, where Jeff has taught her to stand, Maya watches the ball come flying across the net to her left. She returns it with a good backhand. The trick is to anticipate every move by watching the ball all the way across the court. It's a matter of concentration. If people paid attention, nothing should surprise them. No one should be at the mercy of their own feelings. Even if feelings blow across the horizon, as large and unpredictable as tornadoes, people should know when to take shelter and wait out the disaster.

Maya tosses the ball for her serve and lets it drop. A big white car is parked in front of the house across the street. Whoever is in the car starts beeping the horn.

"Come on," Jeff yells, "hit the ball!"

There's another beep. Maya serves the ball into the net. Jeff takes one from his pocket and serves. They continue playing, but the noise doesn't stop. The car is to her left, beyond the other two courts and across the street. With the light shining on the window, she can't tell whether it's a man or a woman behind the wheel. No one comes out of the houses on the block. When Jeff drops a short backhand near the net, Maya lets it go and starts walking toward the car.

When she is halfway across the next court, the car door opens and the driver gets out—a woman with a mane of red hair down her back, cut in the layered style that was popular twenty years ago. She must be six feet tall. In her lacy white tank top and tight black jeans, she towers over the car as she sticks her hand in through the open door and beeps the horn again. She isn't here for the people across the street.

"Jeff!" she yells. "Jeff!"

Jeff doesn't move. The woman's car is on his forehand side. He must have seen it long before Maya did.

Maya walks back to their court and stands at the net. "Who is that? How does she know your name?"

"That's Nancy," he says, just as another beep resounds across the courts. He bounces the ball he's been holding.

"Nancy who?"

"Nancy Schiller, my ex-wife."

"But there is no Nancy Schiller. She's married to someone else in Colorado. That's what you told me."

Jeff catches the ball. His face is red. "She got divorced. When she went to court, she changed her name back to what it was when we were married. Don't ask me why."

"Why is she here?" The woman is looking at them. What she sees is Maya at the net, with her former husband staying back two feet behind the baseline, where every player should position himself to play the whole court to his advantage.

"She's living with her parents on the south side."

"How do you know?"

"She came to see me last week at school."

"You didn't say." The woman is shouting louder now. "But I guess it's none of my business."

Jeff says something Maya can't hear.

"What?"

He lobs the ball at her. She remains standing.

"Come on. Step back from the net."

"I can't play like this."

Taking another ball from his pocket, Jeff turns abruptly to the side and hits it against the practice board on the fence. Nancy is still screaming, but he doesn't miss. He keeps hitting the ball for a long time. Finally, he reaches too late with a backhand; the ball bounces and rolls away. He stops, breathing hard.

"You'd better go talk to her." Maya hasn't moved from her place near the net. "You can't let her go on like this."

Walking toward the fence, Jeff retrieves a ball Maya hit earlier and turns back to the practice board. The ball thumps against the board and rattles the metal fence. These noises are punctuated by the beep of the car horn and Nancy's voice, yelling out "Jeff!" The result is like a crazy rap song. Maybe marriage is a demented duet. Jeff and Nancy remind Maya of old married actors who make one final comeback together in made-for-TV movies and magazine ads. If Jeff were not her husband, she would put her arm around his shoulder and lead him to the street where Nancy is waiting. She would say, "Talk to your wife. She's desperate for your attention."

Only Nancy doesn't need Maya's help. She has reached into her car and dragged out one of the floor mats—a black rubber square that looks oddly like a flag. Holding it over her head with both her hands, she starts waving it back and forth, still calling Jeff's name. She is like someone waving for help from a scene of disaster, using burnt clothing, seat cushions, whatever she has available. Maya imagines Nancy's red hair going up in flames, turning into jagged tongues of fire. Nancy continues to scream. "Jeff! Get over here. Jeff! We need to talk!" Her voice is beginning to crack.

"Listen to her," Maya shouts across the court. "Will you please go talk to her?"

Jeff keeps hitting the ball. He is just as grimly determined as Nancy is. He must have had years of practice at tuning her out: every time they fought, Nancy must have screamed and thrown things while Jeff stood silent, refusing to acknowledge her anger. Their bouts might have resembled the childhood game Maya used to play: rock, scissors, paper. Only, in this version, the rock will get scratched as it crushes the scissors; the paper can cover the rock but it will tear; in the middle of slicing the paper, the scissors will snap in two.

Leaving the park from the other gate, away from the street, Maya walks around the neighborhood, tracing a big square that ends at her back door. She runs upstairs to the spare bedroom, whose windows face the park. Through the blinds, she can see Nancy's car on the street. Jeff comes trudging across the courts. While the two talk next to the car, Nancy lets the floor mat dangle from her hand, a flag at half mast. Jeff fidgets, moving the racket from one hand to the other. Finally, he goes around to the passenger side and gets in. Nancy puts the floor mat down and takes her seat behind the wheel. The car pulls away from the curb, passes the house, and disappears around the corner.

Going to the bedroom closet for her clothes and then to the shower, Maya is retracing Nancy's footsteps from years ago, connecting the same invisible dots between the same rooms. In the shower, she is standing exactly where Nancy must have stood under the stream of hot water. Once, when Maya had just moved in, she found a long strand of reddish blond hair in the flour bin. Faded and brittle, it had been lying dormant, as moths do. The larvae of grain-eating moths are invisible as you scoop the flour into a bag at the grocery store; six months later, when you find them, the moths are already full grown and winged. A frenzy of tiny brown fans in a miniature whiteout, they demand to be set free.

The security door, which is broken, is open. Maya runs up the stairs and knocks. When Yuko opens the door, the music sounds louder. Yuko puts her hand on Maya's shoulder and pulls her into the doorway. "Hey, how are you doing? Everything okay?"

"Not really."

"I didn't think so. You look upset. You want to talk about it?"

"Later."

Yuko nods. "Let's go to the kitchen. I was making dinner." Over her old cutoffs and a T-shirt from the health food store, Yuko is wearing the tie-dyed apron Maya made her last summer. It has swirls of yellow, orange, and green on a deep blue background. "I was doing some serious cutting. You can help me with it."

"All right."

In the kitchen, Yuko has a cookbook open on the counter, its spine weighted down with a green coffee cup they had when they lived in the dorm together. The cup looks like the trunk of a bamboo tree. The cookbook is the kind that has cheerful pictures on every page. Humpty-Dumpty sits on top of the ingredients list, surrounded by green peppers, carrots, onions, celery, and garlic, all with spindly arms and legs. "Here, you can start with these." Yuko hands Maya a knife and two green peppers. She opens the fridge and takes out a carton of eggs.

Maya slices the peppers in half. Yuko cracks four eggs into a white bowl and whistles. "Look at these." She holds the bowl toward Maya. Eight yellow yolks stare back at them, connected two by two with almost invisible membranes. They look like small planets spinning in tandem. "Twins, each one of them," Yuko says.

"Yeah, like all chickens don't look exactly the same anyway."

"But I never saw anything like this before. Did you?"

Maya shakes her head.

"Do you think it's safe to eat them?"

"Of course."

Yuko pokes the eggs with her fork and begins to stir them. "How can chickens tell their chicks apart?"

"I don't know. Are you trying to tell me a joke?"

"No. I really want to know. You're right. They all look the same."

"Maybe not to themselves."

Yuko laughs. "Yeah, for all we know, they go around wishing their beaks were as long as the next chicken's or their necks were as plump." She puts the bowl aside, takes a couple of garlic cloves, and whacks them with the flat of her knife. The skins fall away, curled like shed chrysalides.

Jeff and Nancy are driving somewhere in the city, but they seem so far away. Maya dices the peppers and then the onions. The music playing on the stereo drifts into the kitchen—a new compilation of old James Taylor songs. Back in high school, Maya and Yuko had a business: they baked and decorated cakes. They had an ad in the yellow pages and were written up in the *Star-Tribune* when the paper did a feature about young people. JUST DESSERTS: CAKES FOR SPECIAL OCCASIONS their business was called. The best cake they made was a large sheet cake for a garden party. Maya—who did all the detail work while Yuko took charge of the mixing—photographed the woman's flower beds so the cake could be a miniature of her garden. They worked in Yuko's mother's kitchen, laughing and talking, listening to the stereo. They must have cracked a thousand eggs in those years. Maya wishes she had painted two young girls in a sunny kitchen surrounded by eggshells broken perfectly in two, the matching halves turning into a pair of wings.

"Nancy sounds like a real piece of work," Yuko says, when Maya tells her what happened. "You should be careful. She might be dangerous."

"I'm sure she's just eccentric. She had a big shag haircut, like the seventies."

Yuko rolls her eyes. "Jeff should have warned you about her being in town. Then you wouldn't have had to find out in such an awful, bizarre way. You'd have been less upset."

"He must have thought she'd only see him that one time. I wouldn't have to know about it then."

"Oh, come on. He was married to this woman for a long time. He should have known how crazy she was. She's not the type of person who gives up and goes away. She sounds like a stalker."

"Maybe I shouldn't have left him with her and walked away."

"Don't say that. You have to look out for yourself. It's stupid of Jeff to get into a car with someone who is screaming and carrying on, but there's nothing you can do about it."

Maya looks into her bamboo-shaped coffee mug. When they first met, she had liked Jeff for not sounding bitter about his first marriage. Though he admitted he and Nancy had been unhappy, he remained respectfully vague: he didn't talk about her faults or dwell on self-pity. Maya assumed that his marriage had ended as well as a marriage could end, but all along, the opposite had been true: Jeff and Nancy had never stopped fighting. Even though she was clear across the street and he was pretending to ignore her, he was aware of every move she made, every inflection of her voice. Nancy knew she had his attention; otherwise she would have gotten back in the car and driven away alone. They were picking up where they left off six years ago. Twenty years from now, they'll still be fighting, unable to leave each other alone. When Jeff said that love can't be explained, he must have been speaking from experience. Maya calls home, but no one is there.

Finally, at nine, he answers the phone.

"Hi, I'm at Yuko's. I called earlier but you were gone."

He doesn't say where he has been. "How could you just walk away from me?" he asks instead.

Maya doesn't answer.

"Imagine how you would feel if an old boyfriend of yours came looking for you, and I left you to face him alone—actually turned my back and walked away like I wasn't even your husband."

"I don't have an old boyfriend who'd wave his floor mat around to get my attention. But if I did, I would expect to deal with him myself. It's not your job to protect me."

"You sure think it's Yuko's job to protect you from all kinds of things."

"That's different. I grew up with her."

"Why don't you stay with her then? Don't even come back."

"Fine. Good night." Maya hangs up the phone and walks out of the living room.

Yuko is up on the roof, smoking a cigarette and looking at the comet.

"Jeff told me not to come home."

"Are you kidding?" Yuko squashes her cigarette. "What an asshole."

"I should have waited for him. He was upset that I walked away."

"He has no right to be upset. He can't expect you to wait and worry while he drives around with his psycho ex-wife. That's totally unfair and selfish."

To Maya, it isn't so simple; not everyone wants to be alone at a bad time. Still, she is glad to have Yuko take her side so completely. Maya used to tell Jeff when she felt hurt by her mother, her customers, or a bunch of kids screaming at her out a car window, but Jeff always pointed out how she might have provoked their anger and listed the things she should have done or said to defend herself. He would speculate about how the other person might have been justified in lashing out at her. "I'm just trying to be fair," he'd say. "You weren't necessarily blameless." Maya stopped telling him anything because she found herself changing parts of her story to avoid his criticism. Her own conduct had to be impeccable before she could win his sympathy. She can tell Yuko the whole truth about any situation because Yuko will be angry on her behalf no matter what. "That's awful," she will say. "People can be so mean. Are you all right?"

Yuko points to the sky. "The comet looks different," she says. "It's not as bright."

"No, it's not. We probably won't be able to see it in a couple of days. It could be hundreds of years before another one comes along."

"Great. I can tell everyone I got divorced in the year of the comet."

"I might be saying that too."

Yuko steps closer and hugs Maya. "It'll be okay," she says. "Jeff might be confused right now because everything happened so suddenly. If he doesn't change, though, you'll be all right without him. You don't have to be with a guy who can't stand up to his ex-wife. You deserve better than that. Jeff should get his act together real soon."

"Maybe he's doing his best."

Yuko makes a faint hissing sound between her teeth. "That's not good enough," she says. "You don't have to wait around. We left for college together. This is another version of the same thing. Moving on, being on our own." Yuko tilts her head and smiles. "I'm not saying you have to leave, but if it happens, we'll do some kind of a ritual. A ritual of moving on together."

"That sounds good."

The summer they left Minneapolis, Yuko drove the Barracuda with all of her and Maya's belongings. With no room left for a passenger, Maya had to take the Greyhound bus the next day. When she arrived in Milwaukee, Yuko was waiting at the terminal. They ran screaming to each other, embraced, and cried. The waiting area was crowded with families with children whose clothes looked as if they hadn't been changed in days. Outside, men and women were panhandling on the sidewalk. They were all floating through life, managing at least to get by. She and Yuko were free to do whatever they wanted to do for the first time.

Before that day, there were years when Maya thought she could never leave her mother's house. Time moved so slowly when she and Yuko were children, every season or school year stretching almost forever. Now, each year adds only a fraction to the decades they've already lived. Climbing down the ladder to the back porch, Maya remembers the black ladder Georgia O'Keeffe painted in the middle of a desert landscape—a ladder to the sky. She pictures the women standing around the fire pit on summer solstice. Few if any of those women will now be with the men they cast their love spells for. Perhaps what counts is not the wish for love but the ritual itself—the coming together of women, the need for courage. As Yuko steps into the hallway and holds the door open, Maya imagines following her into a new life.

— 9 —

Yuko is sitting on her futon with a cup of coffee and a cigarette. The clothes she wears to work—jeans and a jean jacket, a green bandanna wrapped around her head—remind Maya of college. Maya crawls out of the sleeping bag on the floor. Her mother's cypress-wood dresser is against the wall. The books Yuko had in the dorm seventeen years ago are on the shelves next to the dresser. Maya feels as though she and Yuko are trapped in some strange nightmare—the kind in which all the people from the different periods of their lives are mixed together in a crowded house and no one is happy.

"Did you sleep all right?" Yuko asks.

Maya nods.

Yuko places a key ring on the orange crate she's been using as a coffee table. "This is for you. You know you can come here any time."

"I don't know what I'm going to do."

Yuko puts out her cigarette and walks over to Maya. They sit side by side on the sleeping bag without speaking.

"You don't have to rush into anything," Yuko says finally. "What I was saying last night about moving on together—I don't want you to feel pressured by it. I've never been a big fan of Jeff's, that's true. But who you're married to makes no difference to me. If you and Jeff work things out, you shouldn't feel like you've let me down. I'm sorry if I came across like I wanted you to leave him."

Maya puts her arms around Yuko. "Don't worry about it. I don't feel pressured."

"I just don't want you to get hurt."

"I know. I'll be all right."

After Yuko leaves, Maya gets back inside the sleeping bag and closes her eyes. Down the street in every direction, cars are starting. Some of them start up smooth and easy; others sputter and cough. It's been a long time since she heard so many people leaving for work all at once. Her neighborhood is mostly duplexes and single-family houses. The noise she is hearing now, in this neighborhood of old brownstones, is oddly communal: so many people—unrelated and unfamiliar to one another—doing the same thing at the same time. There are many ways she can be alone and not alone.

Maya heads home at nine, an hour after Jeff goes to work every day. He might have left her a note on the kitchen table. *It's impossible to work out our differences. Don't come back.* Or, *I'm sorry, let's talk.* Perhaps tonight they will sit in the living room after work in their usual spots: Jeff in his armchair under the light, Maya in the straight-backed chair near the door. Once, Yuko's brothers made flash cards with all the things their parents said to admonish them: THINGS HAVE TO CHANGE. EVERYONE MUST BE MORE CONSIDERATE. WE'RE TALKING ABOUT RESPONSIBILITY HERE. They laid the cards on the table before their father came home to give them a talking-to. Maya could boil down her talks with Jeff to three or four sentences too, but unlike George Nakashima, Jeff won't laugh.

Turning the corner onto her street, Maya sees two cars in the driveway. The big white car from yesterday is parked behind Jeff's station wagon. She drives past her house, trying not to slow down or look. At the end of the block, she takes a side street to the freeway.

Several boxes of Nancy's clothes and books are still in the attic. She could have come to get them, and Jeff might have stayed home from work to help her. But she could have been there all night, too. If Mrs. Nordstrom were still living next door, Maya could find out the truth. As they sat sipping tea under Mrs. Nordstrom's wedding pictures and her silver spoons from around the world mounted on the wall, the old woman would whisper, "I know it's none of my business, but I want to tell you something." Mrs. Nordstrom had told Maya that Nancy had been gone almost every weekend for years before she finally moved out. On Friday afternoons, Mrs. Nordstrom would look out the window and see Nancy loading the station wagon with her canoe and mountain-climbing equipment; by five she was off, leaving Jeff alone and carless the entire weekend.

On the freeway, a blue pickup truck passes Maya's car and pulls back only a few feet in front. When Maya taps her horn, the driver slows down deliberately. She steps on the gas, swerves around the truck, and gets back into the lane. In the rearview mirror, she can see the driver shaking his fist at her, a young man with a crew cut. He looks like he might be nineteen or twenty. Beeping his horn, he speeds up and passes her again. He sticks up his middle finger in the side window. As soon as he's back in her lane, Maya speeds up and zooms into the left lane. For a while, they keep passing each other with less room between the bumpers each time. Finally, he pumps his brakes just as he pulls in front of her, forcing her to slam on hers. Her tires squeal and the seat belt tightens around her shoulder. She remembers the accident from yesterday. She's lucky not to skid into the ditch and roll over like that red car. When she doesn't pass him again, the driver leans on his horn and takes off, going ninety miles an hour.

Maya's hands are shaking. She has never acted like this before. During cross-country races in high school, runners often made a move in order to pass each other in the last quarter mile. They went all out, breathing with their mouths open, sounding as though thousands of dying birds were beating their wings inside their chest. When someone was gaining on her, Maya could always tell because of that noise. She pictured her opponent falling down on the gravel path from exhaustion, clutching her chest in pain, strangled by her own breathing. Let her win, Maya thought then, already backing off. It was just a race. She never wanted to beat anyone that much. Easing off her pace, she would let the other runner pass, staying several steps behind her until they crossed the finish line. As she stood in the chute with the girl who beat her but was now doubled over in pain, Maya had enough breath left to extend her hand and say, "Good race. Nice finish."

All through the season, Maya came in second or third. "You are a first-rate runner with a second-rate attitude," her coach scolded. If she and Nancy were in the last leg of a five-kilometer race, Nancy would have the same determined grimace on her face that she had yesterday. She'd be the kind of runner who went all out in every race, breathing short, painful mouthfuls of air like knife-points stabbing her heart. Maya would have to back off and let her win. If she didn't, they would both collapse before they got to the finish line. Only a crazy person thinks that winning is everything. Standing in the chute among runners bent over with pain, Maya used to enjoy the extra breath she had held back. It felt solid and good, like a perfect square of ice she could press against her face on a hot day.

The store is quiet all morning. When the door swings open at noon and Eric walks in, Casper is taken by surprise. He leaps from Maya's lap onto the cash register and then to the highest shelf, where he hides inside a large grapevine basket.

"My cat doesn't like anyone except me."

"I'll ignore him." Eric turns his back to the shelf. His black T-shirt has tiny holes like pinpricks on the sleeves. Maya had shirts full of holes and paint splashes when she was an art student. His shirt makes her nostalgic for that time and also for junior high school. In eighth grade, Maya and Yuko made needle holes on an old black umbrella in the patterns of winter constellations. On nights when it was too cold to go outside, they held the umbrella under the light to see the stars. Their constellations weren't placed in the right order; they got confused about which way to turn the umbrella while they pricked the holes, following the star chart in their science book. The result was their own unique galaxy, with constellations rearranged.

"How have you been?" Eric asks, leaning over the counter toward her. "That's beautiful." He points to the necklace of fans she has been making.

"Thanks."

"I was away. My father was sick, so I stayed with my mother for a week."

"Is he better?"

"I think so. He only had a cold, but he's pretty sick to begin with. He has a bad heart and his arteries are clogged. It's hard for my mother."

"Yes, it must be."

Eric looks into her eyes. "I called you from my mother's house. I hung up when your husband answered. I don't know why I did that."

"Hanging up or calling?"

"Both."

"You could have asked for me."

"Your husband wouldn't have been upset?"

"I don't know. I've never had a phone call from someone he doesn't know."

"If I were him, I'd be jealous if a strange man called you." He pauses. "I dreamed about you last night."

"What was I doing in your dream?"

He glances down for a moment. "We were on a dock. It looked like a combination of a few places I know—a dock near my hometown where you can take a ferry to Michigan, another place I know in Maine, and a dock in Door County near my ex-in-laws' cottage. Anyway, this dock was deserted and the two of us were sitting alone on a bench. I knew we had missed the last ferry, but I didn't want to tell you because I wanted to keep sitting there with you."

Maya doesn't speak for a long time. It's as if she too were in that dream, sitting on the bench with him as the waves kept rolling in. The movement of the water around the earth is lonely and constant. The waves surge endlessly to touch the shore, though each touch is brief. If Eric were like her father, he would have sat at the kitchen table in the morning and drawn pictures of the water, the wind in the distance, two people sitting on the bench.

"Do you get off for lunch?" he asks. "I would love to sit down with you and talk some more."

"I can close for an hour and leave a note on the door."

At the coffee shop near the freeway, they are seated at the table by the window. In the parking lot across the street, suburban women are getting out of their vans and walking to the boutiques or the bookstores in a strip mall. Fifteen years ago, there was nothing but cornfields and farmhouses, a gas station, and a general store in the middle of nowhere. Eric stares out the window. He must hate being back here, two hours from his father in the nursing home, his mother living in a trailer like someone waiting in a temporary shelter for a rescue team.

"At least it's beautiful out today," Maya says. People who leave their past in a foreign country can choose any new life. Maya wonders how she ended up being the kind of person who is always ready with an insipid remark about the weather.

"Wisconsin is a beautiful place," Eric agrees. "I wish I could be happier here. Every time my father gets sick, though, I can't help wishing for the end. I can say I hate to see him suffer or it'll be better for my mother, but the truth is, I want to be free."

"Maybe you should just move back east. It's no good being unhappy."

He smiles. "Are you trying to get rid of me?"

"No." She feels her face flush. "I think your parents wouldn't want you to be unhappy."

"My father is too far gone to know the difference. My mother would forgive me if I left. Last night as I was leaving, she told me she could manage alone. I was standing outside, putting my backpack in the trunk. That's how we are in our family. We can't tell each other anything important unless one of us is getting ready to leave. Otherwise, we're too embarrassed to talk."

"Whatever she told you then, she must really mean it. People don't tell you lies when you're leaving." On the day Maya left, her father didn't pretend that they might meet again or hear from each other. "You'll be better off with your mother," he had said. "It's all right if you have to forget about me. I want you to be happy."

"It's too late to do anything for this fall," Eric says, "but I did start thinking about January, or next fall at the latest. I'll probably go back by then, regardless of how things are with my father."

"That's good."

"You won't miss me?"

"We just met."

"So?"

"It's not a good question for you to ask me." Three gulls have landed on the far side of the parking lot to pick at some scraps. Maya watches them. When she turns back, the waitress is approaching their table. She puts down the plates, reversed.

"The other way," Maya tells her.

"I'm sorry."

"It's all right." Maya asks for more coffee so the waitress will come back. Something is happening here that calls for caution. Though the coffee shop is full of people, she and Eric are caught in a small space of silence as if they were on the edge of rapidly changing weather. The light feels too bright and the air is suddenly thin. Maya tries to talk, but then feels as though she were stranded in a rainstorm, struggling to start her car to drive out of danger. She keeps talking, trying to get somewhere. She tells him how she used to waitress at a coffee shop on the east side. He listens, his eyes narrowed in concentration even though she isn't saying anything important.

"After I graduated, it was depressing not to have a real job. My mother expected me to move back home and work at an advertising agency. My boyfriend wanted to get married and move to northern Wisconsin, where he could teach in a one-room country school. I kept waitressing and making clothes because I didn't know what else to do. Then in September I met Peg."

She describes the afternoon Peg came to the coffee shop to have lunch with a friend. She had just quit her job as a nurse to start her business. Peg noticed the woven linen blouse Maya was wearing and asked her where she had bought it. "I made it myself," Maya said. "See the clay buttons? I baked them in a toaster oven. They're a little lopsided." Peg offered Maya a job at the boutique, which was under construction.

"I still have that blouse," Maya tells Eric. "I wear it now and then for good luck."

"I saved some of the paintings from my admission application for an MFA. They're nothing special, but they got me out of Wisconsin to go to art school. It was the first time I left home. I was already twenty-two."

"You lived at home till then?"

"I commuted forty miles to the university extension in Green Bay. I had to stay on the farm to help my father because my brother and sister had already moved out. When I left, one of my cousins was old enough to take my place for a while, but I knew that my parents would eventually have to sell the farm. I felt terrible, though I had no interest in farming. In fourth grade, my best friend Lee Hansen raised a pig that won a ribbon at the state fair. I didn't know the pig was going to be auctioned off to be made into sausages. Lee went on to win all kinds of Four-H awards, but I was devastated. I cried all afternoon." He shrugs. "I was a softhearted kid—my father wanted my brother and me to be tough, but we were both timid and studious."

As a young boy, Eric would have had the same direct gaze. His left cheek would have dimpled when he smiled, making his slightly crooked teeth look endearing. They're not so crooked that a farm family out in the country would send him to an orthodontist. She wonders what it would have been like to grow up on a farm, with a father who didn't care how you did at school. It must have felt so lonely.

"I thought about you every day when I was at my mother's," Eric says. "I started wishing that we'd met earlier."

"It's never too late to make new friends. I'm thirty-five. I still have half my life left."

"More than half, I hope. I'm a year older than you."

"My father was sixty when he died." She tries to smile. "But maybe my mother will live to be a hundred. She might come from hardy stock. I don't know." Kay used to get letters from her sister a couple of times a year, but she never mentioned what they said. As far as Maya knows, her mother hasn't seen her family since she left Osaka.

When the waitress returns, Eric reaches for the check. "This is my treat."

"Only if you'll let me treat next time."

"Good. That means you'll have lunch with me again."

Back at the store, Maya's car is the only one out front. During the week, Peg stops by in the late afternoon to pick up the mail and to chat. She keeps the books and runs errands for Larry's construction business.

Eric turns off his engine. "After we talked last time, I wanted to do some work. This morning I was setting up the studio the university gave me. I'm going back there now."

"You must be in that old warehouse building on the lower east side."

"Did you go there when you were a student?"

"Yes. Ruth—the professor I worked for—had a studio there too. I learned to weave in that building. I lived down the block."

"That makes me feel good about going back, knowing you were there once."

Maya doesn't answer.

"When I was visiting my mother," he continues, "I found some black-and-white photographs she took in her early twenties. Like my father, she grew up on a farm, but she wanted to be a photographer. Her family wouldn't let her go to college or move to the city. So she got married, and pretty soon the only photographs she took were of us kids. But these photographs I found—they're mostly of the places near her parents' farm and of her relatives—they were good. I want to do some paintings based on them."

"That must make her happy."

"She was a little shy about it, actually. In a couple of weeks, when I get something done, I want you to see it. You really inspired me. If we hadn't met, I'd still be sitting at home feeling sorry for myself."

"No, you wouldn't, but I'd love to see what you do."

"You don't mind my stopping here again? I feel a little strange about calling you at home."

Maya remembers the white car parked in her driveway. She hasn't thought of Jeff and Nancy in the last hour.

Eric turns away from her abruptly and stares straight ahead. "I don't know what to do. I can't stop thinking about you." He doesn't say anything more.

They are sitting only inches apart. If she reached out her hand, she could touch his shoulder; her fingers would connect the tiny holes on his black T-shirt the way the lines in her schoolbooks connected the stars in the same constellation. Maya imagines herself in the shaky cabin of a helicopter rising up to the sky. From the windows, the ground below would look heartbreakingly familiar. If she were up in that helicopter, she would not want to stay airborne in search of help that would most likely come too late. She would rather fall through space and meet her disaster head-on. Then she remembers Nancy screaming Jeff's name. Two disasters can never cancel each other out.

"You'll feel differently in a while," she tells Eric.

He looks into her eyes and asks, "Do you really think that?"

"It doesn't matter what I think. You can't talk this way." As she turns to open the car door, he clasps her other hand and draws her toward him. His fingers are cold. "Good-bye," she says, opening the door and pulling away. "I do want to see you again, but not like this."

He waits in his car while she walks away. At the door, she waves without looking back.

Jeff is sitting in the armchair, reading a book. He gets up and meets her in the middle of the room. "I shouldn't have told you not to come home. I was way out of line. I called you at the store around noon to apologize, but you were gone."

"I went out for lunch," she says. Her voice catches and sounds strange even to herself.

He puts his arms around her and hugs her. "I shouldn't have been so angry on the phone."

She rests her forehead against his chest. "So what's up with Nancy?" she asks, after a while.

"Nancy shouldn't make any difference to us."

"That's not what she thinks. She wants you back."

"How do you know?"

"Come on, the whole neighborhood knows." Maya pictures Nancy's car in the driveway. But she says instead, "She was screaming your name yesterday for at least twenty minutes."

"Let's sit down." Jeff takes her hand and leads her to the couch. "You're right. Nancy asked me if we could be married again. But I said no. I'm married to you now. I went to her parents' house with her last night because I didn't want to hurt her feelings. But I also went because I was mad at you for walking away." He pauses but doesn't say anything about this morning. "Nancy has a four-year-old daughter. She came back to Milwaukee so her parents could help raise her. She's in a very bad spot. She feels like she's a total failure and no one cares about her except her parents. If it cheers her up, I wouldn't mind seeing her now and then as a friend. But I need to talk to you about it first."

"Why? I can't help you with your problems with Nancy." Maya can't keep her voice from sounding cold. Right this moment, she could be at an important turning point where every word she says could change the direction of her life. If she says the right things, she and Jeff could go back to the way they were in the first year of their marriage; or they could spare themselves years of unhappiness by parting now. It's like landing on those squares in a childhood board game, where a ladder extends with an instruction: "Go back to the beginning" or "Skip forward to the next turn." Only she doesn't know in which direction the game is played. Is it better to go back to the beginning or to skip forward, to go up a new ladder or slide down an old one? "I don't know what you want me to do," she tells Jeff.

"Nancy and I parted badly. I was tempted to avoid her, but I can't. She's going to be living twenty minutes away. It's probably healthier for us to get together now and then to talk."

"Well, then you should," Maya says.

Jeff leans down and peers into her face. "I want you to understand. Nancy and I never had a chance to discuss the things that went wrong between us. We were miserable for years and then she left me suddenly. It would be good for us to talk so we can forgive each other. Every time we tried to talk before, we ended up having a big fight."

"Like at the tennis court yesterday."

Jeff frowns. "It's going to take us some time to change."

"I don't understand why you want to spend time with someone who screams at you."

"It isn't all her fault. She gets upset with me and then she gets even more upset with herself. Then I make things worse by trying to ignore her. I can't just blame her. I did some wrong things, too." He sighs. "Look. I once thought I was going to spend the rest of my life with her. Just because things didn't work out, I can't turn my back on her when she needs a friend."

"If you feel so strongly about it, why even ask me?"

He takes her by the shoulders. "I'm asking because I don't want to hurt you. If it really bothers you, I won't speak to her ever again."

"It shouldn't be up to me."

"But it is. I'm married to you, not to her."

Maya sighs. "I can't tell you not to see someone from your past."

"I'm glad you feel that way," he says. "If you didn't, it would be like me asking you to give up seeing Yuko."

I would leave you in a second if you did, Maya thinks. She says, "One condition."

"What's that?"

"Don't come home and tell me what the two of you did, where you went, and what you talked about."

"Why not? I don't have anything to hide. I was going to tell you everything she and I talked about last night."

"I don't want to know."

"Aren't you curious?"

"Maybe I am, but I don't think you can really tell me everything. There might be things you won't tell me because you think they're not important, but then I'll find out and be upset. It's better if we agree to say nothing in the first place. Otherwise, no matter how honest you intend to be, there'll always be something you skip over."

Jeff doesn't respond.

"Your problem with Nancy is none of my business," Maya adds. "You can't expect any help from me, but you don't owe me any explanations. I trust you to do the right thing."

Jeff pulls her closer. "I appreciate your trust, then. I won't take it for granted."

Her face buried in his shoulder, Maya closes her eyes tight. The jagged edges of yellow light inside her eyelids remind her of fire. Nancy is waving her flag of despair while a helicopter approaches above. Far away, Maya's father continues to paint inside a burning building. Maya pictures Yuko taking the scissors to her long black hair, Dan picking up his own plate and placing it in front of Meredith like an offering, herself and Eric sitting in his car this afternoon. Maybe everyone is on the brink of some disaster, but Maya doesn't want to think about it. She tries to put aside the feelings of doom she's had since yesterday afternoon, when Nancy stepped out of her big white car and started calling Jeff's name. With caution, she and Jeff can steer their way out of this bad stretch. All they have to do is keep looking ahead. It's all right to ignore everything that falls by the way-side—they're other people's disasters. Her father gave her a single image, like a prophet's dream, to take her into the future. Sometimes there is only one way to move ahead: don't look back, don't glance to the side, just keep going forward regardless of what you see out the corner of your eye.

— 10 —

Kay's house in Minneapolis had been built during the Great Depression. In the basement, there were three windowless rooms that must have been intended for storing root vegetables and canned goods. Later, the people who owned the house during the Cold War might have stocked these rooms with bottled water and hermetically sealed food and prepared them as fallout shelters. By the time Bill and Kay bought the house, people had stopped believing they could survive a nuclear holocaust by holing up in the basement, though at school during bomb drills, Maya was instructed to crawl under her desk and cover her eyes so the nuclear flash would not burn out her retina. Kay and Bill had nothing to store in the basement except a few cans of insecticide.

For her time-outs, Maya was sent to the smallest of the three rooms behind the furnace. The punishment could come at any time. If she waited too long to answer a question or spoke too soon, too loudly, or too softly, her mother's arm would come flying toward her and her strong, cold fingers would latch on to Maya's wrist. Bill would mutter, "Take it easy," "Everyone calm down," or "Let's slow things down a minute." Paying no attention to him, Kay would drag Maya down the stairs. As Kay yelled and yanked Maya's arm, Maya stayed absolutely quiet and concentrated on her steps. If she dawdled and caused her mother to stumble, they would fall headfirst on the concrete floor, her wrist still clutched in Kay's grip.

In the basement, Kay threw Maya into the room and locked the door from the outside. Her steps punched up the staircase, swept across the kitchen, and became muffled once she reached the living room. Sometimes, Maya could hear Bill and Kay arguing. She waited until all was quiet before sitting down on the floor. Kay had taken the bulb out of the overhead light, but Maya wasn't afraid of the dark. The running watch Yuko gave her on her eleventh birthday had a yellow light she could turn on by pushing a button. If she knew telepathy, she could flash the circle of light on and off around her wrist and send a message to Yuko. Down the street in the Nakashimas' house, Yuko would sense Maya's words without having to take her eyes off her homework or a game of Monopoly she was playing with her brothers.

Even without telepathy, the watch helped Maya pass the time. She would pick a color and try to think of as many things in that color as she could in three minutes. Or she would give herself ten minutes to remember the names of all the cities and rivers she saw in Japan, the painters and the sculptors her father had liked, the food he used to cook. She made a list of the third-grade students in her class in Osaka, the neighbors on their block. She could walk from house to house in her mind or stand next to each row of desks in the classroom and see who sat where. Only the same kids would not be at the same desks anymore, and the old men and women who walked with canes might have gone to live with their children in another city. Nothing stayed the same, in Osaka or anywhere else. Every semester in her geography class, there were new countries added to the world atlas.

The Zen masters in her father's stories were always trying to teach the same lessons to the young warriors who studied with them: *Be patient, because everything changes in time.* The truly enlightened people were quiet. The most revered masters, who meditated every day, could slow down their heartbeats until they only had to breathe once every five or ten minutes. Sitting perfectly still in the lotus position, their hearts scarcely beating, they had dreams of beauty and peace. Maya counted her pulse as she sat with her legs folded. Her heart beat slow and steady. By taking deep, even breaths, she could make her pulse go down from sixty to fifty-five, fifty-two, fifty-one. But no matter how she tried, she could never make it slower than fifty. Forty-nine was the magic number. The day her pulse matched that number, she might be granted an important wish. Her mother would decide that she and Bill would be happier if Maya wasn't around. They would give her money to live wherever she wanted to for the rest of her life. Maya didn't know where that would be, except that she would have a beautiful house, and Yuko and other friends would visit her there. By the time she was so enlightened that she could stop her own heartbeat, finding a place to live would be easy.

In an hour, maybe two, her mother came downstairs and opened the door. Her face streaked with tears, Kay would whisper, "I'm sorry this is so difficult for both of us. We have to try harder to get along. You and I—we have only each other." Maya let herself be hugged because, if she didn't, they would have to start over from the beginning, with her mother screaming and carrying on again. Some afternoons at school, Mr. Lloyd, the choir director, made the class practice the same passage over and over, each time sounding worse. As they walked home, Yuko would mutter, "It's useless to go over that stuff. The only way we're going to sound better is if we got rid of Tracy Hoagland, Mary Lou Price, and half the tenor section." With Kay's arms clasped around her shoulders, Maya felt as though she were being strangled. If she didn't stay quiet, they would be just like a choir doomed to repeat the same terrible noise over and over because it had all the wrong people. While Kay went on about how they had no one except each other, Maya imagined being alone in a beautiful house by the sea.

On her drive down to Evanston, Maya keeps thinking about that basement. As she sat in the dark, trying to imagine a perfect home where she would be happy, she did not dream of being allowed to go back to Osaka to live with her father. When she made up the house in which she would live alone, she pictured Yuko, Yuko's family, and several other friends visiting her. The house would have a white patio overlooking the sea, surrounded by flowers and tropical birds. Maya and her guests would have dinner, listen to music, dance, laugh, and talk. But her father never appeared in the house of her daydreams. Even there, she had to find explanations about why she didn't have to invite her mother. She didn't imagine that she would magically turn out to be someone else's daughter or that her father would show up one day to take her home. In a few years, she stopped making any pictures in her mind about the future that included her father. The letters he sent back unopened were like leaves falling off the trees in autumn. They were unmistakable signs that any reunion Maya imagined was as false as the feeling people get on a warm day in September that just this year, summer might not end.

The Romantics were wrong: Imagination is as doomed to failure as any human faculty. The year Maya worked as art editor of a college magazine, her friend Lori submitted a story about a girl who had a summer job in a factory. "The story is based on my summer job," Lori explained. "Only, in the story, the smart and good-looking machinist falls in love with the character based on me. He keeps hurting her, though, because he resents her for being a college girl. In real life, I had a big crush on a machinist who took no notice of me. His indifference made me miserable all summer. The story is my fantasy." Lori laughed when she said that. She had a self-deprecating sense of humor Maya admired. But even in a story in which she could have made anything happen, Lori could not imagine a nice guy falling in love with her stand-in. Some things are so bad, and their badness so deeply etched in a person's memory, even imagination cannot alter the facts.

Just as Lori could not imagine meeting a nice man who returned her love, Maya could not imagine her mother being a calm and rational person or her father being able to take her back.

Maya follows the freeway as it splits and veers toward the northeastern suburbs. If Kay had sent occasional news back to Osaka over the years, Minoru would have had something other than his imagination to rely on. On his sleepless nights, he wouldn't have wondered if Maya might be hurt or sick, if she might have gotten mixed up with the wrong kids at school, if she might have married someone who was cruel to her. Knowing nothing, he would have feared the worst, just as she imagines his lonely death because she has nothing except Mr. Kubo's short letter. Imagination is a road that dead-ends in one direction but goes on forever in the other, wrapping itself around the earth's circumference. Though the best of what people imagine cannot overcome the sad reality, the worst may be imagined many times over, each time a little more clearly, with added touches of desperation. The most painful details of her father's life may be no worse than what Maya has imagined already and can go on imagining. If only she could know the truth, she could move forward past this sad time and her uncertainty about everything.

At the party at Peg's house, Lillian had said Maya's "Heavenly Garment" jacket was still in her window because several women kept coming back to try it on. "They're working up the gumption to buy it," Lillian explained. Now the jacket is gone. There are only spring dresses and crocheted cardigans in the window. Lillian goes into the back room and returns with a pot of tea and two cups. They drink the tea, standing across the counter from each other, while Lillian examines the fan necklace and the earrings Maya made to match.

"They're beautiful. Do you want me to price them, or is there a price you want to get?"

"You do it."

Lillian puts the necklace and earrings back in the box. "Do you need these back in case I don't sell them by a certain date?"

"No. I'm done with them. I never have to see them again."

"That's good. Last week someone wanted me to track down a customer and borrow back a shawl she made a year ago."

"I would never ask you to do that." Maya keeps a record of everything she makes so she won't have to know who buys it or what happens to it. If another customer wants a similar piece, she will recreate it from her notes. Once a garment is out of her hands, she can forget about it completely.

"I sold the jacket," Lillian says, "to one of those women I told you about. Toward the end, she was coming in almost every day and staring longingly at the jacket. I was glad she finally gave herself a break."

Maya pictures the *tennyo* rising up into the sky. Alone in the blue light, she would continue to dance for sheer happiness.

"I'll get my books so we can settle up." Lillian writes Maya a check and slides it across the counter. "Do you want to stay for lunch?"

Maya shakes her head. "I wish I could, but I have to do something." Last night before she went to bed, she promised herself that she would call her mother from a gas station and try to visit her if the jacket had been sold. "Maybe another time," she says to Lillian.

"I'll help you load the boxes if you want to go get your car," Lillian offers.

"Thanks." Maya tries not to look despondent. Even the car reminds her of her last meeting with Kay.

The answering machine picks up after two rings. Kay's voice says, "You have reached the Muellers." After a short pause, Nate repeats the same sentence in Japanese. "We are not home," Kay follows and waits for Nate. The two voices intertwine, each person speaking only four or five words at a time; it's like a strange rendition of the marriage vows.

After the beep, Maya says, "I'm at a gas station someplace in Evanston, but I guess you're not home."

"Maya." Her mother's voice interrupts. "Is that you?"

"Yes."

"Where are you?"

"I was just saying that I'm in Evanston, at a gas station."

Kay doesn't respond.

"I know I should have called, but I decided to come at the last minute to get my things from Lillian's store. If it's an inconvenient time, I'm sorry."

"Which street are you on, exactly?"

"I don't know. I pulled into the first gas station I saw. I didn't notice the name of the street."

Behind her at the counter, a woman is telling the attendant that the pump isn't working. "It's really slow," she says. "You know, I squeeze the lever and nothing happens."

"Listen," Maya says to Kay. "I'll come back another time."

"Do you want to come and visit me now?"

"That's why I was calling."

"You can come then."

"Are you sure?"

"I don't have anything to do all day."

The attendant leaves the counter and follows the woman out the door. Alone in the store, Maya stares at the racks of movies next to the phone. She wonders if anyone really rents movies at a gas station.

"Do you know how to get here from wherever you are?" Kay asks.

"Yes," Maya says. "I'll find my way."

Maya stays in her car for a few minutes, examining the house and the garden from across the street as though she were a private eye. The house is a white stucco colonial with stone steps leading to the pillared entrance. In the front yard, a thick patch of dwarf irises blooms, forming a pale blue nimbus, and a Japanese maple is beginning to put forth its red leaves. Although Maya has seen this tree on her previous three visits, it still astonishes her: such a delicate tree to plant in a garden in the Midwest. All summer long, its small red leaves—their five clefts more pronounced than those of the sugar and silver maples all over the city—will waver in the wind like a multitude of hands. Nate planted the Japanese maple and the irises because Japan is his favorite place in the world and Japanese art moves him to tears.

Kay is at the top of the steps, holding the door open. "What were you doing, sitting in your car?" she asks.

"Nothing. I wasn't there that long." In the foyer, several pairs of shoes are lined up neatly against the wall. Maya takes off her sandals. Her mother brings a pair of brown guest slippers out of the closet and places them on the floor, pointed toward the living room. Putting them on, Maya feels as though she were in a strange game where her feet must follow footprints drawn on the floor.

"Don't just stand there. Come in." Kay hugged her in the basement in Minnesota, but even back then she didn't hold Maya's hand as they walked across the street or smooth her hair with her fingers when they came inside the house on a windy day. When her mother's hand reached toward her, it meant Maya was in trouble. They haven't touched each other since Maya left home.

Once, when Maya tried to hug her, Kay stepped back out of reach. Maya has never repeated the gesture. She follows her mother through the living room into the kitchen. Kay is wearing a beige-colored cotton T-shirt and khakis. Her eyebrows are neatly plucked and her lips painted a bright red. Taking all this in, Maya knows her mother is probably doing the same thing, passing judgment on Maya's purple cotton dress and beaded earrings, her hair tied back in a ponytail, her face without any makeup. She must be thinking that Maya looks washed out and eccentric, like a leftover hippie.

"So, sit down." Kay points to one of the chairs.

Maya seats herself at the table in the corner while her mother prepares tea. The ceramic cup she brings to the table is the Japanese kind without a handle. Maya thanks her and sips the bitter green tea. Neither of them speaks for a long time. Finally, Maya takes a deep breath and starts.

"I need to say something." She has rehearsed this part with Yuko. "I owe you an apology. I should never have left you stranded at that restaurant. I want to apologize once and for all. I don't know why I acted in such an inconsiderate way."

Kay narrows her eyes and squints into her cup. "Maybe you were disappointed in your show and took out your frustrations on me." She closes her mouth and shrugs.

Her own cup suspended between the table and her mouth, Maya stares at Kay. Often, when they are together, Maya has a sensation that a small tape recorder is implanted in her inner ear and she can only understand her mother's words through its instant playback feature. That's why it takes her a few seconds to react to what she heard. Most people, when offered an apology, will gladly share the blame. "It wasn't all your fault," they say. "I should have been more considerate too." Maya lifts the cup to her lips and swallows. During their first year in college, Maya told Yuko, "My mother has never said one nice thing to me. Not even 'Nice haircut' or 'That's a pretty blouse you're wearing.'" Yuko was silent for a long time; then they burst out laughing and could not stop. "For a minute," Yuko said, "I thought you had to be exaggerating. But you know what? You're right. I've never heard her say anything nice to you either." Maya and Yuko made up a game in which they exaggerated the things Kay should have said. "Oh, how nice to hear from you!" they would exclaim, in a sweet voice completely unlike Kay's. "It was *so* thoughtful of you to call. I hope the semester is going well. Have a pleasant afternoon." They would flop on the floor and laugh until tears came out of their eyes. *"I'm sorry I hurt your feelings too,"* Maya would say in a timid voice if she were playing that game now; *"You must forgive me for having been so thoughtless."*

Maya straightens her teacup on the table. "Well, the show's over now. As I told you, I'm on my way back from picking up my boxes."

"Did you sell anything?"

"Enough." Maya did much better than she'd expected, selling several vests, blouses, and scarves as well as the jacket, but she doesn't tell her mother. The words she doesn't say feel like a protection, a shiny gemstone hidden in her pocket.

Kay stands up. "Did you eat?"

"No. But you don't have to go to any trouble for me."

Kay opens the refrigerator and starts taking out some dishes and bowls.

"Can I help?"

"No." Kay reaches into the freezer for something wrapped in plastic.

"What's that?"

"Rice. We cook a whole pot for our dinner and freeze the leftovers. It's easy to warm it up in the microwave."

Maya takes the various boiled and pickled vegetables from the bowls, avoiding the bits of beef and chicken that are mixed into everything. Her mother picks up bite-sized portions, which she eats with her rice. This is the kind of lunch Maya's father used to make. Kay is talking about how hard it is to find good Asian eggplant out of season. All the years they lived together, Kay's lunch was cottage cheese with peach halves or rye crispies with tuna salad, washed down with a glass of Tab while she read her political science journals. Now she chatters about what she and Nate have been doing, where they have been eating out. No one would guess that she has had any life other than the one she is leading. She says *we* and *us* as though these pronouns, from the beginning of the English language, had never referred to anyone except herself and Nate.

While they are clearing the dishes, Kay says, "So we're going to Japan in August. Nate's been wanting to take me there all this time."

Maya puts the bowls in the sink. Behind her, Kay is wiping the table with a dishrag. "What do you mean he's *taking* you there? You make it sound like you've never been there yourself."

"Not to the places we're planning to visit. We're going to stay with his old AFS family in Nagoya. We'll be there for a month and travel around from there. For me, it'll be like going to a foreign country. The only place I really know in Japan is Tokyo, but I was just a child. Nate was in Nagoya for a whole year in high school, and he's been back several times since. He's the one who really knows the country." With the dishrag in hand, Kay heads back to the sink. Maya returns to the table. She can't talk or hear anything while Kay turns on the water. In a while, Kay leaves the dishes in the sink and comes to sit across the table from Maya. "Nate wanted to take me to Japan the first year we were together, but I feel better about going now." She lowers her voice even though no one else is listening. "You can guess why."

It's just like that night at the restaurant. Kay is sitting across the table and nodding a little in the way people do when they want the other person to agree without discussion. *We don't have to talk about this because we both know and agree*—that's what her expression means. "You're wrong," Maya spits out. "You could have gone to Japan without running into my father. You could have avoided going to Osaka if you were so afraid of seeing him. You didn't have to wait until he was dead."

Kay makes a sour face. "I don't think you understand how unhappy I was there once."

Maya stares at the plump gray-haired woman across the table. She is not the same person who left red marks on her wrists from clutching her too tight as they climbed down the basement steps. That was years ago in a different house. "Even if you were, it's unfair to blame my father and make it sound like he was some kind of a monster. You were unhappy in Minnesota, too. You spread your unhappiness around and blame other people."

Kay draws in a sharp breath and does not exhale for a long time. Maya expects her to pick something up from the table and throw it, but she just sits there.

"I wish you'd left me alone," Maya says. "I hated living with you."

"If I hadn't gotten you out of Osaka, you wouldn't have had any kind of a life. Even your father agreed you'd be better off with me."

"That's because you made him feel bad."

"It wasn't easy for me to send for you. Bill and I might have gotten along better if I'd been alone."

Though the Nakashimas invited him to their Christmas dinner, Bill didn't come. When Maya saw him the next day, his pale blue eyes looked watery and unfocused. "I didn't hurt Bill. You did. Still, you should have left me with my father. I would have been happier with him."

Kay leans forward and glares at her. "You never really knew your father. You were too young."

"How can you say that? I was with him the whole time. You were seldom home even before you left us."

Kay's nose crinkles when she frowns. "Your father chose his work over you. If he had wanted to give you a better home, he could have gotten a steady, normal job. Instead of being so proud, he could have asked his father and his brother for help. They had money and influence. They could have found him a real job, a second marriage, anything. But your father wasn't willing to change his life for you. He didn't love you enough to give up being a poor artist. He sent you to me so he could live his own life. He didn't choose you."

Maya has the feeling she's often had with her mother—she has been shrunk into a tiny insect buzzing around their heads. With her insect eyes, she is watching her mother's mouth open and close, but all she knows is insect language. If she doesn't concentrate, she will be blown away or squashed under her mother's fingers with the nails painted a dark red.

"You're wrong," she manages to say. "My father let me go because he loved me. He gave me up because you convinced him I'd be better off with you. Letting me go was a sign of love."

"That's pathetic. He let you go because it was convenient, because he'd rather be an artist than a father."

"I don't blame my father for being an artist. That was the one thing he couldn't give up even if he tried."

"Why not? I gave up my job when I met Nate. I gave it up because I loved him. Why couldn't your father do the same?"

Being a political science professor isn't the same as being an artist. Besides, by the time Kay resigned from her position, she was already fifty-five, old enough for an early retirement. She was not giving up something she was in the midst of. But Maya doesn't want to argue anymore. No matter what she says, her mother will have something more to say. "I need to head home," Maya announces, getting up and pushing her chair back. The legs scrape against the floor. "It's getting late."

Kay follows her without a word. As they walk down the hallway, Maya remembers the knitting needle stabbing her back in her dreams, the metal ruler descending on her head. She quickens her steps in the floppy slippers and almost stumbles, but she doesn't slow down.

In the living room, the afghans Maya wove to match the couch are nowhere to be seen. Kay must notice her looking. "Those blankets you sent us," she says, "they were too scratchy. I put them away. If I'd known you were coming, I might have brought them out just for you. But this was so sudden."

Maya shrugs. She was going to use only soft, washable wool to make the afghans. But she couldn't resist putting in a few strands of dark-gray mohair threads because they made all the muted blues and greens come together; without them, the whole thing looked pointless and bland. She should have known how sensitive Kay is to any thread with a coarse texture.

In the foyer, Maya takes off the slippers. Stooped over, she has to fumble with the straps of her sandals. When she straightens up, her mother is standing next to the door with her hand on the knob. Like a gate-crasher being shown the way out, Maya leaves without saying good-bye.

When she gets home, the red light is flashing on the answering machine in the kitchen. Maya pushes the button. It's Dan, asking Jeff if he wants to go golfing with him and Meredith on Saturday. Maya reaches for the message pad on the fridge. The yellow pad already has something written on it—the word *Hi* with a big exclamation point, the letters stretching long and tall and taking up the whole space. The pencil mark is thin, so the word looks like a long shadow cast at daybreak or dusk. Maya doesn't know why Jeff would write that. It has to be some joke she isn't getting. As she turns away, she notices the photograph tucked under the dinosaur magnet from the museum. All she can see under the green ceramic T. rex is a bright yellow bottom edge.

Maya moves the magnet aside. The photograph fits perfectly in her hand. Its bottom half is taken up by a yellow crocheted blanket in which a baby is wrapped. The woman holding the baby, the blanket covering parts of her arms, is Nancy. She looks fuller-faced than when Maya saw her at the tennis courts, and her cheeks are rosy. The baby must have been only a few weeks old; her face is red and wrinkled, her eyes dark and opaque. Holding her in a sunny room, Nancy is smiling, radiant with happiness. In the corner of the photograph, Maya can see the tip of the shadow cast by the person behind the camera—her mother on a visit, perhaps, or her second husband. On the back of the photograph, words in black ink say, *For Jeff, from Nancy and Brittany*.

Cradling the photograph in her hand as delicately as if it were an egg, Maya examines the light falling on Nancy's hair and her white blouse. It's a beautiful image, and she can see why Nancy would want Jeff to have it—she is giving him the best of who she is, a loving mother. Maya tries to see herself grabbing the opposite corners of this photograph and tearing it. The edge will waver slightly, the shiny surface ripping more unevenly than the white back. The line will run right down the image, splitting Nancy's face and the baby's face in two. Maya stands there thinking about it for a long time. When she practiced her high jump on the track team, her coach used to tell her to visualize as she approached the bar: make a picture in her mind of every movement of her arms and legs going over. If you can see it, he said, you can do it. Visualization helped with the bars she could have cleared anyway, but there was a limit to what the coach called the power of the mind. Eventually, she got to bars she couldn't clear no matter what she visualized, because they were simply too high. She could picture herself flying up to the sky and her leg would still catch, sending the bar clattering down. The power of the mind cannot overcome the laws of gravity.

If she put the picture back on the refrigerator, Jeff might not notice it right away. Even if she left and came back, there is no guarantee that he would find it and put it away. Instead, he might see it as he was setting the table for their supper or getting her a drink. He would take it down and look at it, and by the time he turned back to Maya, his face would be full of pity or guilt. He might feel compelled to offer explanations or apologies. The whole scene would make her feel like someone standing in the way of another woman's true love.

Holding the photograph in her hand, Maya goes upstairs to the spare room and opens the closet. Hanging on the pole are her and Jeff's heavy winter coats and jackets in the plastic sheaths from the dry cleaner's. Maya puts the picture in one of the empty shoeboxes from the shelf above the coats and slides it on the floor to the back of the closet, where it is hidden behind the longer coats. In six months, when it is cold enough to bring out these coats again, she may be gone, living somewhere else, or Nancy may have given up and moved on. One of those things will have happened before then. Maya wishes the closet was like a crystal ball, a cup of fortune tea, or a sky full of flying birds so she could augur the future by the arrangements of the coats on the rack. A small forest of winter colors in April, the coats offer her no answers.

Instead, Maya pictures her father on that winter day when he took her to the airport. Surely her mother was wrong to suggest that he didn't love Maya because he refused to give up his art. There are things people cannot do no matter how much they try to imagine doing them. He could no more become a businessman than she could tear someone else's picture or hold on to her lead in the last stretch of the race with another runner struggling for breath right behind her. People cannot do things against their nature.

Standing alone in her own empty house, Maya thinks of her father returning to their house on that afternoon. After Maya had walked through her tunnel into the airplane, he would have gone up to the observation deck and waved to her even though he knew she could not see him. He would have stayed until the airplane taxied off and tilted up into the sky, turning into a silver charm—the kind a woman might wear on a chain around her neck for good luck. Then he would have taken the train back to the house and entered its quietness. He wouldn't have cried; he wouldn't have thrown or broken things the way her mother did in her anger. Instead, he would have gone into Maya's room and opened the closet. The day before, he had packed Maya's suitcase with her favorite dresses, sweaters, skirts, and trousers, folding them neatly, tucking in the sleeves so that each little figure bowed at the waist, embracing itself. Now, with her gone, he would have stared at the clothes that were left in the closet, all of them facing the same direction on their hangers like children marching off into the woods, leaving their fathers and mothers, the houses where they were once happy. He would not have been able to put the clothes away that day or the next day. It would have taken him a long time to go into her room again. It is impossible to forget someone you used to love—their traces are left forever in the house you shared with them. If they came back suddenly, the love you tried to forget would come back, too.

Maya closes the door gently. Her father didn't have to tell her anything. She knows how to go on living with a quiet and empty heart.

— 11 —

The cold weather has returned, though it is the first week of May. All around the neighborhood, the trees have begun to bud. Half in, half out of their scaly sheaths, the new leaves look like scratchy lines drawn in crayon between the gray-brown branches. Maya stands shivering in the doorway while the furnace starts up, sending a hiss of dry air from the basement.

Mr. Raine is kneeling in the foyer over the metal parts he has taken off the front door. His ad in the phone book said FRED RAINE, LOCK-SMITH—at your service rain or shine. From the leather tool belt he wears over his blue work clothes, Mr. Raine takes out a screwdriver. His brown work boots are scuffed; his white hair is thinning on top. Every week, he must get calls from people stranded in parking lots with their keys locked inside their cars or afraid to go home because an ex-boyfriend has a garage-door opener. Maya wonders if he has ever changed the lock to protect someone from unwanted photographs and notes coming in through the door—fragments of the past like beach glass, the edges worn smooth and made prettier by the passage of time.

The last photograph Nancy left, two days ago, was a recent one of herself and her daughter sitting side by side in front of a mottled aqua backdrop. Nancy was wearing a tight black dress; the child was in a white dress with a flouncy tiered skirt. Maya held the photograph in her hand for a long time, unable to stop looking at it. Nancy and her daughter reminded Maya of the same person split in two in an allegorical painting: she was the body with its adult temptations, the little girl was the pure, angel-like soul inside. Though they were dressed in opposite ways, they both had the same bright red hair cut in layers, big ear-to-ear smiles, pretty green eyes. On the back, Nancy had written, *To Jeff, with love from his family. Nancy and Brittany.* The name of a studio downtown was stamped under her message.

Like a history lesson, the photographs have followed a chronological order. After the first one of Nancy with her newborn child, there was another of Brittany being fed something orange—mashed carrots or pumpkin—out of a baby food jar; next, she was in a high chair holding her own spoon over a green plastic plate. Then there were several snapshots of her crawling, standing up, starting to walk. Nancy posted pictures the girl had colored, one of which had a unicorn solidly filled in with black, the strokes of the crayon going both horizontal and vertical, crisscrossing over the slender body of the animal. She left notes on pink stationery about how they had gone to the park or started the baby swimming class at the Y. All the notes ended with *We can't wait to spend more time with you. Love, Nancy and Brittany.*

When there were only two or three photographs, Maya could have put them back on the fridge and gone back to her studio, giving Jeff a chance to discover them in her absence. But after she came back, Jeff would have to show the photographs to her and they would have to talk. Or he would have to hide them and pretend that they never existed. Maya wasn't sure which would be worse. If he wanted to talk, she would have to act as though she were seeing the pictures for the first time. If he didn't say anything, she would notice him glancing toward her with guilty looks. She hesitated until there were too many photographs and notes for Nancy to have left on the same day. Like so many things Maya didn't do, putting back the pictures ceased to be a possibility while she was still thinking of all the ways things could turn out so she could make the perfect decision. She had no choice but to go on accumulating Nancy's messages in her shoebox as though the two of them were sharing secrets.

When Nancy left the last picture from a studio in Milwaukee, Maya knew that the first round had been completed. The studio picture was taken in the last few weeks. It brought everything current, to the sum total of where they were now. After that, Nancy would have to leave entirely new pictures—she would bring recent snapshots including Jeff, or else she would return to the past she and Jeff had shared, chronicling their marriage in the way she had Brittany's life. Snapshot after snapshot, Jeff's past would reassemble itself in the shoebox Maya had hidden.

"You've got to call a locksmith," Yuko said, when Maya told her what was happening. "How do you know this woman's not going to walk in someday and hurt you?"

"I don't think she cares about me. She already acts as if I didn't exist—she comes in whenever she wants and leaves notes on the fridge."

Yuko narrowed her eyes and tilted her head a little. "Are you sure she's leaving that stuff for Jeff? She's like an animal marking its territory. Maybe the pictures are meant for you."

"No." Maya tried to laugh it off. "She saw me at the tennis courts. I'm sure she's dismissed me as being no real competition." Still, she couldn't help picturing Nancy inside the house. As she stopped in the living room on her way in, Nancy might examine the shawl draped on the straight-backed chair, a book left on the table. She must see that Maya's presence in the house is already fading away. Like the neighbors who heard Nancy beeping her horn and screaming in front of their houses, Maya is no more than a helpless bystander. But people who create a spectacle are nothing without an audience. Nancy is acting like the girls Maya and Yuko knew in high school—the very popular ones—who stared at the other girls for a few seconds and then pointedly looked away. "Those girls," Yuko had said, "they want to have it both ways. They can look down on us all they want, but they need us, too. They can only be better because we're here to be worse."

"Maybe you're right," Maya admitted to Yuko. "Nancy wants to ignore me, but at the same time she's showing off to me, too."

Mr. Raine finishes the front door and goes to work on the back door. His truck, parked on the driveway, has the word LOCKSMITH painted in big red letters. If Nancy was driving by, she would get the message. She would understand that if she wanted to write to Jeff, if she wanted to have him back, she would have to pursue him where Maya wouldn't have to know: she could not expect Maya to be both witness and obstacle.

When Jeff comes home, Maya is ready with the two extra keys taped to the lid of the shoebox. Side by side, the keys look like primitive fig-urines or charms. She opens the door as soon as he pulls up. He gives her a hug, puts down his book bag, and runs upstairs to change into his sweats. He returns to the living room and sits down next to her on the couch but doesn't see the shoebox on the coffee table. Maya points to it.

"I changed the locks, front and back. See the keys?" She puts her finger lightly on the two keys, secure under cellophane tape. "The locksmith just left. What's inside the box is why I changed the locks."

Jeff sighs but makes no move to open the box. Too late, Maya wishes she hadn't closed the lid. The shoebox looks unnecessarily sinister, as though it contained something dead—a bird, a kitten—unrecognizably mangled.

"They're just some photographs and notes she left for you. I took them off the fridge and put them in the box. Maybe I shouldn't have."

"You changed the locks because of Nancy."

Maya nods. "I found these things on the fridge. Maybe she told you about them and you were wondering what happened to them."

She can't help blushing. "You didn't ask and I didn't know how to give them back. I didn't mean to interfere."

Jeff shakes his head. "Why didn't you say something? We could have talked. You didn't have to handle this by yourself."

"What is there to talk about? She has a right to contact you, but she doesn't have to leave you notes where I can find them. I don't want to be involved in what's going on between you. She should leave me out of it."

"There's nothing going on." Jeff glowers at Maya and won't say anything more.

"If there's nothing going on, why are you so upset?"

"I'm upset because you won't talk to me. Every time something goes wrong, you act on your own. You don't give me a chance to explain. You assume the worst and come up with some weird solution. You're worse than Nancy. At least she screams at me about what's going on in her head. You do things without telling me."

"If it's so much better with Nancy, you should go back to her."

"You know that's not what I mean," Jeff says, reaching toward her. Maya leans out of his reach. "You have no reason to be jealous." He sighs. "The other day I told her I was committed to you and couldn't go back to her, ever. She started to cry." Jeff pauses, but Maya doesn't say anything. "I felt terrible about making her cry. Nancy's in rough shape right now. She's really down, to the point where I'm worried about her safety. If she did something drastic, I could never forgive myself. I'm asking you to be patient. I need your understanding. Instead, you go your own way as if we weren't together. You pretend that what happens to me doesn't affect you at all."

Maya pictures Nancy crying at a coffee shop—putting her elbows on the table and covering her face so all Jeff can see is her hair falling over the table. He must have wanted to reach his hand to smooth her hair or pat her shoulder. Maybe he did, or else he politely looked away and lifted his coffee cup to his lips, wanting to give her some privacy. The waitress would have stood in the corner and wondered what was wrong with the couple at her table, why the man was making his girlfriend cry. Oblivious, Nancy would have kept crying, pressing her elbows harder against the table to support the weight of her misery.

Maya shakes her head, trying to clear the pictures that clutter up her mind. "Remember you weren't going to tell me about your meetings with her? I really don't want to hear."

"That has to change. I need to be able to talk to you. Nancy's in much worse shape than I thought she was. It's going to take me a long time to work things out with her. Right now, she says the only time she's happy is when she's with me. She needs me even though that's wrong. I want her to settle into some kind of a life here and leave me alone."

"That's never going to happen. Look at her notes and tell me if you really think she's going to give you up. If she's the kind of person who's afraid to be alone, she'll always try to latch on to you. How do you know she's not manipulating you by pretending to be so depressed? Her notes just sound chatty. They don't seem that depressed to me."

"For someone who doesn't want to know the details, you must have read her notes pretty carefully."

She has practically memorized them. But that's exactly why she wanted to know nothing in the first place. She can't stop halfway between knowing everything and knowing nothing. Once she starts, there will be no end until she can picture every detail as though she had been there herself. Knowing something that hurts you is like standing on the edge of a tall building. It's better not to go near the edge because, once there, jumping seems like the only natural thing to do. It's impossible to resist all that empty air below, calling you to fall. If you don't want to jump, the only solution is to stand back a safe distance. Jump or don't jump, know everything or nothing—the choices are clear. But Jeff could never understand. He doesn't even see that, for Nancy, having him back or not seeing him ever again are the only options. Being his friend isn't acceptable to her. Nancy wants Jeff to give his life—all his love and devotion—to her and her daughter. If you feel that way about someone, friendship will never do. It's just like when Dan told Yuko how much he still cared for her. It would have been better if he'd told her she meant nothing to him.

"Listen," she says to Jeff. "I'm sorry I interfered. Don't be angry."

"I just want us to be able to talk about what's going on."

"I know, but there are things that can't be talked about." She places the shoebox on his lap. "I'm sorry I changed the locks, but there are two keys. What you do with them is none of my business." She gets up from the couch. "I'll be outside."

In the backyard, the crinums she planted against the house are shooting up their long green leaves. Their first spring together, Jeff thought something was wrong with the plants. He only half believed her when she explained that crinums get their leaves in the spring and their flowers in late summer. In August, when the pale pink flowers appeared on their long stems, he said, "These are the same plants that had those scraggly leaves?" Some plants save the best for last. If crinums got their leaves and flowers at the same time, as daffodils do, the flowers wouldn't seem to float in the air all on their own. When Maya first moved here, the area behind the house was covered with gravel and a planting of prickly low bushes—it was the kind of landscaping done around suburban gas stations. Dan and Yuko helped her pull out the bushes and replace the gravel with topsoil. Under the gravel, there was a layer of black plastic to prevent the weeds from growing. They had to tear the plastic out, inch by inch. Nothing could be planted until every piece was gone.

Maya turns on the lawn mower and starts from the west side of the house. She goes back and forth, making straight swaths. In Minneapolis, Kay hired a man from a landscaping company to cut the grass even though both Bill and Maya were willing to do it. Following Kay's instructions, the man made diagonal passes with the mower, leaving barely visible diamond patterns on the cut grass. For a day or so after, the lawn looked like a mirage of a giant chess board.

She is half finished with the lawn when Jeff comes out of the house. He stands by the back door. Maya continues to work, toward the house, away from the house, then toward the house again. Finally, Jeff starts walking across the lawn. Maya turns off the mower.

"I think you care more for Nancy than you've told me. If you're wondering whether to stay with me or go back to her," she says, "you should talk to someone who's not involved."

He takes her hand. "What about you? What do you want?"

"What I want hasn't changed. Some days, I'm glad we're together. Other days, I wish I'd stayed alone. But that's how I've felt all along."

"Even at the beginning?" He peers into her eyes as he squeezes her hand.

"Yes, even at the beginning." Maya swallows hard. "I've always liked being alone. You know that."

"But you were happy with me."

"I still am, sometimes. Nothing's changed for me." She pulls her hand away.

Jeff reaches and grabs her hand again. "Listen, I don't want to be with Nancy. All the years we were together, she either took me for granted because she was feeling great or latched on to me because she was unhappy. I never learned to help her without being pulled along by her ups and downs. Now she's back doing the same thing and I don't know what to do. I can't make her happy, but I can't just leave her the way she is. I can only hope she'll let me go once she gets to feeling better somehow. I have to be patient."

"Then that's what you should do."

"But I don't want to hurt you. You just said you were never that happy with me. Do you really mean it?"

"That's not what I said. I always felt torn between being with you and being alone. But for the most part, it wasn't a problem. You left me alone when I wanted you to. You respected my privacy. I'm willing to do the same for you. I'm sorry I interfered by changing the locks."

"You don't need to apologize. You were upset by the things Nancy wrote to me because you thought I must have given her encouragement—otherwise she wouldn't say those things. You were jealous. That's only natural." He stops and looks into her eyes. She looks away. "I'm sorry," Jeff continues. "But you have to believe me. I never told her that I wanted to be with her, or that she and her kid are my family, or anything like that. You have to trust me." His hand clasping hers, he waits for her answer.

Maya pictures Nancy's green eyes, filled with tears, looking into his. "I trust you to do the right thing," she says, pulling her hand out of his and reaching for the lawn mower. "I'd better finish this."

To her right is the cut grass. Behind the lawn mower, an almost invisible line stretches, separating the cut grass from the uncut. Jeff points to a patch of lawn to their left. "Look," he says, "violets."

"Yeah, it's May."

"Let's pick them before you mow them down. I hate to see the first flowers go to waste."

The violets are white with ink-blue streaks at their center. There's a scattering of them all over the lawn, hugging the ground on their short stems. Maya stoops down and begins to pick them. Jeff is a few steps away, working on another patch. In a short while, they each have a small, leafless bouquet. Maya hands hers to Jeff and goes back to the lawn mower. She watches him walk back to the house, a bouquet in each hand. Several flowers have fallen out because their stems were too short. They dot the grass behind him, but he doesn't notice. Maya turns on the mower and walks toward the house, then away. In the distance, the branches blur with new leaves.

— 12 —

On the side of the freeway, flocks of killdeer swoop over the fields, flashing their white underwings in the sun. Though her car windows are closed, Maya can imagine their sharp screeching calls. From year to year, the same birds return, flying and feeding in the ways she knows well: palm warblers flicking their tails as they feed on the ground, American redstarts fluttering butterflylike among the middle branches. Only one in eight young birds survives the fall and spring migrations to return to the place where it was born, but the individual deaths are insignificant—a few shed feathers weighing almost nothing, marking the places where the flock has stopped and moved on.

If she were to live on her own again, Maya might feel like a bird migrating back to a place far away and yet familiar. She would be with a multitude of women traveling in the same direction—Yuko, Lillian, many of her customers and some of the women who own businesses around town. She would join a great migration of women, from solitude to marriage and then back to solitude. The sequence of women's lives may be as much a part of the natural order as the migration of birds. But Maya remembers the unbroken silence of her years alone. If she were to paint a picture of her life before Jeff, she would depict herself sitting in an empty room with a marble monument filling up the entire space.

When Eric comes to the store at noon, Maya is ringing up someone's purchase. As he wanders over to the other side of the store to wait, she is conscious of exactly where he is. Sunlight is pouring through the windows, making the air feel like a fizzy drink. Once the customer leaves and he begins to approach her, she wants to look up and meet his eyes, but she can't. Looking down at his brown hiking boots, she starts talking about the cattle egret she saw on the side of the highway last week. She's telling him how a person can identify the three white herons and egrets commonly seen in Wisconsin by field marks and feeding habits—as though he cared about such things. When she finally looks up, he is standing across the counter from her. Suddenly, neither of them can talk. The morning after his last visit, Maya came to work and found a note under the door. *I'm sorry if I offended you*, it said. *Forgive me.* He'd signed only his first name.

"I meant to call when I read your note," she says finally, "but I couldn't."

"Are you still angry with me?"

"No. I couldn't call because I don't know your last name. I couldn't look you up in the phone book."

"Oakley," he says.

"Like Annie?"

"Yeah." He shrugs. "I never shot a gun, though."

"I thought everyone out in the country went hunting."

"My father took me pheasant hunting once. When he and his friends started shooting, the noise freaked me out completely. I cried and wanted to go home. Then one of the men winged a bird and had to wring its neck. I got sick watching that. My father never took me again, which was fine with me."

"My friend Yuko hates hunters. One year during deer season she borrowed a mannequin from Peg, dressed it in blaze orange, and drove around with it tied to the top of her Barracuda. Her husband—soon-to-be-ex-husband—made her take it down because he was afraid someone might slash her tires or shoot at the car."

Eric laughs. "I want to show you what I've been working on. Do you have some time today?"

"Yes." She nods. "We can go now."

The parking space they find is only a block from the first house where Maya lived with Yuko, Scott, and Dan. She points it out as they walk by. The house has been painted a light yellow; the rotting porch steps have long been fixed. The neighborhood has changed, but the old warehouse building looks the same. Maya has not been inside since she graduated from college. The hallway is painted the same off-white, and Eric's studio is on the third floor, where Ruth had hers before she retired and moved away. The stairway looks unchanged too: uncarpeted, rubberized, industrial gray.

Last fall, when Peg went back to her grade school for a reunion, she couldn't get over how much smaller everything was. The drinking fountain in the gym was a standard-issue drinking fountain, not the big silver square box in the corner that made mysterious grunting noises all day long. She used to dream about her first-grade teacher, Sister Nana, who made kids kneel on kidney beans strewn over the hardwood floor to say their rosaries. In Peg's dreams, Sister Nana flew around the classroom in her black habit, looking more like Dracula than a nun. Peg had to hide in the huge dark closet in the back of the room, and she always woke up just as she was closing the door behind her. After her visit, when she saw that the closet was an ordinary storage room, she never had that dream again. "I kind of miss my nightmare," she said.

On rainy days in Wisconsin, Maya remembers the smell of the dark oiled floor at her grade school in Osaka. In the hallway by the door, there was an umbrella stand with wire rings—like the device that holds single-stemmed flowers in a large vase—in which each student placed his or her umbrella. Outside, dwarf palms were planted by the gate, and peacocks walked about inside their cage. She is not sure if her memories are accurate. She will never be able to revisit the past and see how much smaller everything really was. Eric can go back to his farming community every weekend to see that it has not changed. He must feel relieved when he drives past his old grade school and a scattering of stores, on to the freeway back to Milwaukee. Week after week, he is repeating his getaway. He can be free of his hometown because it's still there.

Eric stops in front of a metal door and turns the key. Maya follows him into a large room with white walls, a gray floor, big windows on one side to admit natural light. Large industrial lamps hang from the ceiling.

On one white wall, Eric has tacked twenty rectangular panels in five rows, each panel the size of a windowpane. The black brush strokes on the panels look like calligraphy, full of dark paint and movement; the white strokes are feathery and delicate. The paint is layered over with cut paper, fabric, ink, and glue, which has left a semitransparent finish. All the panels taken together comprise a winter landscape, black and white with a gravel road; the bare trees in back seem to be receding. What Maya notices most is the texture of each panel— gritty and rough but oddly tender, with the many layers exposed as if under a skin.

"What do you think?" Eric asks.

If she had seen these panels when she was in college, she might have felt hope instead of despair. They would have shown her how a stark landscape can inspire tenderness instead of cold precision. No one's work showed her that possibility back then. What she saw other people do was either unforgivingly harsh and sad or else playful and clever in a superficial manner. She remembers the luminous white light her father captured among swirls of lonely desert colors. With persistence, she too might have found that light in her brush strokes and paint. If she had seen these panels earlier, they might have led her back to the cocoon of canvas where her father told her stories of music that could melt the hearts in hell, of the long celestial dance given as a parting gesture, a kind of consolation for lost love. Even the king of hell was overcome by pity for Orpheus, and the *tennyo* who tricked the young fisherman lingered in the air and danced for him before she flew away. Maya might have sensed a stubborn hope instead of despair in those stories. No matter how sorrowful the ending, each story was sustained by beauty.

"I wish I'd found your work earlier, when I was young. I could have learned so much from it."

"I want to show you how I did this." He goes over to his worktable and returns with a photocopy of a black-and-white photograph. "This is a copy of one of the pictures my mother took when she was a young woman. I enlarged it with a copy machine. That seemed like the right way to open it up a little, to see between the lines." The photocopy in his hand is roughly the same image as the total of the panels, though the similarity is like the family resemblance between father and son, mother and daughter, not like the one between a person's face and his photograph. Eric shows her how he divided the photograph into grids by covering everything but one square inch at a time with white construction paper. "I worked grid by grid, trying to concentrate on each incomplete image. I wanted every panel to be something you can look at and be totally satisfied with."

He moves the paper from one square inch to another, pausing now and then to glance back at her. Maya can see what he was seeing. Every square is a window where starkness and tenderness can come together—in the murky shadings of a pebble or a twig, the black line that cuts across the middle, the white feathering of reflected light. She looks back at the panels and understands how he has retrieved something out of his mother's dreams. Next to the white brush strokes in one of the panels, a piece of gray linen, its edge fraying, is embedded. One single thread hangs loose, never to be tucked in or torn out, protected under layers of glue and paint.

"I thought I was doing this work for my mother, and I suppose I was. But I thought about you the whole time. Every day."

They stand side by side in front of the wall, neither of them able to move. Maya keeps staring at the single thread caught in its unraveling. She turns to Eric and puts her arms around him. "Thank you for showing me your work." He hugs her back hard, his breath warm against her cheek. When they step back, her face feels hot and his cheeks, too, are flushed.

"We should go," Maya says.

They walk out of the room in silence. Halfway down the stairs, he takes her hand and holds it until they are at the door of the building. His hand is warmer than hers; his thumb presses against her palm.

Stepping outside, she feels dizzy. The cold, damp air of mid-spring makes her shiver. With her hand swinging loose again at her side, she is a balloon let go, floating away. When she closes her eyes momentarily, she sees something that takes her breath away. She is recalling the black-and-white photograph Mr. Kubo sent her, of her father in the last years of his life. The image fills her mind like a view from the sky. His face could have been a landscape she knew well, desolate but beautiful. If she could have sat by him in the last months of his life, she would have known every inch of his face, every passage of light and shadow across it, and memorized all the details. She would have learned the shades of meaning in his slightest smile or frown; she would have known him in his weakest and his strongest moments.

She keeps walking, but she is only half inhabiting her body. Back where they parked his car, Eric opens the door for her to get in. She smiles weakly at him, but she is no longer thinking about him or about this moment. Sitting down in the passenger seat, a block from where she used to live, she knows she should have kept writing to her father no matter how many times he returned her letters. She should have sent him photographs, drawings, her schoolwork, pressed flowers from her garden. The sheer volume and persistence of her need would have worn him down. And if that did not work, she could have telephoned him; years later, she could have gone to Osaka and found him in the same house where they once lived. She did not do any of these things because—like him—she was quiet and sad, pure-minded and proud in the wrong way. She could picture the piles of returned mail, hear the silence on the other end of the line, feel the door slammed against her in that old house, and the things she imagined left her utterly hopeless. What was past was irretrievable, she had reasoned. But if she had not been so hopeless, stubbornly seeing all or nothing as her only choices, she might have been resourceful enough to manage a correspondence, even a visit. She would have been with him at the end. The short time they spent together would never have made up for the decades they lost, but it would have been better than the nothing they chose.

Eric is leaning toward her, his hand on her shoulder. "You don't have to say anything unless you want to."

"I'll tell you another time," she says, looking straight ahead. "This has nothing to do with you."

It would be so easy to let the tears come. In his sidelong glance, she can see how he wants to hold her, how he might teach her to take all her sorrow and turn it into a distant gray shade—always there but a source of tenderness more than grief. But it is too late. A long time ago, she decided to find comfort in solitude and peace; alone in a dark basement room, she slowed her heart and prepared herself not to love. When her marriage ends, she will go back to the quiet life she has known a long time.

She pulls back so Eric has no choice but to remove his hand. If they had met earlier, he would have salvaged some tenderness out of her past, as he did out of his mother's aspirations. She would have loved him and told him everything. But now, loving him would only be an escape from the solitude that waits on the other side of her marriage. Her face turned away from him, Maya presses her fingertips into her eyes, and when that isn't enough she rubs them hard with her hand clenched into a fist. As he starts the car and slowly pulls out, the gray concrete of the sidewalk dissolves into a gentle light. Maya remembers the last things she painted in college—stones that rose to the surface of farm fields year after year to be piled onto the hedgerow. Relics from a distant landscape and climate, many of them trapping seashells or fish bones in their layers of history, they were the meaning of the name she had inherited from her father. Maya wishes she had been courageous enough to stay with her painting and learn the discipline of seeing between the lines of landscape. If she could crack open even the smallest gray pebble, so much light would come pouring out.

— 13 —

As the plane had climbed into the sky, Maya could see the blue water of Osaka Bay below. The land curved around it in the shape of a bow, just like in her geography book. *I won't ever see this water again*, she had thought, and started to cry. By the time she arrived in Minneapolis, her eyes were red and her head felt foggy, as though she had spent hours underwater instead of up in the sky. She did not recognize the short-haired woman who stood at the gate in a navy blue pants suit. She hadn't seen Kay for three years. Back home, her mother had worn pastel-colored dresses with sprigs of flowers printed on them, her hair trimmed shoulder-length. When the woman wrapped her arms around her and began to cry, Maya took a deep breath and held it as though she were diving into a deep well from which she might never come back up alive. Even though she understood everything Kay said to her, Maya did not speak for two days. She thought about the Chinese brother who could drink a whole lake. When he was holding the lake inside him, surely he was unable to utter a word.

Calling her mother from her kitchen on Mother's Day twenty-five years later, Maya still has the underwater feeling.

"Hello, Muellers," her mother says into the phone.

"Hi, it's Maya."

Kay's voice changes from businesslike to impatient. "I can't talk for long. We're just going out the door for our morning walk."

If someone else had called, Kay would never be so blunt. Maybe, for her, being a mother means a right to be rude. "I'm sorry to intrude. I was only calling because it's Mother's Day."

They are quiet for a long time. This is the first time Maya has called since her visit.

Kay clears her throat. "Are you going out for Mother's Day?" she asks.

"Why would I? I'm not a mother."

"That's true."

"Well, have a nice walk. I'll call again another time." Kay doesn't respond, so Maya hangs up.

Maya sits down at the kitchen table with a cup of coffee. In a while, Jeff comes downstairs in a button-down shirt and dress pants. This year he has not asked her to go to Mother's Day brunch with him and his parents.

"Tell your parents I said hi," Maya offers, while he is pouring coffee into his travel mug.

He looks back and blinks. When his mug is full, he wipes the counter even though it's perfectly clean. "I'm not going to my parents'," he says, as he comes toward the table. "Nancy asked me to go to church with her and Brittany. There's a special Mother's Day program for kids."

"You don't need to tell me."

Jeff pulls out the chair and sits down. He puts his hands, folded together, on the table. It's as though he were already praying. "I'm feeling more and more confused. I don't know what's going on."

"Only you can figure it out."

"Is that all you have to say?"

"What else can I possibly say?"

"If some guy tried to take you away from me, I would do everything I could to stop him. I would ask you not to leave me."

Maya looks down at her own hand around the coffee mug and remembers Eric's fingers laced with hers as they went down the stairs at the studio. "I don't know what to think. Maybe we should spend some time apart."

Jeff reaches across the table and grabs her wrist. "Don't give up on me. I want to hold on. But I need a little encouragement."

With her free hand on top of his, Maya gently pries his fingers off her wrist. "I can't hold on for you. You wouldn't feel any better if I were begging you not to leave me. You'd only feel more torn." She gets up. "I promised to help Yuko clean her apartment. I have to go."

"Are you coming back?"

"Yes. I wouldn't leave without telling you."

"Are you sure? We have to talk if you want to leave."

She nods. "The same thing if you do."

On the old paper lining they pull out of the cupboard, faint broken circles mark the places where former tenants must have put their coffee cups, turned upside down. Most of Yuko's plates and cups date back to their years together at college. If she were still an artist, Maya would paint them. Precariously balanced on the counter, light reflecting on the smooth and chipped surfaces, each stack is a jumbled mile marker of where they have been. Yuko rolls up the old paper and pitches it into the trash. The new paper is plain white and spotless.

"I hope my mother won't be upset," Yuko says. "I already told her I didn't keep anything she gave me and Dan, but when she actually sees this place, she'll be worried. Here I'm thirty-five and I have to ask my parents to stay in a hotel because my apartment's too small. I feel like I'm letting them down."

"You were brave to leave everything behind and move on. Your parents will understand that."

"My father will be okay. He takes everything in stride. It's my mother I'm worried about. She really liked Dan. She's going to miss him."

When Yuko's parents visited last Thanksgiving, her mother, Reiko, cooked the turkey. Dan, who was supposed to be helping, stuck the meat thermometer in the turkey's thigh. Later, he laughed. "The bird was upside down. The oven was hot, and I felt disoriented. I couldn't see where the breast was. I'd have been helpless without Reiko." No one that afternoon could have known he was already seeing Meredith. When he insisted on driving across town to find a store that was open, to buy a few salad fixings they could easily have done without, he must have been looking for an excuse to get out of the house and visit Meredith on his way. After Yuko found out about their affair, she kept going over the things she and Dan did in the last three months. "Everything I remembered came back with a big mental asterisk. At the bottom of each page, there would be a footnote saying, 'And he was already in love with her when you were doing this with him.' The same damn footnote over and over."

"Your mother won't cry over Dan," Maya tells Yuko. "She liked him before. But now is a different time."

Yuko smooths the new lining with her fingers.

"You're lucky she's your mother. Imagine how mine is going to be if I leave Jeff. Even though she never warmed up to him, she'd start talking like he was the greatest person on earth. She'd make him sound like an important prize I lost."

"Yeah, she probably would."

"It's the opposite of what you or Peg would do. I always knew you guys didn't like Jeff but you tried to hide it till lately. Now, you both think I might leave him, so you're not afraid to tell me."

"Well, that's how it should be, don't you think? Your friends should always act like the guy you're with is a prince and the guy you left—or the one who left you—is a total loser."

"I agree."

Yuko picks up one of the mugs and peers into it. "Clean enough." She blows at it and shrugs. "So how are things, anyway. Have you decided what to do?"

"Not yet."

"Is Jeff still seeing the psycho ex-wife?"

"Yeah, she stopped leaving him pictures and notes once I changed the locks. But I know she still wants him back. He went to church with her this morning."

Yuko shakes her head but doesn't say anything right away. In the silence that follows, Maya remembers the afternoon she'd gone with Eric to his studio. As they stood looking at his painting, their shoulders almost touching, she could believe that her whole life would have been different if they had met earlier. Yuko puts down the cup and peers into Maya's face. She has no idea what Maya is thinking about. Those few minutes in the studio, Maya was in a sudden state of grace. Even though that didn't last, she can't share it with anyone except Eric. The memory of that afternoon floats past her like a vision, but its beauty gives her only a temporary reprieve. When Yuko reaches and touches Maya's arm lightly, Maya feels as though a wall has sprung up between them, and only she can see it. She tries to throw her voice across the wall to the other side.

"As he was getting ready to leave, Jeff told me he felt really confused. He asked me to help him hold on. I think he's afraid of being pulled back into his first marriage." Maya pictures Jeff standing in the path of a tornado. "I can't help him."

"If Jeff had so much baggage from his first marriage, he should have told you in the beginning. Then you wouldn't have married him." Yuko scowls. "When you were single, guys I knew from bands often asked to meet you. Those musicians—they weren't exactly a happy lot. Remember, you never wanted to go out with them because they were so obviously troubled. That made sense. It's hard enough to get along with people who are stable. So why choose guys with big problems? You might have dismissed Jeff for the same reason."

"That's possible."

Yuko smiles teasingly. "All the guys I knew were neurotic when we were younger. Some have mellowed out and turned into decent people. Maybe if you're alone again, I'll introduce you to one of them."

"Oh, I don't think I'd want to be with anyone else if I got divorced." Maya takes the cups from the counter and hands them over, two by two, for Yuko to put away. The stoneware makes a faint clicking noise. On the morning she had tea with Eric, Maya couldn't look him in the eye without blushing. She couldn't talk without getting nervous. She wanted to tell him everything she knew and thought about. Listen, she could say to Yuko now, there's a man who comes to the store. I might be falling in love with him. She would sound just like her mother or Dan: a person who runs from one commitment to another, afraid to be alone.

At the restaurant downtown, the tables are crowded with people dressed in their Sunday best. Women wearing corsages sit accompanied by their husbands or grown children. The restaurant is too formal for young families. Jeff must be sitting down to lunch with Nancy and Brittany somewhere on the south side—a sunny, noisy room full of children coloring pictures on paper place mats.

A young waiter approaches the table, holding two long-stemmed red roses as well as the menus. He hands out the menus and lays the flowers on the table next to the silver. "Happy Mother's Day."

"But we're not mothers," Yuko protests, with a puzzled smile.

"We give flowers to all the ladies on Mother's Day."

Yuko cranes her neck to examine the other tables.

"Thank you." Maya smiles at the waiter.

After he goes away, Yuko says, "That's so stupid. I don't want a flower on Mother's Day. They should do away with Mother's Day and have Daughter's Day instead. Then every woman can celebrate."

"I don't know if I want to celebrate being my mother's daughter."

"Do you think we'll regret not having had kids?" Yuko asks, after a while.

"I don't think so."

"I used to feel envious when I saw women in the park playing with their kids. If Dan hadn't been so set against it, I might have become a mother. That might have been a good thing."

"Maybe you'll get married again and have kids."

"No." Yuko shakes her head. "Whatever feelings I had about wanting kids—they faded away. Now I notice the women whose kids are screaming and carrying on. I feel sorry for them. Things could go wrong even if your kids never act out. They could fall off the swing and hurt themselves. Someone could come and kidnap them. There wouldn't be a moment of peace if you were a mother."

Maya pictures a park full of children running around, riding the swings, climbing over the jungle gym. If she were a mother sitting on a bench, she wouldn't be able to tell, from the pitter-patter of the feet and the high-pitched voices, whether the children were playing happily or fighting and crying. She would only hear a jumble of anxious noise. What would prevent her from getting up from the bench, walking to her car, and driving away alone? Last winter, a man left his infant son in his car parked outside his office in subzero weather. He had forgotten to drop off the baby at day care because it wasn't part of his morning routine; his wife usually did it. By the time he remembered, it was too late. People can mean no harm and still hurt their children. Maya and Jeff used to argue almost every week about having children. "I'm not saying we absolutely have to have kids. I'm disturbed that you won't at least consider the possibility. You're so closed-minded," Jeff said. "But I already know that I never want to be a mother. I've known that about myself for a long time. I told you before we were married," Maya responded. "You shouldn't take it personally, like I don't want to have *your* kids. I like being alone during the day. I don't want to give that up." "That's the most selfish thing I've ever heard," he spat out. After nearly a year of fighting with him,

Maya scheduled a tubal ligation. She didn't tell Jeff until she came back. They argued about it for a week and then dropped the subject because there was nothing more to say.

"I have no regrets about being childless," she says to Yuko.

On the white tablecloth, their roses look like well-dressed dolls that children admire but never touch. Red is the color of motherhood. In Osaka, on Mother's Day, children wore red carnations to honor their mothers. If you had lost your mother, you were supposed to wear white carnations in her memory, but Maya never saw anyone do that. One Mother's Day after Kay was gone, Maya went to the museum with her father, and on their way on the train, they saw many children with red carnations pinned to their dresses and shirts. Her father took her hand and pulled her closer to him, but neither of them said anything. If she could paint a picture of herself and her father from that day, she would put white flowers on their lapels as they stood hand in hand on the crowded train platform.

— 14 —

From the wooden bench outside the store, Eric waves as Maya parks her car next to his and gets out.

"I was going to call if you didn't show up in an hour," he says, standing up.

"We're not open on Mondays. I came to weave."

"I know."

She walks up to the bench.

"I'm going to my mother's place. She's in Oregon visiting my sister and her family. I promised to cut the grass and fill the bird feeders. I would love it if you could come with me."

Maya has just started weaving a large piece of linen to sew some dresses and vests for the store. The color she chose is the blue of cathedral windows—of portals opening up to the sky. It's a beautiful blue, but she's suddenly unsure about spending the whole day looking at it.

"We can be back by three or four, whatever time you were planning to be home. There won't be any trouble."

"I'm not worried about the time."

"Will you come then?"

"All right, but I have to check on my cat. Wait here."

Casper is sitting by the door. As soon as Maya steps inside, he rolls over on his back and begins to purr. Next to him on the floor are two mice, smaller than usual. One has no ears, and the other has a gash across its back. She kneels down and rubs Casper's smooth belly. "You're a ruthless hunter," she tells him. "Let's make sure you have enough food upstairs so you don't have to eat mice."

He runs up the steps behind her, heeling like a dog. Maya refills his water and food bowls on the studio floor. Casper sticks his long white face into the food bowl and starts munching, but he isn't so easily fooled. By the time she's halfway down the stairs, he is right beside her, running with his tail up in the air.

"Sorry, I have to go." She picks up the mice from the floor and puts them in a bag. As soon as she steps outside, Casper starts crying and scratching the door. She had to get him declawed to protect the clothes in the shop. He can only make a muffled noise, like the soft hiss of a broom across the floor.

Eric is waiting in his car. Maya puts the mice in the trash can and gets in.

"Casper's not too happy about this," she says.

"Too bad." He grins. "I am."

The trees along the freeway are bright green with new leaves. The foliage has changed the landscape, drawing the eye to the masses of color instead of the intersecting lines and angles.

"When you left that note on the floor the other day," Maya tells Eric, "it was in the same spot where my cat leaves the mice he catches. It gave me a start."

"We're both giving you peace offerings."

"I suppose so."

"I could have used your cat at the last house I rented in Vermont. The mice in the attic made such a racket I couldn't sleep through the night. It was like rodent Olympics up there. Soon they started coming into the kitchen. The only thing I left on the counter overnight was ground coffee in a metal container with a plastic lid. The mice chewed through the lid, got into the can, and ate the coffee. At first, I set the humane traps you can take outside to release the catch, but the mice ate the bait without springing the trap. After weeks of feeding them peanut butter, I started having dreams about mice, so I knew it was time to act."

"What did you do?"

"I set those traps that break their necks." He glances sideways at her, as if to check her reaction.

"Before we had Casper, Peg set out poison. The traps are more humane. They die instantly. That's not so bad."

"The woman I was dating left me because I set those traps. She cried over dead mice." He laughs. "But we weren't getting along so great anyway. The mice were catalysts, nothing more."

Maya laughs, even though it's almost a sad story.

"After we broke up, I was killing a dozen mice every night in my great mice massacre. By this time, it was the end of May—a year ago now. I put the dead mice near the hedge in the backyard, where I saw a lot of ants. I thought the ants might strip the carcasses clean and leave me the bones. Maybe I was going crazy, but I wanted to sketch the mouse skeletons. The humane traps that didn't work came with instructions in French, don't ask me why. I'd saved the instruction sheet. I was going to cut up the sheet and layer them over the sketches. I even thought of using the actual bones somehow. You probably think I'm sick in the head."

"No. I think bones are kind of pretty." Her father used to strip thin flakes of white meat from the small steamed fish he made for their lunch in Osaka. With his chopsticks, he peeled the mottled brown skin in one piece, then picked the meat off the bones to put on her plate. They sat under the yellow light of the kitchen lamp and ate the soft, salty morsels with rice. At the end, there was a perfect fish skeleton, a clean shape of a leaf, and the skin rolled up, like a tiny garment. Some mornings in his journal, he drew fish skeletons, bird feathers, a butterfly dropped on the doorstep by the cold. "I don't think anything is automatically ugly or grotesque," Maya says.

"You're a woman after my own heart. Why didn't I meet you earlier?"

Outside the window, next to a farmhouse, the sun is shining on a clothesline full of towels and sheets. The sheets flap in the wind, absorbing the warmth of the sun, the movement of the air, the sound of traffic. A person sleeping on those sheets might dream of cars coming and going on the freeway, of different lives far away. A mother or a father might smooth a pillowcase, fresh from the line, over a plumped pillow and make a wish that the children would hear the distant call and strike out on their own. Maybe that's what Eric's mother used to do. Surely, Kay was wrong. It isn't pathetic to say that Minoru let Maya go because he loved her, because he wanted her to be happy elsewhere. Any woman living on a farm along this freeway might wish the same for her son or daughter. Love isn't always about holding on. Letting go can be the ultimate act of love and mercy. "So what happened in Vermont?" she asks Eric. "Did the ants give you the bones you wanted?"

"No. An hour or so later, I looked out the window. My yard was a sea of black wings. There must have been fifteen crows pecking at those mice. When they were gone, there was nothing left. The crows ate everything."

"You didn't think it was a bad omen, did you?"

"I loved seeing those birds. So I kept putting out the mice every morning."

The crows in his yard would have resembled a black tide flowing in, then ebbing back into the sky. In another life, she and Eric might have lived together like the humble good characters in the fairy tales her father told—those the ants helped by collecting scattered grains of millet or the ravens rewarded with golden apples. They would have been content even with the smallest gifts of beauty from the birds and the fish: white bones, black feathers, insatiable hunger.

"I might go back to Vermont," Eric says abruptly, when they have been driving for half an hour.

"For the summer or for good?"

"I don't know. A friend of mine called yesterday. He was an alternate for a one-year teaching job in Indiana, and the other guy backed out at the last minute. He heard that I was looking to come back, so he asked me if I would house-sit for him while he's in Indiana. All I have to do is pay the utilities and do some repairs he'd been planning to get done—some carpentry work I can do on my own. It's a way I can get back there and start over."

"That sounds good."

"Does it?"

"Of course."

"Will you come and visit me?"

"I don't think so. You can't ask me that." Her voice catches in her throat and wavers. She takes a deep breath and doesn't say anything more.

Eric puts his hand over hers, which is clenched into a fist on her lap. "I'm sorry. This has been on my mind all morning. If I decide to go, I have to be there by the last week of June. That's only a month from now. When my friend called, I almost wished he hadn't. I told him I'd call him back tonight. I hesitated because I was thinking of you."

"Promise you'll go. Don't stay here and be unhappy."

"But I'll be unhappy *there* now," he says.

"Not for long," she insists. "You'll feel better once you're away."

"I don't think so. But you can believe that if you want to."

"I do." She opens her hand and lets her fingers intertwine with his. By the time he is settled in Vermont, she might be alone. If she told him the truth now, changing the course of her life might be as easy as following the road as it curves first to the right, then the left. But Maya pictures Nancy waving her floor mat beside her car. Love is a burning wreck smoldering on the side of the road. Maya wills herself to close her eyes and swerve around it.

Off the freeway, past a small town, they follow a narrow two-lane highway into the countryside. The trailer house is set back from the road. It's a solid structure with a white roof and brown siding, much bigger than the trailers and campers Maya has seen pulled behind trucks. A gravel driveway leads up to a garage built next to the trailer. A rusted metal windmill has been put up behind the house. Its weathervanes make a moaning sound, like the lowing of cattle.

From the back door, a hallway leads past two closed doors into the kitchen and the living room. The house is not the desolate place Maya imagined. The plaid couch in the living room is covered with two hand-crocheted afghans; even the top of the TV set has framed pictures, and the coffee table is scattered with magazines. From the ceiling in the kitchen hangs a mobile made of seashells and feathers—a child must have made it at school. Wallet-sized school portraits are taped on the fridge.

Maya steps closer for a better look. "These must be your nieces."

Eric points to the pictures. "They're all my sister's kids—Ashley, Sarah, and Jessica." Though there are a dozen pictures on the door, they show the same girls at various ages. From picture to picture, their hair and clothes change, but the eyes and the smiles remain the same.

"My sister is the only one with kids. I wasn't married long enough to have them and my brother is gay. My mother gave up on me having kids, but Kevin never came out to my parents because he was afraid of my father's reaction. Now that Dad's too far gone to understand anything, Kevin could just tell Mom, but he feels weird about it. He's kept his secret for so long. He can't tell the truth now without making her feel bad. He has no choice but to go on pretending that he's straight."

"I understand. The longer you say nothing, the harder it is to break the silence. There's always that moment when you should have told the truth.

If you miss it, you may never get another chance. Only you don't always know when you're at that now-or-never time." Maya recalls standing in Yuko's kitchen last week and handing her the cups in silence. Perhaps that was the now-or-never moment to tell her about Eric. *I'm falling in love with someone and I'm scared,* she should have said.

"Families," Eric says. "They can really screw you up. Compared to most, mine is pretty benign. Even my brother is fortunate."

On the shelf above the couch in the living room, three high school pictures stand side by side. The girl, in the center, has long straight hair parted in the middle; she's wearing a pale pink formal with a corsage of white lilies. The two boys have the kind of long hair that clean-cut boys could have in the late seventies—down to their ears but parted neatly on the side. Eric is wearing a powder blue jacket over a white ruffled shirt. His face is clean-shaven, as it is now, and he is smiling at the camera. Maya picks up the frame.

"I should have hidden that thing." Eric covers his eyes with his hand.

"You don't look so bad. You must have been going to the prom."

"I look like a lounge lizard."

She laughs, but it's the same kind of picture Jeff had taken at his mother's insistence. The only difference is that Eric's suit is more overdone because he lived in a rural area and he is more obviously handsome.

"Even my husband has pictures like this at his parents' house."

"Your husband," Eric says, "is a lucky guy."

The house is quiet except for the sound of the windmill in the back. Eric places his hand on the other corner of the picture frame. The moment for truth must resemble the big wave that surfers wait for. Riding its crest, a person could cross a tunnel of blue water to the other side. *I want to tell you something,* Maya might begin; *Jeff and I have been unhappy for a long time.* But she is thinking of her mother knocking on her door at midnight, her car packed with boxes. "I've left him." She giggled. "I'm on my way to be with the man I really love." Letting go of the picture frame, Maya steps away. "I'll help you with your chores," she says.

Walking down the hallway, Maya notices pictures everywhere: on the wall, on the stand outside the bathroom door, on the bulletin board by the telephone. Many of them are of Eric, his sister, and his brother from long ago. No matter how old the three of them get, they are always children splashing in the lake or eating ice-cream cones at a drive-in, along with the children who came twenty years later. Wherever he lives, he will always be one of the children in this laughing multitude. For a few months in Vermont, he will miss Maya, and then gradually he will forget her. Being alone is easier when you know that your mother's love is as unchanging as the pictures she keeps on the walls.

Around the trailer, feeders hang from hooks outside every window. Maya holds the tube and wire containers Eric takes down and tilts them for him to fill with black sunflower and thistle seeds, millet, corn. By the time they are halfway around the house, sparrows and finches are eating from the feeders they have just filled. Maya imagines herself as a small bird that a young man has saved from a trap and set free. Transforming herself into a woman, she would follow him all the rest of her life to pay back her debt. Nothing would stand in the way of her devotion. In this life, she is a woman Eric might recall with vague regret several years from now when he remembers the year he spent back home. "I thought I was in love with her," he would say, "but she was married."

Behind the trailer, the lawn ends after about twenty yards and a swath of tall weeds separates the property from the neighbor's cornfield. Where the lawn ends and the weeds start seems completely arbitrary. It doesn't follow a tree line and there is no marker.

"I'd better cut the grass," Eric says, when they are done with the feeders.

"I can go inside and vacuum. People like to come home to a freshly cleaned house."

"But I didn't bring you here to work."

"That's okay. I don't mind."

The vacuum cleaner is in the tiny hallway closet, half hidden behind the coats and a few pairs of winter slacks. There are only three coats: a long maroon dress coat, a powder-blue down parka, and a denim jacket with a pink flannel lining. Eric's father's coats must have been moved to the nursing home or given away; he is never expected to return. Maya takes out the vacuum cleaner and starts cleaning the kitchen. Living alone in this trailer, married to a man who does not remember the past they shared, Eric's mother must feel the worst kind of loneliness: she is all by herself and yet she is not free. Perhaps that was the way her father felt too. Being a father across the ocean would be the same as living in this trailer, bound to someone who will never return. He sent back Maya's letters because to read them was to hold on to false hope.

At the end of the hallway, Maya pushes open one of the closed doors and enters a room with a large double bed covered with a white hand-stitched quilt. On the nightstand is a photograph of an older couple standing together. The man is wearing a navy-blue suit; the woman is in a pale yellow dress. They both have white hair and rosy cheeks. The woman's eyes are the same shade between brown and green as Eric's.

Three plain frames hang on the wall opposite the bed. The pencil sketches are of bare trees, with the sky above them full of dark clouds. Every detail is decisive and strong, but the shading looks murky and emotional. Maya notices Eric standing in the doorway behind her.

"Those are the things my mother likes the best of all my work. I'm not sure if it's because they're straightforward and uncomplicated or because she knows they're about her."

"The sketches are good. They have a lot of feeling."

Eric steps into the room and stands next to her. "Four years ago, when my parents were still living on the farm, I spent Christmas with them. My father was forgetful and impatient. He snapped at my mother for the most insignificant things. I should have had some compassion, but I couldn't stand to be with him. I was mad at my mother, too, for taking his verbal abuse and saying nothing. Many afternoons, I had to get out of the house and drive to an apple orchard several miles away. I stayed out until I couldn't see anything. I was sketching just to get away, but later I thought, Maybe these are about my mother being alone."

The trees are in the foreground, their black branches darker than the shades falling fast behind them. Instead of melting away into darkness, the branches stand out as if they had grown more solid with the diminishing light.

"At least that's how I wanted to imagine her life without my father."

"I'm sure your mother understands." Maya pictures darkness rising from the trees and filling the room. "Come on," she says, taking his hand. "You must be thirsty."

Inside the refrigerator in the kitchen, there is nothing except a glass pitcher of clear liquid—water, it must be—on the top shelf. She pulls open the freezer and finds a dozen round disks wrapped in aluminum. They're deep-dish pie tins, the kind restaurants use to wrap up leftovers.

"What are these?"

"Meals-on-wheels. Someone from Manitowoc delivers them three times a week, but my mother seldom eats them. She's too polite to say anything, so she just sticks them in the freezer."

Maya closes the freezer. Inside the fridge, a pure, cold light from the bulb illuminates the clear water, the only thing his mother wants to be nourished by.

Eric lets go of her hand. "I'm ashamed of myself. I want to romanticize my mother's life with sketches of trees, when actually she's an old woman living alone in a trailer. She won't eat because she wishes her life were over."

"Don't blame yourself."

"I can't do a thing for her, and I'm running away."

"You're not running away. She wants you to go. She's letting go of you because she loves you."

When Eric looks down, his eyes are red. Maya puts her arms around him and kisses his cheek. His skin is warm with a faint taste of salt. She remembers a story her father told her about a warrior who sent a handful of sea salt to his enemy, who had exhausted his own supply and was dying. The two men were supposed to meet in battle the following day. The warrior wanted to save the other man's life, even though he was willing to kill him the next day with his sword. People long ago must have been so much more capable of finding their way through a maze of emotions—pity, generosity, a desire for justice and fairness, love.

Eric holds her tight, one arm wrapped around her waist and the other gently cupping her face. She closes her eyes and feels his fingers smoothing her hair. Slowly, he begins to kiss her cheek and then her eyebrows. She hears a sigh but she can't decide which one of them has made it. Outside, the windmill is creaking. Turning her face aside, she kisses the palm of his hand and looks up at him.

His eyelashes remind her of something fragile under glass—a shed flower, the torn wing of a dragonfly. Everything about his face seems utterly familiar. In the instant it takes her to memorize all the small shadows that fall across his closed eyelids, she has made up her mind. When he leans down toward her, she stands on her tiptoes to meet his kiss. She is falling through layers of air and water toward him. She clings to him as he touches her face and presses his lips against hers. When they stop, she knows they are coming up only for a short breath. She doesn't say anything. She kisses him again.

Holding tightly to each other, they enter the narrow hallway and keep walking. When he opens the door to the spare room, Maya remembers the afternoon she walked down the corridor that curved toward her plane in Osaka. There is no way she can turn back, now as then. She steps into the room and lies down with him on the blue quilt on the bed by the window. As he unbuttons her blouse, each twist of his fingers draws a little circle and an X that might mean *kisses, hugs*. Outside the window, a bird feeder hangs from the hook; behind it, she can see the cloudless sky so far away. Across that blank stretch of blue, house sparrows are darting back and forth. Just before they land on the feeder, they stop in midair and flutter their wings, as if to right their aim. Each sparrow eats hungrily, spilling the empty sunflower hulls like tiny black wings. Under their chins, the males have thumb-sized imprints of black, shaped like mysterious continents on a map. She will always remember this place, this patch of the sky, though she will never be here again.

She shrugs out of her blouse and holds on tight while they kiss. Under his T-shirt, her fingers trace the warm skin of his chest and slide smoothly down his stomach. They continue to kiss while she tries the belt buckle, unbuckling it easily with one hand. In the warm place where their lips come together, she doesn't have to say anything. Each kiss is a word they speak in silence, the slow movements of their tongues like calligraphy known only to them. Soon, they've shed what was left of their clothing. With his hand on the small of her back, he pulls her hard toward him, cradling her with the other arm as though she were both fragile and strong. She keeps on kissing him as their bodies come together, her silent words saying, *Don't stop, don't be afraid*. They lie still for a few seconds, their mouths and legs locked tight, his hand gently stroking her long hair, before they begin to move together. In those few seconds, Maya imagines the future. When she comes out of this room, her life will never be the same. She will be as alone as she was when she watched the sky tilt blue outside the window of her plane all those years ago. Only this time she won't cry or feel regret.

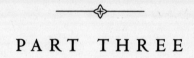

PART THREE

— 15 —

Cornfields stretch in every direction behind the gas station. The lot has three pumps and an old-fashioned phone booth with a door. Only someone hopelessly far away from home would use the booth. Their shoulder pressed against the plastic wall, they would hear the phone ringing hundreds of miles away in another climate.

Inside the store, deli containers of bait are stacked next to the soda cans in the cooler. "This is my hometown." Eric laughs. "You can buy night crawlers anywhere."

"Are you a good fisherman?" Maya asks.

"My brother and I used to fish in the pond near our parents' farm. We stopped because neither of us liked cleaning the fish."

"You don't like to inflict pain."

He tightens his fingers around her hand. "I don't want you to be hurt by what we did."

"I'm not easily hurt."

"I don't believe that."

"You'll have to. Otherwise, you'd feel bad."

"I want you to come with me to Vermont."

The soda cans behind glass are bright red, green, and orange. Each row is neatly lined up, the same colors following each other all the way to the back. Eric is about to say something, but Maya places her index finger on his lips. "Please. Can we not talk about this right now?"

He opens his mouth and moves his tongue slowly across her finger. If her fingertip could make music, it would sound like a violin solo underwater. "You didn't make love to me like that without caring about me," he says, when she tries to pull away.

Instead of answering, she opens the cooler and takes the nearest cans. "We should go."

The man behind the cashier looks up as they approach. Maya puts the soda cans on the counter. The man pushes his gray hair out of his eyes and squints at her.

"Hi. Gas over there and these sodas," Eric points to his car outside.

Without speaking, the man takes the twenty-dollar bill Eric has pulled out of his pocket. As he turns away to make change, Eric puts his arms around Maya and kisses her. "I love you," he whispers, and kisses her again. With his hand on her back, he turns as if they were slow-dancing and places himself between her and the counter. They are still kissing when the man slams the change on the counter. Eric takes his time collecting it, one arm wrapped around Maya's waist. They walk away, still holding each other.

"*Thank you* would have been the right thing for him to say," Eric whispers, as the door closes behind them. "I'm sorry."

"People always stare at me in small towns. I'm used to it."

"People should only stare at you because you're pretty."

"He was just curious."

"The first time I saw you, you were standing by a window talking to one of your customers. You looked so delicate and pretty. The woman you were talking to was towering over you. I wanted to stand next to you and put my arm around you like this."

"You thought that when you were with Sylvia?"

"Yes. Sylvia noticed me staring at you. Maybe that's why she got so mean."

"No." Maya shakes her head. "Sylvia's always moody and mean. That's just how she is."

Dusk is falling when they get back to Peg's store. Maya has been lying across the seat with her head on his lap. Half asleep, she could feel his fingers smoothing her hair and stroking her face. When the car stops, she sits up. Neither of them speaks for a long time.

"I don't want to let you go," he says finally.

"You have to."

"Will you be all right?"

"I think so."

"When can I see you again?"

"I don't know." She opens the door. "Promise that you won't call or come looking for me."

"Why not?"

"I'm not sure if I can see you again." She pushes the door wider.

Eric puts his hand over hers. She doesn't resist when he pulls her back toward him. "I don't know what your situation is at home, but I don't think you're happy there. I want you to come with me."

"I can't do that. But you have to call your friend and tell him you're moving back. I won't be able to forgive myself if you don't go."

"I can't imagine being there without you."

"If you stay, I'll never see you."

"Do you mean that?"

"Yes, absolutely." She gets out of his car without another word.

The familiar highway at dusk looks like a foreign territory. Off the exit, her own neighborhood comes up first, but Maya keeps driving. She parks in front of Yuko's building and runs up to the fourth floor. No one answers the door, but the spare key is on her key ring. She unlocks the door and goes in.

Several boxes from department stores downtown are scattered around the living room. Yuko's parents have been in town since last week. Maya sits down on the floor and closes her eyes. She can see Eric's face as though he were only an arm's reach away. "I've wanted to touch you like this for so long," he said. When he lay on his back and held her above him, the wrinkled blue quilt under them reminded her of the waves of the sea. All afternoon, she felt as though they were swimming and flying at once. Even the tiny shower stall, where they stood shivering and kissing as the water turned cold, resembled an underwater chamber or a capsule inside a spaceship. If they'd met earlier, she might have slept in his arms every night and dreamed about secret rooms where she could stay, breathing perfect air under the sea or up in the stratosphere. When Eric kissed her at the gas station, her hair was still damp from the shower; they stood surrounded by the faint apple smell of the shampoo, as though they were holding each other inside an invisible net. In the car on the way home, he traced the shape of her cheekbone, the curve of her lips and eyebrows, as though he meant to memorize her face by touch.

Maya turns on the desk lamp Yuko has placed on the makeshift shelves and picks up the telephone from the floor. She dials the number and hears the phone ringing. As usual, the machine comes on.

"Jeff," she says, "it's me. Pick up."

"Where are you? It's almost eight o'clock."

"I'm at Yuko's."

He doesn't respond. She can sense the silence thicken around them. It's as though they were sitting next to each other one final time.

"I can't come back. I'm sorry."

His breath scratches against the phone when he sighs.

"I know we promised to talk if one of us decided to leave. But I can't. I don't know what there is to say."

"I'm not surprised. With you, there's no discussion ever. It's time for you to go, so you go. You couldn't care less that I'm not ready."

"But you would have been ready sooner or later."

He doesn't answer.

"You aren't ready. That's not the same as saying you want me to stay. We were coming to the same decision. What difference does it make whether we talked it over or got there separately?"

"I want to ask you one thing."

"What?"

"Did you ever really love me?"

"I don't know."

"It's a simple question. Yes or no."

"I didn't love you in the way I should have."

"Well, that's all I needed to know."

Before she can say anything, he hangs up. She puts down the receiver and pushes the phone away. She pictures Jeff sitting alone in the kitchen. On the table, the violets they picked from the lawn faded overnight; the petals shrank into fragile sheaths that resembled insect wings. In ten years, Maya will have almost nothing to say about Jeff. So many of her good memories from the last four years are about being alone in the house: making bread in the late afternoons while she waited for him to get home, gardening on summer mornings while he read the paper in the living room. They are only about him indirectly. Once, a divorced woman who came to the store said about her marriage, "There was nothing really wrong with it, but there wasn't much right with it, either."

In his apartment, Eric, too, might be staring at the telephone, trying to will himself to call his friend in Vermont, believing Maya has gone home to her husband. If she called him now and told him that she was at Yuko's, he would ask her to come to him. She would tell him that her marriage is already over. In a month, she could follow him to a place where no one would know her. When people asked her where she was from, she could reply, "Oh, Wisconsin and Minnesota and, before that, Osaka." She would smile mysteriously, implying that there was more to the story but she wished not to discuss it. Her mother uses that smile when she tells people that she grew up in

Canada. Inside her own head, Maya would hear the screech of the tape fast-forwarding through her life before Eric. The thousands of evenings she and Yuko had driven around town looking for something to do and come home perfectly contented after just a cup of coffee, the weekend afternoons she'd sat in the store with Peg, their numerous parties, and the hours she'd spent weaving in her studio—all would become a blur of vague memories. In her new life, Maya would be no one except through Eric. Like an invisible friend a child makes up, she would be nothing even to herself.

Maya wonders what Yuko would think if she told her the truth. "You're out of your mind," Yuko would say. "You can't move across the country with someone you've just met. Maybe you love him now, but what if you changed or he did? You'll end up alone in a strange place." So far, the two of them have been proof that a friendship can outlast any change. Since the first hour they sat next to each other in Miss Larson's class, their friendship has felt like a perfect duet: Yuko's rich alto intertwining, conversation after conversation, with Maya's tremulous soprano. No matter what changes they have gone through over the years, their voices have kept weaving around the same basic harmony. Maya cannot separate her own thoughts from Yuko's anymore than she can distinguish the voices from the sound they make together. Every opinion she has, even those they don't agree about, has a part that comes from Yuko. If she went to Vermont with Eric, her life with him might be the same way. Year after year, she would feel the different variations of that moment he touched his warm fingers to her wrist in his kitchen and her heart beat so fast she could not speak. If their feelings for each other were as unchanging as the friendship she has with Yuko, Maya would come to believe that she was always meant to be with him and no one else. Yuko would then become nothing more than a childhood friend whom Maya might visit once or twice a year. That must be how most married women think of their old friends. For them, any friendship with another woman, no matter how close, is only a rehearsal; once they are married, their husbands are the center of their lives, and everyone else is just someone from the past. Kay must have thought so every time she started a new life with a new man. After each marriage, she became a different person, while Maya's father spent the rest of his life drawing in his diary and painting in their old house in the shade of trees. He chose loneliness over happiness that requires erasing the past and forgetting who you used to be.

Maya gets up and goes out the back door to the roof. The comet is long gone. Instead, in the southern sky, there are two planets. One is brighter than the other, but both shine hard and cold without flickering and blinking like stars.

When Yuko comes home, Maya can hear her steps on the metal rungs of the ladder.

"I'm sorry I wasn't here," Yuko says, hugging Maya. "I went out to dinner with my parents."

"I figured that. I'm glad you gave me the key."

"Let's go downstairs," Yuko says.

In the kitchen, Maya sits down at the table while Yuko makes tea. The note she left is still on the counter: *I'm up on the roof. I made my decision.* Yuko pours the tea into two cups, hands one to Maya, and sits down. The sharp ginger flavor of the tea reminds Maya of the Thai restaurant they used to go to in Minneapolis. Maya has lost count of all the times they have sat together like this. Their sophomore year in high school, Yuko found a picture postcard of two very old women in identical straw hats and gingham dresses seated in front of a birthday cake. Even though one woman was much taller than the other, their wrinkled faces—with eyes almost disappearing into their sockets and lips stretched into loose, big grins—looked very much the same. Yuko tacked that postcard on the wall in the kitchen where she and Maya baked their cakes. "This is us in eighty years," they used to say, and laugh.

Yuko is smiling at Maya in an uncertain way, waiting for her to speak. Maya puts down her teacup but doesn't know what to say. Leaving a marriage is one thing: without Eric, even without Nancy,

Maya and Jeff might have come to the same end sooner or later. That isn't true at all about her friendship with Yuko. Without Eric, Maya would never consider moving away from Yuko only six months after Dan left her. She and Yuko could travel, share a house, or go into business together like some of the women from Peg's town. Theirs would be a good future, an equal measure of solitude and friendship. If she hadn't met Eric, Maya wouldn't want anything else. But the moment she thinks about him, Maya feels as though she were only half here, drinking tea with Yuko. The other half of her is still in that room, her arms clasped tight around him. Maybe that's what's wrong with love: being in love can make you hurt everyone except your lover; a person in love is even more selfishly alone than someone who chooses simple solitude.

"I take it that your decision was to leave Jeff," Yuko says.

Maya nods. "I already called him and told him I'm not coming back. He hung up on me, but he didn't try to stop me."

"You're not disappointed that he didn't try to stop you, are you?"

"Of course not."

"That's good. Dan wanted me to cry and beg him to stay, I'm convinced of it. Even though it was his idea to dump me, he wanted me to say I was miserable, too. He wanted us to have that one final agreement before he could leave me."

Dan's actions might have been the result of a warm heart gone wrong. Perhaps he couldn't tear himself away because he was overwhelmed by pity. Maya can't recall a time when she was overwhelmed by any feeling toward Jeff. Every time he seemed upset about something that happened at school or at his parents' house, she turned away politely, believing she was giving him privacy. This afternoon, when Eric's eyes were red from the tears he was holding back, she wanted to put her arms around him and hold him close until the hurt look was gone. There's an expression she's heard many times and dismissed as an exaggeration: *My heart went out to him.* Just like that, she felt her heart jump out of her body, leaving behind an empty skin. Everything about her felt transparent; a single match could light up all the dark corners.

"I need to stay here for a few days," she tells Yuko.

"You can stay longer than that."

"I might go away, though. If Peg can give me a month off, I'll go somewhere to be alone. I'll come back in July to settle things with Jeff and look for an apartment."

"Where will you go?"

"I don't know. Somewhere." She can hardly visit her mother for two days. If Lillian lived anywhere but in Evanston, she could stay with her, but her place is too close to Kay's.

"You can visit my parents," Yuko offers. "They'll give you a key to the cottage if you want to be alone. No one goes there during the week. You can take your cat, even. I'll come up to visit you." Yuko frowns uncertainly. "Unless, of course, you want to be absolutely alone. Then I won't bother you."

"Oh, Yuko, of course I'll want to see you. I didn't mean it like that." Maya touches Yuko's arm.

Yuko smiles. "Good. I don't want you to turn into a hermit."

The Nakashimas' cottage is an hour north of Minneapolis on a small lake. It will be easy to stay there until Eric has gone back to Vermont.

"Do you want me to ask my parents? They're here for another day. I can bring my mother to the shop if you'd rather ask her yourself."

"I'll talk to Peg tomorrow and arrange for the time off first." As she puts her arms around Yuko's shoulders, Maya thinks of the note she will leave for Eric on her way out of town. If she doesn't tell Peg where she is staying, he will never be able to find her.

The blue sweatshirt and pants Yuko lent her are too long, making Maya look floppy, like a rag doll, but she has enough clothes in the loft to go away for a month. "I'm leaving Jeff, and I need a retreat," she will tell Peg. "I don't want anyone but Yuko to know where I am. I'll call you so you won't worry." If Peg needs someone to fill in, she'll suggest Jennifer, who's been complaining more and more about working for Sylvia.

Maya turns the wheel around the last bend in the narrow road. When she sees a car parked in front of the store, she doesn't immediately understand. Then she notices him sitting on the bench, exactly where he was yesterday. Maya looks back over her shoulder. The road is too narrow to turn her car. In high school, in driver's ed, everyone had to drive backward for one hundred yards. Maya loved the high whine of the gears and the scenery reversing itself. She could drive backward faster and more decisively than anyone else in her group. But Eric is running toward her. He stands next to her car and taps on her window until she turns off her engine and pushes the door open.

He steps back to let her out, but the next moment his arms are around her and he is holding her tight. His lips graze her hair when she turns her face away from his kiss. She doesn't realize that she is crying, until she hears him murmuring, "I'm sorry." He is touching her cheek and his fingertips are wet.

"You broke your promise." She wants to say more, but she can't. Instead, she is clinging to him and thinking, *This is all wrong.*

"Do you remember the dream I told you about?" he asks, after they sit down on the bench.

"About waiting for the ferry?" She rests her head against his shoulder. Through the tiny holes in his black T-shirt, she can see his skin like distant stars.

"We were sitting on a bench like this." He tightens his arm around her shoulder. "I didn't tell you before, but we were kissing in the dream. I was hoping we'd missed the last boat because I wanted to go on kissing you. I didn't want to stop."

"I guess I knew that." Maya leans up and kisses him. She is letting herself back into his dream. She imagines the water lapping at the shore, gulls screaming in the distance. It could have been the lake, or the ocean, or the blue water of the inland sea she saw from the plane. She pictures tears falling from the sky and turning into the blue salt water below. "Was it like this?" she asks, kissing him again and again.

"Yes. When I dreamed about it, that wasn't the first time I wanted to kiss you. The morning you brought me back here in your car and hugged me, I wanted to. I couldn't think about anything else for hours afterward."

"Why didn't you kiss me?"

"Because I didn't want you to think I was bad. You'd just told me that you were married. I guessed that you weren't happy. You looked so sad when you pointed out your finger without a wedding ring."

"I stayed at Yuko's last night. I didn't go home. I never will." Maya looks down and kicks some pebbles with her shoe. "But I meant to go away without seeing you. That's why I came in early. I was going to ask Peg for time off. I would have left you a note but I wouldn't have said where I was going."

"I knew you were saying good-bye to me last night. I came to wait for you because I figured you'd have to get things squared away before you could leave. You wouldn't just take off."

"I wouldn't?"

"No. You'd never do that to Peg or your cat, or even to me."

"Leaving you the note would have been the hardest part." She looks away. "Now I don't have to do that because I've told you everything I would have written. I can't tell you anything more. I'll be gone by the end of the week."

He puts his hand under her chin and turns her face gently toward him. "Do you love me?" he asks.

"Yes."

"So why won't you come with me to Vermont? Are you afraid because we only met last month and it's such a long way to go? If you are, we can stay here until you feel ready."

"That's not what worries me." Maya takes his hand in both of hers. "I can't go because it's wrong. I don't mean because I'm married. Jeff and I haven't been very happy for a long time. His first wife is back in town, and she wants to be with him. We'd have gone our separate ways sooner or later. Afterward, I'd have lived alone, spent time with my friend Yuko, worked for Peg, and been content with my quiet life. If I left with you, I'd feel like I was running away instead of being alone to face things." She pictures her father at his kitchen table with a pencil in his hand. He is drawing the long tunnel of solitude that stretches between this life and the next. "I just can't go with you," Maya says.

Eric leans toward her until his forehead is touching hers. It's what her father used to do to see if she had a fever. "You feel a little warm," he would say, going to get a thermometer, or, "You feel just fine. Nothing wrong with you."

"Don't go away. At least be with me until I have to leave. You don't have to come with me if you don't want to."

"I don't know."

His hand behind her neck, he pulls her toward him. "You can't deny how you feel." Maya imagines the Nakashimas' cabin, the lonely lake at night. She can hear the creak of the floorboards under her steps. That, or somewhere like that, is where she is headed eventually. But for now she can't stop kissing him and wanting to feel his fingers touching her hair.

"Promise you'll go back to Vermont," she manages to say, "without me."

"If that's what you want at the end of June, I'll have no choice."

"And you won't try to talk me into going with you."

"No."

"I won't be able to tell anyone about us. Not even my best friend, because I don't know how to tell her. You'll be my secret."

"I don't care about anyone else." His hands on her shoulders, he looks into her face. "Will you stay?" he asks.

"Yes," she answers. "I'll stay."

Inside the barn, Casper is waiting at the top of the stairs. As soon as he sees Eric, Casper streaks down the steps with his tail puffed up.

"I was going to take Casper if I went away. He'd have been miserable without me."

"He wouldn't have been the only one."

"I found Casper a month after my father died. I wanted to believe that my father had sent him to console me. A long time ago, my father took me to a weaving cottage, where we saw a beautiful black cat. Casper could have been his counterpart, all white instead of black. I loved traveling with my father. I was so proud to be with him."

"I wish I could go back into the past with you," Eric says. "If there was a time machine, that's what I'd want to do—go back and see all the important moments of your life."

Holding hands, they walk up to the loft, where she gets her clothes from the closet. He's still holding her hand as she heads for the shower. He only lets go to take off her sweatshirt and pull his own T-shirt over his head.

"Before yesterday," she says, "I never took a shower with anyone because I was too shy."

"You weren't very shy with me yesterday."

"The faucet's tricky. The hot water makes a very annoying noise. It whines, but in a very high pitch."

"I don't mind," he says, pulling open the shower curtain.

Five minutes later, she's not even hearing that high-pitched noise anymore as she leans back under the stream of water, her back toward him as he washes her hair.

"I haven't had anyone wash my hair since I was four. I scarcely remember it." All she recalls is leaning against the kitchen sink in her pajamas with eyes squinched shut, ears covered, while her father poured a thin stream of water from a basin. From this distance in time, it feels like a brave act of faith. "At my house, it was my father who took care of me when I was little. My mother wasn't around much. She was taking classes and teaching at a university. Some days, I didn't even see her. I didn't miss her, but my father was a modest man, so I had to be on my own to take a bath or dress myself."

"You'd have thought we were shameless. My brother, sister, and I used to swim naked in a little plastic pool in our backyard until we were eight or nine. Our mother was too naive to be embarrassed." He turns her toward him and hugs her. "You're beautiful."

She reaches behind her and shuts off the water. The sudden quietness surprises her. Opening the shower curtain, he takes the large purple towel hanging on the rack and drapes it around her hair. The towel hangs over her shoulders, covering her almost down to her waist.

As he pulls her, still draped in purple, toward him, Maya remembers a woman in a magic trick she once saw. The woman lay down in a box, and the magician draped a cloth over it. He began his countdown and then sawed the box in half. When the cloth was removed, the woman reappeared, miraculously unhurt, though the box remained cut in half. During those seconds in between, the woman was in a secret place known only to herself and the magician, hidden, safe, and invisible.

In the foyer, Jeff's faded running shoes are placed next to black patent-leather sandals with spike heels. On the antique hat rack Maya and Jeff never used, a floppy black hat perches like a crow. Maya crosses the foyer and climbs up the stairs, with Yuko following. At the top, she points to the spare room.

"My winter coats are in the closet in there. If you can grab them and throw them in the backseat, I'll get the rest of my clothes from the bedroom."

Maya pulls open the closet door and finds a black camisole and boxer shorts hanging from the hook. The glossy synthetic fabric looks fragile but it's probably tougher than anything. In the burn test that textile specialists use to identify fabric swatches, it would curl and shrink into itself with hardly a flame. Maya's clothes haven't been moved or touched. She gathers a whole row of dresses into one of the black plastic bags she brought. When the bag is full, she takes it to the stairway landing. Yuko is halfway down the stairs with an armload of coats.

"When you're done with the coats, you can take the bags down. I'll put them here." She returns to the closet, where she collects the rest of the hanging clothes, then starts with the folded clothes on the shelves. One after another, she takes the bags and sets them on the landing so Yuko will be kept busy going up and down the stairs. She doesn't want her to come into the room and see Nancy's camisole and boxer shorts. Maya and Yuko have never owned underclothes like these. In the four years she lived here, Maya always got dressed in the bathroom with the door shut, unless she knew that she was alone. She slept in clothes she sewed for herself: cotton and flannel nightgowns with long full skirts, linen pajamas with pretty shell buttons and precise cuffs on the shirt-sleeves. Jeff hated the thick, quilted bed jacket she wore to read in bed. "It looks like you're wearing a tent. It's not exactly alluring," he complained. The bed jacket has patterns of moons and stars, gold and silver against a deep blue background. The clay buttons she made are shaped like the planets. She'd had no idea how dowdy and foolish her clothes must have looked to someone who was used to black camisoles and spike heels.

The plastic bags bulge as though they contain garbage instead of clothes. Complete strangers used to stop her on the street to compliment her on what she was wearing, and she felt proud instead of shy. She never expected to feel ashamed of her clothes.

In the bathroom, boxes of rouge and makeup brushes clutter the shelf above the sink. A pink hair dryer is still plugged in. The bathtub has some plastic toys: a blue shark, a windup swimmer, a pair of yellow rubber ducks that remind Maya of her own childhood. Yuko is standing in the doorway. Maya takes down the oak jewelry case Dan made for her.

"I can get that," Yuko says, reaching for the case.

As their arms come together to form a double V around the case, Maya feels her throat tighten.

"It's okay," Yuko says. "Dan did a good job on this. I'm glad you have it."

Inside the case, Dan made various compartments for her earrings, necklaces, and bracelets, assembled from beads by herself or cast in silver by the jewelers she traded pieces with. Her whole history from the last ten years is contained in the box, but there is no reminder of Jeff. The only piece of jewelry that connected her to him was her wedding ring, lost several months before Nancy arrived back in town.

After the clothes and the jewelry box, all Maya has left in the house are the odds and ends in the kitchen drawer and her bicycle in the garage. Throughout her marriage, many of her things were in the loft above the store, and it seems only natural that she's moving there. "I'd feel better about the store with you there all the time," Peg said. "Remember when those kids knocked down a bunch of mailboxes and stole a case of beer from Natalie's garage? You and Casper can keep the place safe. Free rent is part of the deal." Peg smiled and held up her hand when Maya protested.

Maya follows Yuko down the stairs and opens the garage door. "I just have a few things in the kitchen. I'll be right out."

On the kitchen table, next to some picture books, there is a wooden puzzle where a child has to put brightly colored cutout pieces back into the board, matching the shapes. The yellow triangles, red circles, and blue squares remind Maya of landscapes painted in the first part of the century. Almost before she was old enough to read, her father taught her how the purple road and the green sky Gabriele Munter saw in Germany and the pink and blue mountains Georgia O'Keeffe painted in New Mexico were transforming themselves into triangles and squares, into pure geometry. "Look at the way that sky cuts into the road," he would say. "Most of that composition is taken up by a shadow. All the lines come at the same angle." While her mother made her learn English, her father taught her the language of colors and light, of shapes and lines and angles. Even in their short time together, he gave a legacy. Maya never looked at any landscape without noticing the fields of color, the shapes of light, the alignment of the world. Nancy's daughter, when she is twenty, will see the wheat and cornfields outside the city and remember this kitchen where she learned the names of colors and shapes from a wooden puzzle. Maya picks up a yellow triangle that has not found its proper place. With its sharp point turned straight up, it fits perfectly into the shape cut out of the wood. She runs her fingers over it and closes her eyes. If she knew the right benediction, she would say it. *May you learn the colors in peace. May you grow up in beauty. I give you my blessing and my good-will.* The yellow triangle will come back, again and again, in a pool of sunshine next to a window, the brightness at the heart of a lily where the petals are fused.

Mr. Kubo's letter is still in the kitchen drawer. He has not written her a second time. Maya pulls out the drawer and empties its contents into a bag. Spools of thread, coloring pencils, a disposable camera— everything falls on top of the letter at the bottom of the bag. In the garage, she picks up her bicycle pump, binoculars, and helmet. Yuko has already put her bicycle on the roof rack. Maya shoves the last items in the car and then reaches into the glove compartment for her garage door opener.

Standing in the driveway, she takes her two house keys off the key ring. With the opener aimed at the door, she presses the button. There's a whirr, and immediately the door starts coming down. Maya throws the opener and the keys into the garage and watches them slide across the concrete floor. They remind her of pebbles skipping across the waves.

"You don't have to live here alone unless you really want to," Yuko says, when they've unloaded the bags. "If you think it's spooky to be out here, you can always come back to my place."

"It's not spooky. I'm comfortable here."

Even the couch, where she is sitting with Yuko now, reminds her of Eric. The morning he had come to the store, she got dressed and ran downstairs when she heard voices. It was nearly eleven, and two women from Illinois were browsing through the store unattended. "Sorry. I was upstairs and didn't hear you," Maya said. Her face turned hot when one of them looked at her and smiled. When she went back upstairs, Eric had fallen asleep on the couch, and Casper was perched on the shelf across the room, looking down at him with his shoulders hunched. "Your cat looks like a gargoyle," Eric said, opening his eyes. "He must be your guardian spirit." When Maya sat down on the edge of the couch, Eric pulled her toward him. "Are your customers gone?" he asked. She nodded. "Good," he whispered. "I don't think it's going to be very busy today." Since then, she has gone to stay with him every night; most afternoons, he comes and sits in the store, working on his drawings and collages at the café table while she tends to her customers. Maya told Yuko that she changed her mind about going away. "Taking off from work didn't seem like such a good idea after all. I still need to be alone to think, but I can do that without going all the way to Minnesota." She must have sounded so wishy-washy.

Casper is scratching the door in the bathroom, where she's locked him up. "I'm not alone," Maya says to Yuko. There's someone I need to tell you about, she might begin; I didn't go away because of him. But when Yuko turns to her with a slight frown, Maya says, "There's Casper." The comment sounds lame even to herself.

Yuko laughs. "You and that cat. It must have been destiny that brought you together. He's devoted to you."

"He's my guardian angel."

"Come on. He's more like the devil. I'm his godmother, and still he makes that awful noise at me. I should have named him Damien or Beelzebub. You told me he'd settled down."

"I thought he did because he runs away from the customers. But he must consider the upstairs to be his territory. That's why he doesn't want you up here." Casper has taken to sitting at Eric's feet, regarding him warily with his blue eyes.

"Do you want to go get something to eat—or see a movie?" Yuko asks.

"Maybe another time," Maya answers. "I'll take you out to dinner for helping me, but I don't feel up to it tonight."

Yuko pats her shoulder. "You're not feeling so good, huh?"

Maya shakes her head. "I'm all right," is all she can say.

"You want to be alone. I understand. You know you're doing the right thing," Yuko says, as she gets up from the couch. "Everything will be okay."

The envelope her father sent is on the worktable. With her fingertips, Maya traces the pictorial letters he had written, spelling her name in Japanese. He had named her *Mayumi*, true arrow, because the name suggested strength and fidelity: a person who can fly like an arrow, straight to the heart of the matter. She has turned out to be more like the single arrow from another proverb: a single arrow is easily broken, but three arrows can withstand any force. She and her parents are three arrows that got separated and broken, one by one.

On the back of the envelope is a picture she drew last week. Sitting in the studio alone after Eric had gone to run an errand, she had wanted to record what was in her head, as her father had done every morning. She kept thinking of the sparrows that plummeted out of the sky and swarmed to the feeders outside the window at Eric's mother's trailer, so she drew them upside down, the way she saw them while she was lying down on the bed in that small room. At the top of the picture is the feeder, with its circle in the center and the straight lines of perches. Birds seem to be swimming up to these shapes and lines instead of flying down—they are fluttering upward, trying to surface with their necks outstretched and wings pulled back.

Her lines are shaky. She will never draw with confidence again. All the same, from the bag she brought from Jeff's house, she takes out the envelope that contains Mr. Kubo's letter and turns it to the back. With a pencil, she draws the phone booth outside the gas station near the highway. It's a square box in the middle of cornfields, which she indicates with jagged vertical lines, adding the roads intersecting in the front. The box resembles something dropped from the sky. Perhaps it longs, in vain, to be lifted back into the air. If she had called her father, she would have felt like someone inside that booth. It would have taken courage to stand in the middle of nowhere, dial the number, and wait, with the whole silent world listening in. A person named for a flying arrow should have had that courage.

Maya reaches into the first envelope and takes out her father's drawing and the black-and-white portrait of him. The lines in his sketch are decisive and strong. He drew the flames of hell as though he had seen them, not simply imagined them. In the photograph, his eyes appear sorrowful, his forehead etched with deep lines of loneliness. He would have looked less pained, Maya is sure, if he had never gotten married and had been alone all along. His solitude then might have been tolerable or even satisfying, a peaceful life dedicated to work. But once a person falls in love, being alone is never the same. In the last two weeks, Maya and Eric have only been separated for five, six hours at a time, and yet every time he comes to the store or she goes to his apartment after work, one or both of them says, "I missed you." One afternoon, he went inside a store to buy some tea while she waited in the car. When he opened the car door, he said, "There was a long line, and I started getting this terrible feeling that you might be gone when I came out. I almost walked out without getting the tea. I didn't want to miss out on any time I could be with you." The rest of Maya's life will be like those ten minutes he was gone. Alone with a gray road stretching before her outside the window, she won't find the comfort she used to feel in her hours at the loom, on the path by the lake, in the store surrounded by shawls and dresses. For the first time, she will know the solitude her father endured.

Eric is waiting for her in his apartment. "I wish you'd let me help you," he said, when she left to meet Yuko. "I can't," she answered, "but I'll be back as soon as we're done." Maya gathers the things on the worktable—the two envelopes, the photograph, her father's drawing, Mr. Kubo's letter—and takes them to the kitchen. She pulls the utensils out of the top left-hand drawer and places the letters and the pictures inside. This is the one thing she can keep from her four years with Jeff. The drawer under the sink is where she will keep all her unfinished business to mull over late at night when she can't sleep. A few pictures at a time, she will sketch the images that come to her. In time, layers of faint pencil marks will accumulate inside the drawer like fossils. Perhaps she herself will be turned into stone. If there is a goddess of solitude, as there are goddesses of love and wisdom, she must be like the Medusa of her father's stories, a woman whose unflinching stare could turn a person to stone. The goddess of solitude has been with Maya all along; she has watched over her childhood and all the years Maya lived alone before her marriage. When Eric is gone, Maya will have no choice but to go back to her. The courage that failed her before may finally come to her then. Though she could not step into a box out in the middle of nowhere and send her voice wavering across the ocean to her father, she will face the silence of his death without running away.

— 17 —

Every night for the last week they have woken up together between three and four, in the middle of a conversation they hadn't finished.

"You've never felt like this about anyone else," he said, "so how can you let me leave without you?" Instead of answering, she touched his hair, pressed her lips against his throat, and heard him sigh. "Until I met you," he insisted, "I thought I was perfectly happy alone. Now I think I must have been lonely without you. I must have missed you even before we met."

She kissed him before he could say another word. Until now, she did not know that desire is an unfailing way out of difficult talk, a shortcut through everything she cannot say. When she and Jeff came to the silence at the end of their argument, there was nowhere to go. Now she holds Eric's hand and kisses his fingertips as though each word she can't say might stay, like evidence, caught between the lines of his fingerprint.

On summer solstice, light lingers in the sky past nine. Everything in Eric's apartment has been packed except for the few pieces of furniture he sold to a young man who's coming to pick them up tomorrow afternoon. By then, he'll be halfway across Indiana. Sitting next to him on the front steps with her head on his shoulder, Maya remembers the night they struggled up these steps together, his arm around her waist as though he'd gotten hurt in an accident. Nighthawks are circling overhead. They fall a long way before soaring up again, their white wing patches shining. Maya has put her binoculars and field guide inside Eric's suitcase. He'll find them when he unpacks at his friend's house three days from now. Out in the woods in Vermont, birds will come to him with the field marks she showed him on their walks along the bluff: white eye rings, yellow wing patches, a faint orange wash over the breast—each mark will be a message from her even after they have lost touch.

Eric opens the box of sparklers he bought on his way home from his mother's last night. Maya was sleeping when he came back at eleven. "I wish I could make you fall asleep just as I'm leaving," he said. "I'd hypnotize you and take you to Vermont." Now, as the sky darkens, he hands her two of the sparklers. Watching him strike the match, Maya remembers her father lighting bottle rockets on summer nights. He always made her stay back a safe distance. Their favorite kind had a small parachute that came down at the end, a messenger from the sky. The sparklers in her hands begin to hiss softly. Eric gets two more and tips them toward hers. The buttons of fire move from her sparklers to his, splitting themselves. In the dark, there are four webs of light.

"We used to do this out on the farm. There were fireflies in a ravine in the back on summer nights. I thought the light from my sparklers was flying away and turning into those fireflies."

Maya pictures three children by the ravine, surrounded by the irregular flight of orange light. The sparklers would have made the same noise she is hearing now, and there would have been crickets in the grass. She wants to get a clear picture of everything he has told her. On the walls in his mother's trailer, the photographs of Eric's childhood are tacked next to those of his nieces. In Maya's mind, the three children by the ravine are across the street from herself and her father lighting their bottle rockets in their yard; the butterflies her father caught and then set free soar into the air next to Eric's fireflies. Perhaps memory can spread like the light Eric imagined as a child— bright sparks freeing themselves from the source and coming to life as they depart.

Her sparklers are almost extinguished. Just in time, Eric reaches into the box for another pair and holds them to the ones about to go out. The fire moves from one pair to the other, this time without splitting. He offers her the new sparklers with their orange webs. No matter how much it hurts when he leaves tomorrow morning, she wants to remember this moment when she is almost perfectly happy.

The only things left in the bedroom are the bed and a lamp on the windowsill.

"We can go to your loft if you feel better there," Eric says. "It looks desolate here."

Maya shakes her head. She can already picture herself waking up tomorrow night. She is going to sit up with a start, stunned to be alone without him. Yuko left her house because she did not want to be haunted by memories. By tomorrow night, this room will be completely bare. Maya would rather leave the ghosts of herself and Eric here, in an empty room at first, among other people's furniture later, in a place that will belong to neither of them.

"I want to stay with you here."

The blue blinds on the windows and the lines on the hardwood floor remind her of the nudes Bonnard painted against the checkerboard of a tiled floor, the steep diagonal angle of a bathtub, the long vertical downsweep of curtains. The figures looked oddly fluid amid the overlapping gridwork of the surrounding composition. The woman leaning over the tub or drying her hair resembled the soft light that moves across a room on winter mornings—unfettered but tenuous, a temporary brightness against the solid geometry of the world. Eric has turned off the overhead light, leaving only the lamp on the windowsill. He is holding out his hand toward her. The shadows in the room have changed already. We are here for such a short time, Maya thinks, as she takes his hand and steps toward the light.

Standing next to Eric's car at seven the next morning, Maya glances back at her own car, parked behind his. She will be the first to go.

"Will you let me know if you change your mind?" he asks. "I'll drive back to get you. I don't want you to come out alone. Your car's not going to make it all the way to Vermont."

"I'm not going to change my mind." She holds him tighter.

"I have a vision of us driving across the country. Your cat would meow across Indiana, Ohio, Pennsylvania—those big states between here and there. You'd look so worried and serious, and I'd do everything to reassure you."

"I'm going to call you in a month to say good-bye. Until then, I won't write or call. You know I love you. That's what I want you to remember."

"You won't let me call you?"

"No."

"Can I write to you at least?"

"I wish you wouldn't. I need to start being alone. It's what I'm going to do for the rest of my life. It'll only hurt me to get letters from you. I don't know if I can bear to read them."

"You're crazy, you know that?" He pulls away long enough so she has to look up at him. His eyes are red.

"I know it sounds crazy. But going with you doesn't make sense to me. Being alone does."

"I don't know anyone like you. That's why I love you."

"I know that, too."

When they kiss, it's as if their lips and hands continue talking when nothing more is left to say. All night, they kept waking up with their arms and legs tangled together. Soon after they finally fell asleep, the alarm went off. In silence, they went into the shower, where Maya couldn't tell if it was water or tears she felt on her face. She kisses him one final time and pulls away.

"Be careful driving," she says. "I'm worried about you. We didn't sleep very much." We'll never have another sleepless night together, she thinks. She strokes his arm, wishing her touch could protect him on the road to Vermont and everywhere.

"I love you," Eric says, as she walks to her car.

He is behind her when they get to the freeway. As she turns onto the northbound ramp, she can see him in her rearview mirror, driving straight across the overpass to the southbound side. She beeps her horn as though they were saying a happy good-bye. He waves but does not beep back. Halfway down the ramp, she looks up at the overpass, but he is already gone. In the line of traffic heading north, she finds a space between a purple pickup truck and a blue sedan. Almost bumper to bumper in the morning rush hour, the traffic still keeps flowing fifty miles an hour. From the sky, the cars would look like strings of beads moving through an assembly line. The invisible needle descends, stitching her to the fabric of summer trees and roadside flowers.

— 18 —

After the Fourth of July party at Peg's house, the air outside is warm and humid. Peg follows Maya to the Civic parked on the grass. The moon has a faint yellow rim above it, as if it were holding an umbrella. Maya's father used to say that a moon with an umbrella was a sign of approaching rain.

"Anytime you get lonely up there"—Peg points in the direction of the big barn—"come on over."

Except for the slight breeze rustling the leaves of the trees and the corn in the fields, everything is quiet. As Maya pulls her car onto the dirt road, Peg waves as though she were departing on a long journey. After the road curves, there is nothing around the car except the fields. The headlights fan out into the dark. In the distance, an orange flare shoots up from someone's fireworks. The light breaks into streams of green and red as it fades away. Out in Vermont at his friend's house, Eric, too, might be thinking of the sparklers they lit on his front porch. "I'm still seeing the sparklers," she said to him as they fell asleep, and he answered, "Me too." She imagined tiny webs of fire imprinted on their closed eyelids forever.

The last time she drove away from Peg's house after a party, she was taking him home. Though that was three months ago, it seems like a lifetime away in another place; out in the country, summer is nothing like early spring. In her memory, every day she spent with Eric is like a coastline that curves curlicue after curlicue to touch the water, each minute stretching beyond ordinary measure by coiling tightly around itself. But the coastline is only a small part of the map. Thirty-five years of Maya's life had already happened before the night she met Eric. By then, her course had been unalterably set. Ever since she left her father's house, Maya has known she was meant to live alone. Solitude has been her calling the way devotion is for other people. Nearly all her father's stories had the same ending: love, no matter how deep, cannot alter anyone's destiny.

Eric sent her a drawing, in red ink, of himself and Maya holding each other in the middle of nowhere. The lines at their feet might be grass, ripples in the water, or flames in a lake of fire. His hand disappearing in her long hair, her face upturned toward him, they looked like currents of light tangled together. Around the figures, he'd placed blue and pink squares the size of fingernails. The squares were cut out of the cloth Maya wove to make the jacket for her show. She had given him what was left and told him the story of the heavenly garment, but he had arranged the squares so that the meticulous sequence of colors from blue to pink was broken. The effect was that of a sky shaken up and made brighter, as if a rainbow had been mixed back into pure light. He didn't include any words, but she knew everything he must have been thinking and remembering. "Your father must have loved you so much," Eric had said, when she showed him the picture of the tunnel. "I wish I could have met him." She put Eric's drawing in the kitchen where she kept her father's and her own drawings. If the dark space inside the kitchen drawer were a universe of its own, the pictures would cleave together in time and become a shiny black rock.

Maya parks the car in front of the barn and steps out under the stars. The Milky Way is a belt of white light stretched across the sky. *Ama no kawa*, her father used to call it—the River of Heaven. This time of the year, the two stars separated by the river, Altair and Vega, move closest. On the seventh of July every year, Maya and her father strung colored pieces of paper from bamboo branches with their wishes written in ink. He told her the story of the two stars. Vega, a weaver, and Altair, a farmhand, were lovers who neglected their work because they were too much in love. As punishment, they were placed on opposite banks of the River of Heaven and allowed to meet only once a year by crossing the river on a swan's outstretched wings. On that night, they could grant the wishes of the people living below. Maya cannot recall wishing for anything specific. The words she and her father wrote were large and all-encompassing: *happiness, safety, peace, strength*.

Separated from her lover for an eternity, the weaver is still at her celestial loom. Maya imagines her weaving a silver cloth of starlight, an indigo garment of the night. Vega is a gentle goddess of solitude, lonely but resigned, not at all like Medusa, whose gaze turned people to stone. The star is somewhere near the Swan, in the constellation called Lyre. But the sky is full of stars Maya has forgotten. The weaver could be any of the bright stars along the Heavenly River. Maya raises her hand in its general direction, saluting the vast empty space between the earth and the heavens.

When she opens the door, Casper is waiting. He follows her up the stairs and clings to her as she gets ready for bed. In the bathroom, he perches on her shoulder while she brushes her teeth. He does not notice his own reflection in the mirror above the sink. He rides on her shoulder to the middle of the loft, where she pulls open the futon that she folds up and pushes against the wall every morning. The day after Eric left, Maya borrowed Larry's pickup and drove to the futon store on the east side. She hadn't been able to sleep the night before on the couch. Every time she closed her eyes, she saw Eric's face as though she could still touch him if she only reached out her hand.

Casper is at her side, nudging her to lift the thin sheet she is lying under. He raises his paw and taps her face over and over until she lets him crawl in and curl up against her neck, his face flattened against her throat. Falling asleep to his purring, Maya remembers the night she almost ran over him. Out on the highway, he had shown her that a whole life could begin from a chance meeting, a near calamity trans-formed into a lucky accident. Casper knew how to stretch his body on the road at her feet and be lifted through the crack in fortune that opened up to save his life. He might have been trying to teach her to trust. It's a lesson she has learned only halfway. No matter how much she trusts Eric's love, she can only picture herself letting go and mov-ing on alone.

Yuko is waiting outside her apartment building in a yellow sundress. She has gotten another haircut. Her hair barely covers her left earlobe; on the back and on the right it's shaved close, exposing her nape and right ear. The haircut makes her head look like a single daisy in a glass vase—a beautiful and sad flower.

"Are you all right?" Maya asks, as Yuko gets into the passenger side.

"Yeah." She lifts her feet to point to her black sandals. "Do you think I should have worn nylons and regular shoes?" Her toenails are painted red.

"No, the sandals look fine."

"I didn't know how to dress for this. I didn't want to look stupid, but I haven't worn nylons for ten years. I didn't want to put them on."

"You don't look stupid at all."

"Not even Emily Post can tell you how to dress for your divorce." Yuko stares down at her sandals again as Maya pulls back into traffic. "I wish I were more like you."

"Like me, how?"

"You're always poised. You're good at being alone."

The traffic is heavy enough so Maya doesn't have to look Yuko in the eye. During the month she spent with Eric, she only saw Yuko twice. Maya pictures Eric's hand reaching toward hers across the table, the sunlight on the white ceiling above their bed, the warblers flying in and out of the maple trees in the park where they spent their Sunday mornings. Perhaps she wouldn't have told Yuko very much even if the circumstances had been different. Everything she and Eric saw together was meant only for them. There's a portion of her mind that's sectioned off, a place where there is no room for Yuko. That's the greatest betrayal of all.

Dan is on the steps of the courthouse, dressed in a navy-blue suit and a red checkered tie. Maya has not seen him in a suit since her own wedding four years ago. He must have been spending a lot of time in the sun. His hair is bleached white; his eyebrows have almost disappeared.

When Yuko hugs him, the folder she's holding gets scrunched between them. They have been meeting once a week at a coffee shop on the south side—a place neither of them has ever been or is likely to go back to—to file the papers on their own. Yuko's mother talked her into accepting Dan's offer to refinance the mortgage and give her half the equity. "My mother says it's unkind to reject his offer," Yuko explained. "By taking nothing, I'd be leaving him with a bigger debt to me, a heavier burden of feeling bad. She's absolutely right. That's exactly why I wanted nothing. I'm still tempted to stick him with a mega-debt of guilt so he won't be able to sleep at night. It's like emotional voodoo to make him waste away. Some part of me would be satisfied with that. But like they say, what goes around comes around. No one gets over their unhappiness by making other people miserable. If I help Dan feel better, I can lighten the baggage between us and make it easier for both of us to move on. My mother made me see that."

Kay would never give any advice worth listening to. Maya has called her mother since she moved out but hasn't told her anything. If she can stall for another month, Kay will be gone to Nagoya. By the time she comes back, Maya can have everything settled with Jeff. "It's all done," she can say then, "no use discussing the details." But in the meantime, Maya has been avoiding Jeff too. The whole thing is like a crazy game where she keeps landing on the same square that makes her lose her turn. She can't tell her mother anything until she's settled things with Jeff, but then again, talking to Jeff is more difficult because, if she did, she'd have to tell her mother sooner.

Dan turns to Maya. "Hey, how are you doing?" he asks. As she steps up to hug him, she remembers the day he dropped out of college with only eight weeks left in his last semester. Maya was sitting on the porch when he came back, so she was the first person he told. "I sat down to my philosophy exam, stared at the questions for five minutes, and walked out without writing anything. Then I went to the registrar's office and withdrew from all my courses," he said. "I don't need a college diploma to boost my confidence, like so many people do." Maya hugged him that time without saying anything. Now she has nothing to say again, and she keeps patting his back just like before. "It's good to see you," Dan offers. "Yes, likewise," Maya answers. Dan means well, no matter how thoughtless he sounds from time to time. He's like someone who's tone-deaf or dyslexic: his mistakes are caused by faulty wiring in his brain or a bone in his ear that vibrates to the wrong pitch—he wants so much to be forthright and honest.

Inside the courthouse, a woman in a black suit shows them to the courtroom, where the doors are open and four people are seated at two separate tables before the judge. All four stand up, gather the papers on the tables, and come walking out, two by two.

"Where's the other attorney?" the clerk asks Yuko.

"There is no attorney. I'm the one getting divorced." She lays her hand lightly on Maya's shoulder and says, "This is my best friend. She's here for moral support. Can she come in with us?"

"Your friend can sit there." The clerk points to the chairs in the back of the room. Maya takes her seat.

Yuko proceeds down the aisle toward the two tables where the previous couple sat, each with an attorney. Halfway there, she stops and asks, "Can my husband and I sit together? We don't want to sit at separate tables." Dan is behind Yuko and the clerk, walking with his head hung low.

"Sure," the clerk says. "Go ahead."

Yuko gives the folder to the clerk, who takes it to the judge. Then she waits for Dan to catch up. He's trudging along, his face completely drained of color. Yuko tilts her head a little, smiles, and takes his hand. Together, they walk to one of the tables and sit down. The judge examines the folder and then introduces himself. For the fifteen minutes it takes to complete the hearing, Yuko and Dan sit stiff-backed in the chairs, answering the questions, still holding hands.

"Do you agree that the marriage is irrevocably broken?" the judge asks Yuko.

"Yes," she replies in a clear voice.

The judge asks Dan, who swallows hard before saying "Yes," almost choking on the word.

Maya looks down at the floor and takes a deep breath, thinking of all the people who have come through this room, answered the same question, and marched out together for the last time. If she could record what went on here every hour and then play the tape at a faster speed, it would be an endless procession of misery.

The judge stamps the papers. "A copy will be sent to each of you in a few weeks," he concludes.

Yuko and Dan come walking toward Maya. She follows them out the door, where four people are waiting, two and two, apart. No one's talking. A little farther on, Yuko and Dan stop, let go of each other's hand, and wait for Maya. Their faces are wet, and Maya's too. Standing in the dimly lit hallway, in front of some stone busts, the three of them hug. It's the last huddle to prepare them for what is to come—the rest of their lives. Maya holds on tight to her friends.

Yuko is the first to let go. She wipes at her eyes and sniffles. "Well, I'm glad that's over."

They head for the exit, the three of them walking abreast. As they push open the heavy doors, a blast of warm air hits them. The next moment, they are standing on top of the steps outside, dizzy with the sudden warmth and light.

"It was freezing in there," Yuko says.

Dan stares at her and blinks. "I'm so sorry," he mumbles. "I really am."

Maya is afraid that he will start telling her, once more, how sad he is, but Yuko doesn't give him a chance. "Don't be," she cuts in. "I want to stop being angry at you. I want you to be happy."

"Can we be friends?" Dan asks.

"Always," she replies.

"Good." He nods. "I'll call."

"You do that." Yuko doesn't say, *I'll call too.* She will never be able to call his house, where he lives with Meredith now.

"And you." Dan nods toward Maya. "Are you okay?"

"Sure," she answers. "I'm living at the store; Jeff must have told you. Pretty soon, I'll be back here." Maya points to the courthouse and shrugs.

Dan sighs. "Hard as it seems, we have to believe that everything happens for the best. A new beginning for all of us." He squints into the sun, his jaw square and tight. The next moment he is running down the steps, then down the sidewalk toward wherever he's parked his car. He doesn't look back. He keeps running. Come back, Maya wants to say; stay with us. But her throat won't open up to let the words out.

Yuko is staring after him, narrowing her eyes as though the sight pained her.

"Come on." Maya puts her arm around Yuko. "Let's go home."

They start walking together, Maya's arm around Yuko's shoulder. You are the greatest person in the world, she wants to tell her. Taking

Dan's hand in the courtroom, Yuko guided him to the place where he longed to go but was afraid to.

"What you told Dan," she manages to say, "encouraging him to be happy, saying that you didn't want to be angry—that took a lot. You should be proud of yourself."

"And it was so hard to do." Yuko begins to sob.

They're halfway down the steps. Maya stops and strokes Yuko's back with her hand. "I know," she murmurs into Yuko's hair. "I know how hard it was."

Yuko's tears are warm on Maya's blouse. There is no one she has known and loved for as long. "Yuko," she says, "you know I'll always love you."

"I know," Yuko replies, but she continues to cry.

As they walk down the steps, Maya is thinking again of the afternoon Eric held her and kissed her at that gas station. Every second, the man behind the counter seemed farther away. Eric's fingers, touching her hair, were stirring up the apple scent of their shampoo and weaving it around them like a net of protection no one could break. Maya was completely at rest in that moment; until then, she thought, she had never been perfectly happy. It was as though a small noise she'd been hearing all along had suddenly stopped and she could finally hear a silence that was also a pure sound. She could never give Yuko that same feeling, in consolation or love. Surely, a friendship like theirs is better than most marriages, more solid and lasting, and yet, in all the years they will spend together, she will never make Yuko as happy as she was in that brief moment at the gas station in the middle of nowhere. She and Yuko will not come to each other's door at a day's end, their voices intertwining as they say, "I missed you. I thought about you all day long." Yuko is crying because she too knows that Maya's love can never replace what she has lost. Maya tightens her arms around her and whispers, "I'm so sorry." One step at a time, they climb down, making sure their feet are touching solid stone.

— 19 —

The interior of the gas station is completely dark and the doors are locked. Maya walks back past her car to the phone booth. The phone book—the size of the *National Geographic*—is tied to the booth with cotton twine. The map inside shows the surrounding area: the freeway, the county highway, the road she is on. She hesitates only a second before grasping the page and tearing it. It comes out with a fine-toothed edge, as even and straight as a zigzag seam from her sewing machine. With the map on the dashboard, she drives down the county highway.

As she parks her car down the road from the trailer, the sun is rising over the flat stretch of land. Already, large flocks of house finches and house sparrows are at the feeders outside every window. A pair of cardinals moves in and out of the low bushes, making their chipping calls. In the cornfield to her left, song sparrows are announcing their territories. Their song—two long notes followed by a series of fast, buzzy beeps—is supposed to be a quaint invitation: *Maids, maids, put on your teakettles.* Eric laughed when she told him. "They're saying what?" "Listen," she insisted. "Pretty soon you won't be able to hear it any other way." Maya raises her new binoculars to her eyes and pans the field, spotting one male perched on a fence, his tail bobbing, his mouth open with the song. All around, mourning doves are flying up, their wingbeats making a keening sound.

Maya writes down the names of the birds on a notepad. *County Highway NN, between Lyons and Cooper*, she scribbles above the list. *Trailer house with feeders.* The old brown car on the driveway must be Eric's mother's. Perhaps she is sitting in her bed, listening to the lilting song of the finches outside her window as she gazes at his sketches from the apple orchard. In a while, she will get up and go to the kitchen, where she will stand surrounded by the pictures of her three grandchildren and of Eric, his brother, and his sister, as children and as high school students going to the prom. Last week at Peg's house, Maya came across the snapshots Larry took at the sheep's birthday party. She went through the entire stack, but Eric was not in any of them. Larry offered her the pictures in which she stood talking to her customers or holding a glass of punch and smiling with Peg, but it was no consolation. On their last Sunday together, Eric took photographs of her. They sat on the bed in the early morning sunlight, close enough for him to lean toward her between the shots and touch her hair or kiss her. "Now, look at me," he would say or "Look down at my right knee for a second." She wanted to ask him to hand the camera to her so she could take pictures of him. But she would not have the copies unless he were to send them to her from Vermont. So she said nothing and let her own image disappear, shot after shot, behind the lens.

Maya picks up the map from the dashboard and examines it. She drives past the trailer toward a road named Oakley, which intersects the county highway and veers right. After a mile, where the road dead-ends on a ravine, she finds the farmhouse, with a barn and a couple of silos. Out in the country, roads are named after families whose farms are nearby. Eric's family has not been gone long enough for this road to get renamed. Sitting in her car twenty yards from where he grew up, Maya pictures three children holding their sparklers near the ravine, splashing naked in the inflatable pool in the yard. Rolling down the window, she catches the whistling of goldfinches. A small flock comes undulating over the alfalfa field like a handful of musical notes. *Seven gold finches*, she jots down on her notepad. *Alfalfa field across the road from the family farm, on Oakley.*

Maya drives past the fields and stands of trees, writing down every bird she can see: red-tailed hawks circling over cornfields, a pair of sandhill cranes foraging in the distance, kestrels perched on telephone wires. It's something she learned to do when she and Peg volunteered for the Christmas bird counts and breeding bird surveys of the Audubon Society. Only this time she is surveying an area chosen for an entirely different reason than the changing ecology. When she woke up in the dark at four, she planned to drive to one of the state parks immediately north of the city. On the freeway, she passed one exit after another and kept going north. Thirty minutes out of the city, she knew she needed to come back to this countryside. Eric once said he wanted to get in a time machine and visit the places of her past. What she is doing now is the closest thing. With her binoculars and her stolen map, she is learning her way through the countryside of his childhood. When she knows this place by heart, she will be able to say good-bye to the history she has made up in birdsong and field marks, his past and hers intertwined in her mind like the hair Yuko once wanted to cast into the fire. Instead of a love ritual, hers will be a ritual of letting go. Every ritual is a paradox. To possess someone, you had to burn their hair. To forget someone, then, you would have to possess their image so completely that you can finally let go. If she had found his photograph, she would have held it in her hand and memorized every detail. She would have studied the image until it was imprinted so clearly in her mind that she could burn the picture and walk away.

On the telephone wire near the crest of a hill, five tree swallows are perched, their slate-blue wings folded like tiny mantles. In a month, they will begin to congregate for their journey south. They are among the first birds to go. Maya watches them scatter and dip over the field, the arc of their flight like countless lines cast into water.

At ten-thirty, there is no one in the store. If she wanted to, she could call Jeff. She'll have to start meeting him soon to file the papers. Maya pictures herself and Jeff sitting at a George Webb's on the south side. Their discussions will be simple; she wants nothing that's his. Maybe they will only have to meet once or twice. Still, she can't make herself dial his number. Always, for her, there is a gulf between thinking about things and doing them. The longer she waits, the more clearly she can imagine how things will be as if they had already happened, and that keeps her from wanting actually to do them—it's like having to go through the same thing twice.

The day after she and Yuko moved her clothes out of Jeff's house, Maya realized she had forgotten the hand-knit sweaters and hats she had taken out of her mother's dresser and put inside the linen closet. That's where her old things are, too: the red hooded jacket she was wearing on the day she left Osaka, the first sampler she wove under Ruth's instruction, Yuko's love charm, some boxes of photographs. She meant to call Jeff and arrange to retrieve them, but now she's waited too long to be able to justify calling today as opposed to tomorrow or the day after tomorrow. She could go on waiting forever and wishing she had done something earlier. In old Buddhist texts, lost souls are portrayed as slouched figures floating a few feet above the earth without their feet. That's how Maya pictures herself: unable to rise up to heaven or come back to the world of the living, she could spend an eternity in a dismal in-between place.

After lunch, there is a steady stream of customers. At two, Maya is helping a woman who can't decide between a couple of hand-painted silk scarves she has looked at for half an hour. Another woman is in the dressing room with ten dresses she has tried on and not liked, though there was something redeeming about each. When Maya comes back after taking yet another dress to her—one similar to but different from all the others—the first woman is standing in front of the mirror, one shoulder draped with a purple scarf and the other with a yellow scarf. Both have orchids painted on them.

"I'm going to buy them both," she says. "When I get home, I'll decide which one to keep. I can always give the other one to my sister. Her birthday is in September." Every morning between now and September, this woman will stand in front of her mirror, unable to decide which scarf to keep.

The woman who was in the dressing room comes up to the counter with a black skirt.

"I didn't see you try that on," Maya says.

"I didn't today. I saw this one last month and tried it on then. None of the dresses worked out, so I might as well get this instead. I'm glad you still had it."

In a month, this woman will come back to look at some fall coats, and maybe that's when she will buy one of the dresses from today. Wrapping and ringing up the two women's purchases, Maya finds it oddly comforting to be in this business. Like a reverse purgatory, a boutique allows a person to make wrong decisions, delayed decisions, or no decisions at all and still not fall out of the circles of contentment. She imagines her years of solitude as a priestess of this peaceful purgatory. It isn't a bad life.

The phone rings shortly after the two women have walked out to their cars. Casper, who has just come down and sat on Maya's lap, scampers up the stairs again.

"Maya, is that you?" the caller asks. She doesn't recognize the man's voice: high, a little nasal. "Didn't you get the message I left?" he continues. "I left you two messages last night."

"Who am I speaking to?" Maya asks. The only message she found on the answering machine down here was from Yuko, who is in Asheville with her band. She played a short riff on her bass and said,

"Did you know they have the annual UFO conventions in Asheville? The mountains are beautiful. There are a lot of galleries downtown. Maybe we can come here together next spring."

"This is Nate," the caller says. "I'm calling you from Chicago."

"Oh, of course." He must have called Jeff's house last night. He still wouldn't know that Maya wasn't living there. Unless Jeff changed the greeting, all it says on the machine is their number, not their names.

"So didn't you get my messages?" Nate asks again.

"I think so," Maya lies, before she realizes how stupid that sounds. "I was going to call you back," she adds. "But it kind of slipped my mind. I'm sorry."

"Well, I'm calling you from the hospital. Your mother was in a car accident last night."

"What?"

"She made a left turn in front of an oncoming car and got side-swiped. That's why I called you and asked you to call me back immediately. I said it was very important. I gave you two numbers."

"Was she badly hurt?"

"Luckily, no. But she could have been. The other car caught hers in the back on the passenger side, and she ended up crashing into a stop sign. She broke her shoulder and got banged up a little. She's sleeping now."

"You didn't say she was in an accident before, did you?"

"Of course not. Why would I say something like that on an answering machine? I was waiting for you to call me back, which you never did."

Maya can't think of a good explanation. "How long will she be in the hospital?" she asks instead.

"Just today."

"Should I come to see her there?"

"It's up to you," he says, in a tight voice.

"Did she say she wanted me to come?"

"Maya, your mother's been sleeping most of the time since they took her to the emergency room and worked on her shoulder. She's pretty shook up. She's in pain."

All the years they spent together in Minneapolis, Kay shut herself in her room when she was ill. Bill had to sleep on the couch in the living room. "Don't fuss over me. I only want to be left alone," Kay would hiss if anyone came near, but maybe she's different about that now. "I'll come down as soon as I can," Maya tells Nate. "Give me the directions."

He doesn't know the names of the streets, but he gives her long lists of gas stations, restaurants, and strip malls she must steer by. "And if you go over the bridge to the country club—I can't remember the name of the place but you'll know when you see it, it looks unmistakably like a country club—then you've missed the last turn and gone too far," he finishes. She stopped writing anything after the first sentence.

"All right. I'll be there in a couple of hours." She hangs up, gets the number of the hospital from directory assistance, and says to the hospital receptionist, "I need directions to your hospital. I'll be driving down from Milwaukee."

Next, she calls Peg on her cell phone.

"Peg, I need help," Maya says. "My mother was in a car accident. I need to go down to Chicago to the hospital."

"Is she all right?"

"Her husband says she is. She wasn't hurt too badly. But I should probably go see her."

"Of course. Stick a note on the door and leave. I'll get there as soon as I can."

The door opens and four women come in, laughing in the middle of some anecdote one of them has been telling.

"Some people just walked in. I can wait. The accident was last night and she's all right, so it's not an emergency."

"I'm in my car downtown. I'll be there in twenty minutes," Peg says. "Hang in there."

When the four women leave, Maya still has one of their charge cards in her hand. She runs out to the parking lot. The women stop when Maya holds up the card.

"I'm sorry," she apologizes, as one of them reaches out of the passenger window.

"Don't worry. Maybe I should thank you for keeping me from spending more money."

Her friend in the backseat chimes in. "No kidding. Alice always says she isn't going to buy anything, and then she gets more than the rest of us combined."

The others are nodding. They all laugh as they drive away. These four women have visited the store many times before; they are school-teachers from Indiana, one or two of them recently retired. They've been vacationing together for years, leaving their husbands and children behind for a couple of weeks every summer. Walking across the gravel lot back to the store, Maya wonders if Kay has any women friends in Park Ridge. She has never heard of her mother going shopping or having lunch with another woman. Kay seldom says anything nice about other people, and the few she's spoken of with begrudging admiration were always men. For women, she has nothing but contempt. "That woman, she's just a housewife," she would declare, "so we have nothing in common." The women she worked with, on the other hand, were all backbiters and brownnosers, according to Kay. "Men are better," she said. "At least, they're more straightforward and honest even when they're selfish." Very few men, unless you are related to them, would visit you in a hospital. If she had been seriously hurt, Kay would have had no one to take care of her except Nate—no woman friend who would come calling with flowers or food and spend hours entertaining her with talk.

Inside the store, Maya puts away some clothes her customers left in the dressing rooms. The white summer jackets hanging overhead, with their empty sleeves spread out, remind her of the white crosses put up along the highway to mark the sites of fatal accidents. Peg's doll, Wilbur, looks like a crash-test dummy. Maya can almost see her mother's shoulder hitting the dashboard or the driver's window. It must have hurt.

Kay must have sat in the car in shock, unable to unhook her seat belt or open the door. Maybe help was slow getting to her, late at night in a suburb. Sitting in the car with her broken shoulder, Kay might have gone over all the things that were wrong in her life—people often do that in the middle of some predicament—and if she did, any thought about Maya would have aggravated her. Stranded in the middle of the street, she might have remembered the humiliation she'd felt at that restaurant in December when she realized Maya wasn't coming back. If she had died, her last thought of Maya would have been a complete disappointment.

After another customer comes in and leaves, Maya runs up the stairs to her loft. Casper is sleeping on the couch, his back rounded, his front paws covering his eyes. She sits down next to him and calls his name. Even asleep, he begins to purr. Still, as she looks around the loft with her loom and worktable, her futon folded and pushed against the wall, Maya suddenly wishes she had never left Jeff's house. The loft is meager and cluttered—the opposite of Jeff's bedroom, with the white pillow shams and a matching skirt around the bottom of the bed, the lacy summer cover his mother had crocheted. Jeff always slept on his left side, his cheek squished against the pillow and his mouth slightly open. In her memory, his face seems so familiar and dear. Their life together was ordinary and calm; there was no room for nightmares or bad memories. How could she have left him and come to live alone in a drafty barn, spending the next decades of her life missing someone she won't see again? Jeff could never hurt her much. The worst she got from him was like a surface wound.

She can hear Peg's footsteps downstairs. Maya gets up from the couch and leaves the loft, closing the door behind her.

"Casper's upstairs with the door closed," she tells Peg, who's hanging the rest of the clothes from the dressing rooms. "He won't be able to bother you."

"Do you want me to go with you instead? We can close the store. People will come back another time."

"No, that's okay. I'll be all right alone."

"Give your mother my best wishes, okay?"

"Thanks." Maya grabs her directions and her keys and runs out to the parking lot.

In Chicago, Maya has no trouble finding the hospital, but, once there, she has to drive around, looking for the right parking garage. Some have gates that require special permits, and others have signs saying EMERGENCY ONLY, OUTPATIENTS, STAFF. Finally she finds a visitors' ramp, parks on the top level, and tries to retrace her steps to the hospital's main entrance.

The building seems to go on forever without any doors. The only entrance she comes across is for ambulances only. Her palms are sweaty and her stomach in knots as she continues to walk. When Nate first told her about the accident, she wasn't all that worried. Because he said right away that it wasn't serious and then sounded so irritated, she felt more defensive than anything, but now that she's outside the hospital—unable to get in—she can't stop thinking of broken bones, bandages, needles, lots of pain. The last time she was at a hospital was a year ago, when Jeff cut his palm open with a Swiss Army knife. That time, she had the presence of mind to run and get a clean towel first. Even though he was bleeding a lot, she could remember enough of her anatomy class to know that the cut wasn't anywhere near a major artery. Driving him to the emergency room, she kept assuring him that at least the wound wouldn't get infected because it was bleeding so much. Blood, she said, was the body's own cleansing system. The worst that could happen, she thought, was that he would pass out and she would need help dragging him from the car when they got to the hospital. Now she's picturing Kay wrapped in bandages like a mummy.

She must have gotten turned around when she came out of the ramp. The main entrance she saw from the car is nowhere to be found. When she finally sees a set of doors, it's near a different parking area. Next to a glass booth, a security guard in his blue uniform is talking to someone who must be equally lost.

At her approach, the guard turns away from the man he's been talking to. Maya is about to apologize for interrupting when the man calls her name. Ten steps away from them, Maya realizes that Nate has gotten a haircut. His hair was long enough to touch his shoulders. Now it's all but shaved, giving his head a bulletlike appearance. He's wearing a purple golf shirt and khakis. "Oh, Nate," Maya mumbles, "I didn't recognize you. I'm sorry."

A wheelchair is parked inside the glass door of the building. Nate takes her by the elbow and steers her through the door. The woman in the wheelchair is wearing an old sleeveless button-down shirt and baggy shorts, both in a pale cream tint that looks as though the color got there by mistake. She has a neck brace, a cast that covers most of her left shoulder and arm, bandages around her left knee. The right side of her face is marked with abrasions—a raw red rash covers her swollen eye, cheek, and jaw. There's a white bandage on her nose, too. Maya kneels next to the wheelchair. Her mother is clutching an orange plastic bag with black lettering—PATIENTS BELONGING'S—the words placed inside quotation marks with the apostrophe in the wrong place. Jeff would have been upset. "How come people don't know how to use apostrophes anymore?" he would have complained. "And why in quotes? Do they mean, the so-called or alleged belongings?" The bag drapes over Kay's right knee, which looks oddly raw because it's not covered with a bandage like the rest of her.

"Mother, I'm sorry," Maya blurts out. "I didn't know you were so badly hurt. Nate told me it wasn't very serious." She is on the verge of crying, kneeling in front of the absurd plastic bag.

Kay stares at her. The neck brace makes her look as though she were stretched out and hung from something. "I'm not badly hurt," she says, but her voice is hoarse and whispery. "I want to go home," she croaks.

"Come on, Maya, get up," Nate scolds. "This is no time for personal drama."

As soon as she stands up, Nate's hand is on her elbow again. He's leading her outside. "You're going to help me find the car."

"What?" Maya pulls away so he has to drop his hand.

"Your mother's been sitting out here for an hour because I couldn't find my car. You can help me. It's the least you can do." He grimaces. "The parking is insane. I was in the lot for forty minutes and couldn't find my car. That guard thought I was in the wrong one, but maybe the whole thing's just poorly set up."

"You didn't look to see where your car was before you left it?" Maya asks.

"How could I?" Nate leans forward with an ugly scowl on his face. He reminds her of the high school boys who taunted her and her friends when they were in middle school. She can't trust someone who suddenly cuts off his hippie hair and starts looking like a skinhead. "I was preoccupied. My wife was in a car accident and her daughter wouldn't return my call."

Maya doesn't say anything as they walk around the building back to the ramp. On the first floor there, she presses the button for the elevator, but nothing happens. The elevator seems to be stuck on the fourth floor.

Nate is already opening the blue door marked for the stairway.

"My car's on the top floor, in section F-Five," Maya tells him. Following Nate into the stairwell, Maya almost gags on the smell of stale sweat and urine. After the first flight of stairs, Nate begins to talk. He doesn't bother to turn his head back toward her, so his voice echoes on the walls and bounces around as though he were shouting at her from inside a boat while she was underwater. She feels slightly motion-sick.

"Anyway, that was no way to talk to your mother." He pauses.

"What?"

"Telling her how bad she looked. You were scaring her. You should have said she didn't look so bad. That would have been more reassuring."

"I didn't mean any harm by what I said."

"You should be more mindful. You should think twice before you say anything to your mother."

"I do think twice, actually," Maya retorts. "I think three, four times before I open my mouth in front of her. That's the truth. So don't tell me I don't think enough. You have no idea."

"You can think all you want and do no good because you're not paying attention to the right thing. You and your mother. You have several lifetimes' worth of debts you keep passing on to each other. You've been together forever because neither of you knows how to forgive and let go. One life, she wrongs you; the next life, you wrong her. You'll have to keep going on like that for centuries until one of you decides to stop."

"I don't know what you're talking about." Maya can scarcely keep her disgust out of her voice, but Nate doesn't seem to notice or care.

"Karma. No doubt you've heard of it."

"Of course I've heard of it. Only I don't believe in all that non-sense."

"I think some people are addicted to their bad karma just like alcoholics and heroin addicts are to their poison. Denial is a big part of addiction."

Maya doesn't say anything for a while. The stairways Escher drew had no beginning or end. They kept going around and around, branching out and then connecting back to themselves, and hordes of people were climbing the steps, believing they were going somewhere. Maybe, in his head, Nate pictures Maya and Kay trapped in an endless stairwell moving through history.

"Tell me something," Maya says, as she and Nate start climbing up the last flight. "Do you say the same things to my mother? Do you tell her that she's been wronging me through history?"

For the first time, he stops and turns to her. He's taller than she, and he's three steps above her. He towers over her, his thin bony face twisted with a big frown. "No," he spits out. "That's not my mission with her. Your mother is a beautiful soul who's been hurt a lot—by you, mostly, but by her other husbands too. My job is to protect and nurture her, not criticize her and make her feel worse. I'm her peacemaker. I was sent to see her through to the next level. She can spend her next lives in the light, with me, instead of repeating the same bad karma over and over with you and those other men." Whirling away, he runs to the top and pushes open the door.

Stepping out of the staircase after him, Maya is momentarily blinded by the sunlight. Nate is no different from Billy Graham and the multitude of other TV preachers who ask people to leave their seats in the stadium bleachers or on their living-room couches, stand up, and accept Christ as their personal savior. Like them, he believes that a single once-in-a-lifetime action can change a person's destiny forever. But fanaticism is math that doesn't make any sense: the bigger the eternal doom, the simpler the action that brings about salvation. Nate must stay awake worrying that he won't be able to save Kay from her bad karma. He will move on to the next level of existence after this life since he's been careful to put a stop to his debts. He's afraid Kay won't be allowed to go to that place with him, she'll be kept back because of Maya and her previous husbands. Nate wants himself and Kay to move together for eternity like a pair of stars in the same constellation, but time is running short. They only have twenty or thirty years of this life left together. If he succeeds in saving her, he'll be able to possess Kay through life, death, and into all the next lives; if not, he will lose her forever. His belief is enormously hopeful and desperate at the same time.

Maya leads the way to her car without speaking. In spite of his bullying, she might pity or even admire him. Only a week ago, she hugged Dan at the courthouse. She could forgive him because he was well-meaning in spite of the wrong things he couldn't help saying. The same might be true of Nate, but if forgiveness means seeing other people as handicapped—doomed to rudeness and insensitivity—what appears like mercy is motivated by harsh judgment instead of generosity. It means consigning others to a place of hopelessness forever. Maybe holding a grudge is more respectful. Maya isn't sure anymore. She unlocks the passenger door and says, "Here. Get in. Let's go find your car."

Nate's car is in another parking garage, on the other side of the hospital. After he gets out of her car and into his, Maya follows him back to the entrance where they left her mother. Parking her car behind his in the circle, Maya gets out to help him lift Kay out of the wheelchair into the car. Kay blinks, as if dazed. She puts her good arm around her husband's neck. Maya stands ready, but she can't offer her hand because if she touched her mother, it might hurt her shoulder more. The only thing she can do is to open the car door for them. Nate lowers Kay into the seat and is about to close the door when Kay raises her hand. She seems to be motioning to Maya, so Maya approaches and leans down toward her.

"I didn't expect you to come," Kay says, her voice scarcely audible.

Maya isn't sure if she means the remark as an accusation or as a bizarre way of thanking her.

"You would have been gone if Nate hadn't lost his car," she replies. Her mother could have been killed last night, and they are already back to saying the wrong things.

"We would have left you a message," Nate says behind her. "We knew you were headed this way."

"That's true," Maya agrees. "I know."

"Why didn't you call back?" Kay asks. When she narrows her good eye, the other eye looks even more swollen.

Maya hesitates only a second. "I didn't call because Nate telephoned Jeff's house. I didn't get the messages. I don't live there anymore."

"What?" Nate says.

"I moved out." Maya shrugs, turning first to Nate and then back to her mother. "I'm getting a divorce. I've been living at the loft."

"You never said," her mother whispers.

"I know. I'm sorry. I couldn't seem to find the right time to tell you."

"And you think this is it?" Nate yells. "Come on, Maya. Your mother doesn't have to hear about this now. You're upsetting her."

Kay sits there without an expression on her face. It's hard to say whether she's upset or not. She has a bandage on her nose and her face is red with the abrasion.

"You are so inconsiderate—" Kay doesn't stop Nate while he goes on upbraiding Maya.

"Look," Maya interrupts. "I'm sorry I brought this up. I didn't mean to upset anyone."

"Do you have a place to stay?" her mother asks.

"Yes," Maya answers. "I just told you I'm living at the loft above the store."

"That's no place," Kay says. She was only there once. She and Nate drove up to see the barn last year—after Maya had worked there for twelve years. They glanced at the space and left without a comment. "You need a real apartment."

"I'm perfectly happy where I am. Believe me."

"See, you've got her all worried about your fricking loft," Nate says. "You should have kept your mouth shut."

Kay sighs. Her face really looks terrible. When the car hit the stop sign, the airbag must have popped open, punching her nose and scraping her skin. Last fall, Yuko's neighbor had a similar injury when his car hit a deer. His face has healed without a trace. Still, Maya imagines her mother's face with scars, her nose permanently crooked from being broken. "I'm sorry," she says again.

"Me too," Kay mutters. It can be an apology or an accusation. Maya stands hovering over the passenger seat. She was going to suggest that she follow them to their house and visit for a while, but she can see that it won't be a good idea.

"I'd better let you guys get home so you can rest," she offers lamely. "I'll call." Neither Nate nor Kay responds. "Good-bye." Maya walks to her car. "I hope you'll feel better soon."

The circle in front of the entrance is one-way. Sitting behind the wheel, Maya waits while Nate leans down into the car and kisses Kay. He closes the door gently and walks around to the driver's side. As he pulls away, Maya stares at the back of their sky-blue sedan. This is how Nate must imagine the afterlife: he and Kay in the safety of their car traveling to the eternity of peace and love, Maya alone in hers, following her separate journey.

The sun is low in the sky, but there is still plenty of light. Peg has hung the clothes and tidied up the store. On the bottom of the steps, she has set Maya's mail, separated from the store mail. Maya climbs the steps, opens the door, and catches Casper when he jumps straight up from the floor to her shoulder. He purrs and licks her face as she carries him to the couch and sits down. For a while, he bats her mail as she goes through it, but then he loses interest and starts chasing a piece of yarn across the floor. Her mail is mostly bills and newsletters with the yellow forwarding sticker from the post office. Every day, Maya still looks for a letter from Mr. Kubo, though she knows it will never come. She puts the mail on the floor, except for the envelope with Eric's initials above the return address. It's the only thing sent directly to the store.

Inside, Maya finds a piece of construction paper. It's covered with white cloth cut into squares like small windows, some of them painted over with black brush strokes. There are twenty squares, arranged in five rows like the panels of the painting Eric showed her. The squares on the bottom have more black than those near the top, but the one at the top right-hand edge has a lot of black again. The impression is of the black strokes falling to the bottom, but in a shaky, jumpy motion. Some of the squares are frayed. There is a bubble of air caught behind one of them.

Underneath the squares is a message written in blue ink. The words are visible in the lattice-shaped space left uncovered by the squares, and also underneath the squares that are white; the faint blue lines look like veins under the thin skin of wrists. She recognizes a part of her name, *May*, and several other words, some of them crossed out. She switches on the lamp that hangs above her loom. Holding the paper up to the light, she reads the words. *Dear Maya, I miss you.* Then there's something crossed out and the squares begin to darken. All she can see are scratch marks of blue ink, scattered like broken twigs or kindling. *I wake up every morning thinking of you*, the sentence must read. *In the yard, the crows*—and then she can make out nothing more under the dark squares, except at the very bottom, *Love, Eric*.

On the back of the construction paper, he has scribbled another message in pencil—the writing is so thin it's almost illegible. *I write you a dozen letters every day and tear them up. I don't know what to say except that I love you. E.* She reads the message over and over and then turns the paper again to the cloth squares. The room is beginning to darken. She keeps staring at the squares, at the words underneath. It doesn't matter that she can't read half of what he has written. She is looking right through a thin skin of sadness into his heart. This morning, she was twenty yards away from his mother's trailer, where they had kissed in front of the refrigerator that contained nothing but cold air and a pitcher of clear water. If she could pour herself a glass of that water, it would be as pure as loneliness itself, but it isn't enough to live by.

I miss you, too, she wants to write. *I wish you were here. I wish we had met years earlier.* Maya stands in the dark, thinking of all the years she could have spent with him. Nate is luckier than he can ever imagine. He has only to worry about being reunited with Kay in the next life and in all the other lives to come. Maya will never see Eric again even in this life. In the light from the lamp, the words keep floating toward her like fragile petals of ash after the fireworks. *I miss you*, the ashes keep falling. *I miss you.*

− 20 −

When the sun hits the window in the eastern corner of the loft, Maya wakes up thinking about the aquarium light outside Jeff's bedroom window. On her loom, the blue cloth is almost finished. After she cuts out the patterns, there will be scraps left on the table, strips and slivers of blue. Like the white squares Eric painted black, they will remind her of the shapes of silence that border unspoken words, their frayed edges unraveling.

As she folds and pushes the futon against the wall, she cannot remember her dream except that she was in a house that was a combination of all the houses she ever lived in, starting with her father's house in Osaka and ending with Jeff's. The resulting structure felt both rambling and caved in, spaces jutting out every which way, like a shipwreck that refuses to go down. Lately, her dreams resemble still shots of empty places. They bring her back to the houses of her past; only there is nothing happening there, nobody is home, not even herself.

On Eric's letter, the white windows illuminate and obscure the words at once. She will call him in a week to say she has not changed her mind. That will be the last time she will hear his voice. For a while

afterward, he might write, but already his letters are like leaves clinging to oak trees in November.

Maya places the letter in the kitchen drawer, on top of her birdwatching notes. After her phone call to him, she will sit alone under
the midsummer constellations, burn everything that has accumulated
in the drawer, and fill the empty space with blank paper to draw on.
Then she will invite Yuko for their ritual of moving on. With a star
chart, they will find Vega, the solitary weaving star, and ask its blessing.
Even then, she won't tell Yuko about Eric. The secret is the only thing
Maya can hold on to: inside her silence, as under the invisible net she
once imagined, she and Eric will always be alone together. She will
never be able to forget him, but letting go has more to do with remembering than forgetting. Once a month, under the stars, she will allow
herself to recall everything about him and every moment they spent
together so that she can look at all the pictures that remain in her mind
and put them aside. Over the years, she will come to remember less
and less. In the end, her memory of him may be reduced to only a
handful of details. That was what her father was doing when he drew a
picture of her in the tunnel: he was allowing himself to recall one small
image in exchange for all the rest he had let go. A long time ago in their
neighborhood, old men and women brewed bitter black teas and
drank them down for their health. The teas contained dried-up leaves
and hard berries that, in large quantities, might have been poison. The
old people had seen their houses burned by bombs and their sons lost
on islands that were tiny dots on the map. They boiled down their
memories to a bitter, bracing liquid and drank it without flinching.

Maya goes downstairs and sits at the counter next to the telephone.
She has to call Jeff because Jeff is never going to call her. Dialing
the number, she wonders how long it will take her not to remember
the familiarity of their sequence on her fingers. Jeff answers before the
machine comes on. He might be sitting in the kitchen with a cup of
coffee, with Nancy smiling across the table at him. Faintly, she can
hear the radio in the background.

"Jeff, it's me. Maya."

He doesn't answer.

"I left some sweaters in the linen closet by mistake. I'd like to come and get them. We need to talk anyway."

"I know," he replies.

"When's a good time?"

"I'm not sure."

"I'd like to do it soon, if you don't mind." Now is the warmest part of the summer. She won't need those sweaters or hats for months. But when she thinks of the black camisole and boxer shorts on the closet door, Maya wants to hold the sweaters in her hands and touch the stitches she had made. People who survive a flood or a forest fire must feel the same longing when they think of the possessions they left behind.

Jeff clears his throat but says nothing.

"How about this afternoon? I can come after work."

"Hold on a second." She hears him walking away from the phone. For a while, there is nothing except the voices on the radio. The footsteps come back, and Jeff says, "This afternoon is fine."

"I'll be there at five." Maya hangs up, thankful to get the conversation over with.

His station wagon is the only vehicle in the driveway. Maya parks on the street in front and goes up to the door. In the flower bed against the house, the lavender she planted three years ago is blooming. The petals have unfurled all the way out, the stalks are past picking and drying; the mature flowers will fall from the calyx, shedding blue specks of dust on the floor. Last year, she cut the stems when the buds were on the verge of opening and braided them into wreaths. Next to the lavender, delphiniums and hollyhocks are blossoming too. Most of these plants will die out before long. Perennials, too, have their life span; they are not permanent.

Jeff comes to the door in an old pair of jeans and a T-shirt he bought last year. The color, called watermelon, is a shade between red and pink. He was going to send it back because it turned out closer to pink than was shown in the photograph in the catalog. Maya loved the color and talked him into keeping it. She wonders how long it will be before he has no clothes she can recognize—two years, three, maybe more.

He pushes open the screen door but does not step back. She is standing in the doorway in the white sundress she sewed and embroidered with flowers, but he will not remember it. Once, as they were leaving a party in winter, Jeff went to the host's spare bedroom and returned with a blue coat she had never seen. "But that's not mine," she said, too surprised to keep her voice down. "My coat is handwoven and it isn't this blue—it's teal." Everyone in the room laughed while his face reddened. That was the last time he offered to fetch her coat. For all she knows, right now she is already just a woman in an unfamiliar dress.

"Thanks for letting me come over."

He moves aside from the doorway. "Do you want to come into the living room?"

"Yes." In the foyer, he has stacked two large cardboard boxes, taped over with heavy masking tape as though the contents might come bursting out otherwise. "Are these my sweaters?"

"I've had them ready since the afternoon you took the other stuff. I noticed right away that you forgot them."

"You should have called. I would have come sooner."

He shrugs but doesn't reply. She follows him into the living room and takes a seat on the couch, while he walks past her and sits down in the armchair. The couch feels larger than before; alone on it, she is a castaway adrift on a raft. Something looks different about the room, too; it seems brighter. The blinds are gone and the windows are bare. Jeff must see her looking. "We're getting some drapes," he explains. "Those blinds kept getting bent."

Maya pictures a child's fingers bending down the metal slats. "I'm sure the drapes will be nice."

For a long time, they sit, neither of them saying anything.

"I went with Yuko and Dan to their divorce hearing." Maya forces herself to start. "It was very simple. I'm ready to work on ours."

"Are you?" He wrinkles up his nose.

"You're ready too. Don't pretend you're not."

"What's that supposed to mean?"

"Nothing," she replies. "I don't mean to start a fight. All I'm saying is that we're both ready to move on."

He leans forward for a moment, as if to stand up. But he slides farther back against the chair instead. "I'm not the one who left. All this time, you've told me nothing. You called me from Yuko's and said you were never coming back. You got your stuff, threw the keys into the garage, and didn't even leave a note. Then you didn't call for a month. Now you're in a hurry. You don't think that hurts my feelings?"

"I'm sorry. I didn't know what to say. I felt awkward about writing you a note and sticking it in the garage."

"You're just making excuses. Why not at least admit that you really hurt me?"

"You couldn't have felt that bad. How hurt could you be when you had someone to turn back to?" She thinks of the way Dan talked as he was leaving Yuko. "It's over between us," she tells Jeff. "That's the only thing we have to agree on now. We don't have to go on about how bad we feel."

"I went back to Nancy because I realized how much better it was to live with a person who loved me, no matter how unpredictable she was or what she put me through in the past. You come across like such a polite, peaceful person, but that's just your facade. You're cold and calculating. I never met anyone so unfeeling. You care only about yourself. You don't want to get close to people. You'll never be happy in your life."

Maya holds up her hand as if she could bat his words away. *You are this, you are that*—that's all anyone says at the end of a relationship. *You will never be happy.* These words are a bucket of ice water thrown in parting, a curse to reduce you to something horrible but pathetic— a witch melting like a cube of sugar. "I don't want to know what you think about me," Maya says. "Whatever opinions you have, just keep them to yourself. I'm not interested." No matter how angry he made her, she could never spit out a list of everything she thinks might be wrong with him; the word *you*, that open sesame of accusations, wouldn't come out of her mouth.

"I'm not interested," he mimics, in a thin, nasal voice.

Maya gets up from the couch. "I'll get some information from Yuko about the mediator she and Dan used. I'll get our papers done. I don't want anything that's yours. It should be very simple."

"You are so businesslike."

Maya shrugs. "It's the only way to be at this point."

"It's the only way you ever are."

"I don't have to listen to this." She walks back to the foyer, where the boxes are. They are so big. She won't be able to carry them both at the same time. Jeff hasn't moved from his chair. Maya considers leaving without the boxes, but then she'll have to come back another time. Till then, they will be here, reminders of how she stormed off in anger. She picks up the first box, pushes the screen door open with her foot, and walks to the car. When she returns, Jeff is standing in the foyer. His face is pale and drawn-looking, except his eyes, which are red.

"Look, I'm sorry about everything," Maya says, stopping a few steps away from him. "I really am." Her hands dangle uselessly at her sides.

"I know you won't believe it, but I wanted you to stay. I was shocked when you called and said you weren't coming back. You know what I was doing when you called?"

She says nothing.

He goes on. "I was writing Nancy a letter, begging her to leave me alone. Seeing her wasn't working out. You were right about that. Every time we got together, it was a little worse for me. She looked familiar but different, like someone I should never have let go of in the first place. She was so happy to be with me. I couldn't help wanting to spend time with her and her daughter, but I knew it was wrong. I wanted to put a stop to my feelings for them and be with you. The first year we were together, I loved being here with you. I think it was the happiest time of my life."

"Please. I don't mind that you went back to Nancy. You don't have to explain."

"I'm telling you the truth."

Jeff's eyes are shiny with the tears he must be holding back. Maya looks away. They won't stand this close to each other again. In five years, maybe even less, she may not know where he is. She wishes he were her childhood friend or her cousin, someone she would know, at least vaguely, for the rest of her life.

"Some days," he says, "I'm convinced that I went back to Nancy in a state of shock. As soon as you were off the phone, I ripped up the letter I was writing and called her. She came over and watched me cry. She was so compassionate."

"Stop. It only hurts to talk like this."

"When you changed the locks, I should have told you that you were doing the right thing. I should have been happy that you did something to show me you wanted to hold on to me. Instead, I got all upset because you hadn't told me you were going to do it. I acted like you shouldn't do anything without my permission. No wonder you left me. I'm so sorry."

"I didn't leave because of that."

Jeff shakes his head. "Nancy knew you had doubts about me. That's why she was so persistent. The night after she saw us at the tennis courts, she drove by and saw your car wasn't there. She came in at six in the morning and confronted me. I told her you were staying with a friend but it wasn't a big deal. She didn't believe me. We talked for hours; she tried to get me to leave you right then and be with her. I wouldn't do it then, but I started feeling confused."

"Listen to me, Jeff. You have to believe that you did the right thing," Maya tells him. "I don't want you to have any regrets. I'm sure you're meant to be with Nancy and not with me."

"That makes one of us. You never realized how much I loved you."

You just told me I was the most selfish person on the face of the earth, she could remind him, but it would do no good. The day Dan told her about Meredith, Yuko wished him dead. "I had a vision of him clutching his chest and keeling over," she said. "That's what I wanted to see more than anything. But I couldn't stop the words I was saying, begging him to stay and work things out because I loved him. My head and my mouth were playing two different kinds of music. I was a one-woman broken jukebox." Jeff is caught in the same confusion, and there isn't a thing Maya can do to stop him.

"When you first came to this house," he says, "you used to take a bath late at night after I was in bed. You'd sit in the tub with the door ajar because I warned you that the steam would make the wallpaper peel unless you used the fan or left the door open."

Maya nods in spite of herself, thinking of the dimly lit room full of steam. For a moment, she too longs for that time. She was alone and yet with him—safe and comforted in this house. She had loved sitting in the warm water and thinking of the things she was weaving at the loft. All that time, Jeff was lying in his bed across the hallway. He had been a protector of her solitude, a witness to her peace.

"You sang so softly you didn't think I could hear you. Maybe you thought I was sleeping. The songs sounded so mournful. I didn't realize till then that you had such a pretty voice, because you never sang, not even when a song you knew came on the radio in the car. I loved your voice. Lying in bed and listening, I thought I had never loved anyone as much as I loved you then." Jeff blinks, and a few teardrops roll down his face.

She had learned those songs in kindergarten and grade school in Osaka. She could only recall them in fragments, mixing up the verses and the refrains. It made little difference because they were simple songs about the rain or the snow, the waves rising in the sea and the moon setting over the horizon. You could take all those songs together, mix up the words, and they would make as much or as little sense as they always did.

"I only wish," he continues, rubbing his eyes, "that I had told you how much I loved you then. I joked around and hoped you would see how happy you were making me. It wasn't enough. I understand that now, when it's too late."

She wouldn't have been happier if he had told her his feelings. If he had said he loved her voice, she would have stopped singing. Always, Maya had wanted to keep something to herself, something important that was hers alone. She sang late at night in the dim bathroom when she thought Jeff was sleeping. She drove up to the barn to weave by herself and was glad that he never came to the store or to the loft—that he was so unfamiliar with her work as to confuse her handwoven jacket with another woman's department-store coat. Nancy had left her best pictures for him, with light falling on her long hair and white blouse, the loving smile on her face as she looked at her baby. She had wanted to give him the most beautiful things about herself. Maya had chosen the exact opposite: to keep some form of beauty known only to her. Until she met Eric, she didn't understand the desire to let go of beauty instead of hoarding it. When she told him about her father lighting the bottle rockets, about the black cat they saw in the weavers' cottage all those years ago, about the hooded red jacket with her name embroidered in purple thread, her words felt like the webs of light spreading from her hands toward him on the sparklers they lit on summer solstice. She had offered him the pictures of her past so he could keep them in his memory even if they never met again. Jeff has no idea how miserably she failed to love him.

"I know I hurt you because I wasn't assertive enough with Nancy," he goes on. "Maybe you stopped loving me because I seemed too help-less. I was still attracted to her after all these years, but it didn't have to turn out this way. I was determined to get over how I felt about her and be with you."

"But things turned out the way they did. We have to accept that and go on."

"I wake up some mornings thinking I've made a terrible mistake. My life's too weird. I'm like one of those amnesia victims. I wake up, it's six years later, my wife is still here, and we now have a daughter. Only I can remember what I was doing before I woke up. I have such strong mem-ories about being with you. I don't feel right about anything."

He talks on, but she has stopped listening. Instead, she's thinking about the morning last fall when she went birdwatching in a state park north of the city. Shortly after dawn near one of the ponds, among some low bushes, she found a Canada goose someone had shot with an arrow. The bird was still alive, with the feathered end of the arrow sticking out of its back, the pointed end breaking through between its legs. The goose kept circling the bushes, bobbing its head, taking tiny frenzied steps. Maya ran to the house on the other side of the park where the ranger lived. When they returned in the ranger's truck, the goose was still in the same spot. The ranger approached with his leather gloves. What he did was quick and decisive. Maya looked away, and the next moment, the bird was under the ranger's arm, limp and out of misery. The ranger thanked her, told her about the poachers he'd been trying to arrest, and drove away. Maya had known all along that the bird would die; the arrow could not be pulled out without tearing its insides. She only regretted that she wasn't able to step up to the bird immediately and put an end to its suffering. A snap of her wrist was all it would have taken.

Jeff has finished talking and is waiting for her to say something. She looks away from him, at the remaining box of sweaters. Whoever packed the box has used the thickest masking tape, overlapped double. Maya thinks of the lips of prisoners or torture victims sealed shut with tape. It *is* a kind of torture to live the rest of your life wondering whether you've made the right choice or not. If his relationship to Nancy sours, Jeff will think of the years he imagines he could have spent with Maya. Late at night, he will stand alone at the window peering at the darkness, longing for Maya and the peaceful, loving marriage he thinks they had in their first year. He'll regret everything he believes he did wrong. Maya will be a ghost in his life—a figment of imagination that keeps him from living with the choice he has made. That may be the unkindest interpretation of what her father has been. His silence turned him into a ghost who kept Maya wandering all these years, floating a few inches above the ground, unable to rise up or come down. It's too late for her to stop that aimless journey. But she doesn't have to be a ghost in someone else's life. What she is about to do is the only act of mercy possible.

"I want to tell you something," she begins.

"What?"

"I didn't leave because of Nancy. I couldn't come back and stay here another night because I was with someone else."

Jeff narrows his eyes. "You're just telling me that."

"I wish I were."

For a long time, they say nothing. He won't believe her unless she can tell him more.

"It was someone who kept coming to the store—I met him at Peg's." Maya pauses, surprised at how much it hurts to give away even that small detail. It's as if she were betraying Eric by reducing him to a shady character in Jeff's mind. She remembers him putting down his camera and kissing her. He might be looking at those pictures right now. "He's gone now," she says to Jeff. "But that makes no difference, I know. I should have told you when I left. I'm sorry."

"You should have," Jeff mutters. "I feel like an idiot now. The whole time I was tormenting myself because I felt attracted to Nancy and I was being so careful, you were doing this. Nancy tried to seduce me that morning you were gone. I wouldn't go along with it, even though it made her cry. I would never have slept with her while you were here, living in my house."

"I wasn't with him the whole time. I left the afternoon he and I became lovers."

"Still, that changes everything. You didn't leave because of Nancy. You didn't even leave because of me."

"That's true. I left because I did something I shouldn't have done. Now you can stop blaming yourself." Maya picks up the box and steps toward the door. "I'm sorry," she says as he leans back to let her pass.

Just as she pushes open the door, he says, "For a second, I thought you were going to mention Yuko. I thought you were going to tell me that she was the one you slept with. You were always sneaking around to see her. I wouldn't have been surprised if you told me that she and you had been lovers all along."

"You don't have to say things to hurt me now."

"No, really," he insists. "Maybe you could never love me, because all along, you were in love with her."

"That isn't true."

"How do I know you didn't sleep with all kinds of people, men and women, those nights you said you were staying at the studio? I had no way of checking up on you. I couldn't even call."

"I didn't have an affair with anyone else. You just have to take my word for it."

"Yeah, but your word is no good. You're a liar, Maya, that's what you are. A cheater." Jeff leans forward toward her, his shoulders hunched and his lips twisted. Maya has the urge to put down the box and hit him in the face. She can imagine how satisfying it would be to leave a red imprint of her fingers on his pale cheek. "You and Yuko. When you guys were growing up, maybe you kissed and touched each other, doing a little exploration of each other's bodies. I'm not naive. I haven't been working with high school kids all these years for nothing.

I know what some girls do—especially shy and awkward ones like the two of you must have been."

Maya thinks of herself and Yuko baking cakes in Mrs. Nakashima's bright, clean kitchen. It's as if Jeff were spitting on the only good parts of her past. "I know you're angry at me," she says, as quietly as she can. "But leave Yuko out of it. She's the only friend from my childhood. She's almost my sister."

"Can I tell you something?" Jeff's voice sounds terrible and thin. "That's just a pitiful fantasy. You're not related to Yuko. You look nothing like her. You only want her to be your sister because all you've got, besides her, is your dingbat mother."

Maya leans hard into the door and strides out, almost tumbling onto the porch. Regaining her balance, she keeps walking, cutting across the front lawn. She hurls the box in the backseat, slams the door, and slides in behind the wheel. In five seconds, she is peeling out into the street with her tires screeching. Only then does she let herself think of the words she wanted to say: *Just like you're not related to that little girl you're going to raise. She looks nothing like you either. I hope you remember that when you're alone with her.*

Those words would have poured out of her mouth like gasoline on fire, igniting everything in its path. Words her mother said to her in her anger, screaming and sobbing on those basement steps, have burned holes in her heart. *You have no choice. You have no one but me. No one else loves you.* Even the things Kay said more recently—about how Maya's father did not love her enough to give up his art—have turned into a noxious fire smoldering somewhere, never entirely going out. In her anger, Kay must have believed she was only speaking the truth, but the line between wanting to tell the truth and wanting to inflict pain is infinitesimal. It's smaller than the tiniest sliver of fingernail used to cast a killing spell. Maya pictures Nancy standing on the side of the road, waving a black flag of distress; this time, she's holding the little girl's hand with her free hand and both faces are covered with soot—the substance painted on the mouths of female infants in remote parts of the world to stop their hunger forever. Maya's words, undetectable as that, could have ended all their hope for a loving father.

Maya drives on, her eyes steady on the familiar roads of the city. She has avoided the harm her parents did, her father with his long silence and her mother with her bitter words—both of them consumed by one kind of despair or another. She pictures a large globe spinning, her hand reaching toward it to calm its motion. This is the one thing Maya hopes to stop: not the debt Nate believes to be carried from one lifetime to another but the restless circles of loneliness spreading from one person to another within this life.

— 21 —

Going down the last hill near the lake, Maya shifts her bicycle into the highest gear. The wind rises and hums around her. Yuko is close behind her when they start, but halfway down Maya is alone, her legs pumping and her hands gripping the handlebar. She hits the dip at the bottom and keeps going, gliding up the hill without having to downshift until the last stretch. The momentum that pulled her down is carrying her up, but now she has to work harder to keep pedaling. Her throat and lungs ache to turn the air into speed. Cycling is the simplest translation of breath into motion.

At the top, she pulls over on the gravel shoulder to wait. Ahead, the lake glitters between the trees on the bluff. Behind her, Yuko is struggling up the hill. She's beginning to wobble, but she's halfway up. If she can keep going, slow but steady, she won't have to get off and walk her bike as she did yesterday. Yuko has quit smoking. She called the night she returned from Asheville and said, "I want to go bike riding with you tomorrow before work. The earlier the better. I'll meet you at the barn."

Yuko makes it all the way up and stops next to Maya. Sweat is pouring down her forehead; her hair is matted under the helmet. Maya holds out her water bottle. Yuko's is empty. "Drink up. We can get some more water in the park."

Yuko tilts the bottle over her upturned face and gulps the water. Handing the bottle back to Maya, she wipes her forehead with the back of her hand. "I'm in sorry shape. My lungs are shot. My legs feel like rubber. All that time in the gym hasn't done a thing for me."

"This is only your third time out. Don't hold back so much going downhill, though. You have to give it everything you've got on the way down, so you can come right back up."

Yuko shakes her head. "Maybe you don't care about breaking your neck, but I do."

"You're not going to fall down. Even if you did, you'd be all right. That's what helmets are for." Maya taps the side of hers and hears a dull thunk, as though her head had turned into a watermelon or pumpkin. *Kabocha-atama*, pumpkin head, kids used to call each other in Osaka. It means thick-skulled, stupid. Maya taught that word to Yuko and her brothers during their first week together. But the bad words she'd learned in Osaka were nothing like the ones they knew but didn't say in English. *Nakimushi*, crybaby, *baka*, fool, *manuke*, slow-witted—none of them had the angry sting of the names the rougher kids in Minneapolis called each other. Kay used to scream at Maya, "You have no backbone. You're so Japanese! Why can't you speak?" Maya has carried her silence with her all the way from Osaka. Her father taught her to say nothing when there was no consolation in words, while her mother spat out all her venom as if being honest and hurting people were the same virtue. Like the fairies at christenings in her father's stories, they offered her gifts that canceled each other out and left her with nothing.

In the park on the bluff, Maya and Yuko refill their water bottles and sit on a bench overlooking the lake. The sun is still low in the sky. The light ladders across the water, the golden rungs shimmering with the waves. In four days, Maya will have to call Eric to say good-bye. Because she has told Jeff, what was between her and Eric is no longer a secret. For the last few days, she's been trying to tell Yuko. Maya pictures a cracked glass with the water slowly leaking out, leaving her with nothing to hold on to.

"So," she says. She pauses and straightens the straps of the helmet, which she's holding on her lap. "I need to tell you something."

"Uh-huh," Yuko answers vaguely.

"It's kind of a big thing."

"Okay."

"It's not easy to talk about." Maya puts her helmet down on the ground next to Yuko's.

Yuko takes her eyes off the lake. "All right. I'm listening."

"When I left Jeff," Maya begins, "there was something I didn't tell you about. I was keeping a secret."

Yuko looks straight into Maya's eyes but doesn't say anything.

"I was seeing someone else—a painter I met at Peg's party in April. I fell in love with him even though I didn't want to. I tried to go away so I wouldn't see him anymore. But I just couldn't."

Yuko doesn't speak for a long time. Finally she asks, "Why didn't you tell me?"

"I don't know. I wanted to keep it to myself. I thought you might be upset."

"So you lied to me instead?"

"If you have to put it that way, yes."

"What other way can I put it?" Yuko stares at her, frowning.

Maya looks away. "He was moving back east at the end of June. I wanted to be with him and not think of anything or anyone else."

Yuko picks up her water bottle but puts it down without drinking. She is scowling. "Let me get this straight. You wanted to go to my parents' cottage to get away from this man. Then you decided to stay and have a fling with him. And instead of telling me, you pretended you weren't feeling so great and needed to be alone. Like that time I helped you move your stuff—you didn't want to go out with me because you wanted to be with him."

"It wasn't a fling. I really loved him."

"Big deal. Call it what you want, it makes no difference. A lie is a lie. I gave you a lot of space because you told me you needed to be alone. I was worried sick about you, but I said nothing and stayed away. All that time, you were actually seeing this guy. You were avoiding me so you could be with him." Yuko shakes her head. "I have to tell you, Maya, I feel used. I would never have treated you that way."

"You have to understand," Maya pleads. She feels queasy and seasick. "We didn't have a lot of time together. He asked me to move out east with him. I said no, and when he said he would stay here, I said I would never see him again if he didn't move. I'm going to call him in four days to say good-bye, but I think of him every day, almost every moment." Maya stops, not knowing what else to say. "I'm miserable," she adds.

Yuko squeezes her eyes shut and holds up her hand. "Don't tell me any more. I don't want to hear how miserable you are."

In the distance, a few gulls are bobbing up and down with the waves. The water crinkles around them, making them disappear and reappear. "Do you think you could forgive me somehow?" Maya asks.

"I don't know." Yuko sighs. "This is too much like what I went through with Dan. I don't know if I can take it."

Maya thinks of the braid Yuko cut off and stuck inside an envelope. She doesn't have a thing to say in her own defense.

"When I found out about Dan, it changed the way I remembered everything we did together. I told you that. Right now, my mind's doing the same thing about you and me. I think of that month and the mental footnote says, 'But all that time, she was lying to me.'" Yuko leans forward, her elbows on her knees, her hands pressed against her forehead.

Maya wants to lay her hand on Yuko's shoulder, but she's afraid Yuko might squirm away from her touch.

"Really, you've acted just like Dan. I don't mean because you cheated on Jeff. That's between you and Jeff. What makes me mad is something else."

"What?"

"You didn't think about me." Yuko closes her eyes again as though she were trying to get rid of a headache. "When Dan first told me about Meredith, I thought he had done this horrible thing to hurt me. He'd betrayed my trust. That's what made me angry at first. But the truth was worse. Dan wasn't trying to hurt me when he called Meredith and asked her to lunch, or even when he slept with her. He wasn't even thinking about me. I was nothing to him. You did the same thing. You forgot about me too."

Maya recalls all the times she sat with Yuko, scarcely able to keep up a conversation because her mind was elsewhere—daydreaming about Eric, remembering the afternoon they'd spent together. She can't say, You're wrong. I never forgot about you. She wasn't really there even when they were together. "I'm sorry," she mumbles.

"Lucky for you, you don't owe me anything. When Dan and I were married, he promised in front of the minister and eighty people that I would always be foremost in his mind, that he would think about me first. You never made a promise like that. I suppose you can lie to me all you want and get away with it."

"Don't say that," Maya begs her. "My lying to you is almost worse than Dan's."

"You're right. You know why?" Yuko makes a sour face. "Because you were always the person I trusted the most. Even when Dan and I were happy and I was crazy about him, I didn't assume that we'd always be together. How could I? One out of every two marriages ends in divorce. My four brothers have been married six times. I couldn't help having those statistics in the back of my mind. With you it was different. I always thought you'd be my best friend for life."

All around in the trees, squirrels are climbing up and down, making chattering noises at each other with their tails puffed up. When they stop for a moment, the park is absolutely quiet.

"Do you want to stop being my friend? Is that what you're saying?"

Yuko looks down. "Maybe," she mutters.

Maya swallows hard. "Please. Can't you just forgive me?"

"Why should I? I've been your friend almost all your life. You lied to me and avoided me so you can be with some guy you just met. Tell me how that's different from Dan's losing his head over the ticket girl and dumping me."

"You're right." Maya has to concede. "I'm no better than Dan. I forgot about you and lied to you. But there is one difference. I don't want to leave you. I want us to always be friends."

"I don't know. I trusted you and you lied to me. Besides, what's to keep you from leaving me after all? Someday, you'll decide to be with this man and you'll forget about me."

"No, I won't. He went back to Vermont a month ago. I'm never going to see him again."

"Why not? That's pretty screwed up if you really love him so much."

"No, it's not. I can't change my life by latching on to a man I just met, no matter how much I love him. That's what my mother did. Nate believes in reincarnation. He went on about it at the hospital the other day. He's right, but not in the way he thinks. When I see my mother, it's like she's already living her next incarnation and doesn't remember her past life with me. I don't want to change like that. It's not honest. I need to be alone, not running away to Eric."

"Do you think you fell in love with him because you were confused?"

"No, I don't think so. It doesn't matter why I fell in love with him. I go to sleep every night thinking about him, and when I wake up in the morning, I'm still thinking about him. I've never been this way. You know that."

"Oh, Maya." Yuko puts her arms around her. Leaning into her hug, Maya realizes that she's on the verge of tears.

"I wish none of this had happened. I'm so unhappy."

Yuko hugs her tighter. "If you're afraid to be with him because of me, don't be. I'm hurt that you forgot about me. But I guess I have to get used to it. What choice do I have? Besides, if you go away, it won't matter what I think. We won't see each other very much."

"But I don't want to forget about you. I can't go to him because it's wrong. I don't want to be like my mother." Maya pulls away from Yuko's embrace and sits back on the bench.

"You'll never be like your mother."

Maya doesn't answer.

"This is nuts." Yuko shakes her head. "Why am I trying to talk you into being with this man? I'm supposed to be upset with you."

"And you are. It's all right."

Yuko thinks for a while. "I'm confused because you're in love with someone," she says. "All of a sudden, we're in a place we've never been before. I don't know what to think."

"Yes," Maya agrees. She imagines herself and Yuko entering a dark, unfamiliar forest. The trees don't look like the pines and oaks they know by daylight. The moon is no help for telling directions. Together or apart, they are bound to lose their way.

"When Dan introduced you to Jeff," Yuko says, "I knew right away that Jeff could never really understand you."

"That's why you never liked him."

Yuko nods. "To me, from the very start, you were a mysterious girl from a faraway place. As soon as Miss Larson brought you into our class, I piped up and said you were my cousin, but that was just a gamble. I wanted you to choose me as your best friend. I was thrilled when you did. But we were different. I told you everything, good or bad. I might keep things to myself for a while, trying to figure them out on my own, but eventually I'd confide in you. When something upset you, you were quiet. You talked to no one. I got used to that." She shrugs. "Remember a few years ago when you took me birdwatching? You tried to show me the shape of a bird's beak or whether it had a ring around the eye, and all I could think was, It was a little yellow bird and it was beautiful. I didn't care if I could identify any of those birds by name. I liked being outside, watching them fly by. You got irritated with me—but for me, being with you was a lot like birdwatching with you. I didn't understand everything about you, but I was happy to be there. Jeff didn't know you enough to see that. He treated you like you were just an ordinary, quiet person. He didn't see how special you were. Still, when you told me you were going to marry him, I said nothing. You know why?"

"Because I already had my mind made up. It would only have upset me if you'd gone on about his faults."

"That's part of it, but my motive wasn't that pure. I made a selfish calculation." She takes a deep breath. "I said to myself, 'That guy's no competition. She'll still love me the best.'" Frowning, Yuko pushes her bangs out of her eyes.

Maya remembers the lilies Yuko brought her fifteen years ago. The bright yellow petals, perfectly curved, had made Maya want to cry because she was afraid the flowers were a kind of farewell gift. She had done everything to make Dan fall in love with Yuko, and it was finally working. "I felt the same way once," she says to Yuko. "When you fell in love with Dan, I was afraid you'd forget me and spend all your time with him. I was jealous even though I never let on. I would have moved out if you started coming over to see him and ignored me."

"I knew that," Yuko says, "but this is different. By the time I met Dan, you knew all kinds of people who loved me—my parents, my brothers, my grandparents—so it wasn't hard for you to think of Dan as just another person in my life. For me, this is a first. I've always been devoted to you, knowing there was no one else. I didn't think your mother or Jeff really counted. I'm not saying you didn't have any other friends. I don't mean to make you sound like a poor orphan girl."

"I know what you mean. I was alone."

"Yes, and you loved me the best. Now, it's going to take me awhile to get used to this new situation. I sense the change here." She places her hand on her chest. "I feel different, a little empty."

"It won't be different. I'm alone again."

"But I don't want you to be. I shouldn't want you to be."

"Why not?"

"Because I want you to be happy. You love this man. You think of him all day long. I can never make up for his not being with you. You'd rather be with him than with me. If that's true, I have to let you move on. That's a hard thing for me to accept. Maybe that's why I'm so hurt."

"I'm going to call him in four days to say I'll never see him. He knows what I'll say. What was between us is already over."

"Not in the way you feel."

"No."

"Or the way he feels."

"Probably not. Just the same, I have to be alone. My mind's made up."

Yuko shakes her head. "Why don't I feel happy or relieved when you say that?"

"Because you're a good person, Yuko. That's the truth. You would let me go if you thought I'd be happier living far away with someone else." She leans forward and puts her arms around Yuko. Yuko hugs her back and starts crying. "It's all right," Maya says.

"I don't think I'm crying for me." Yuko sniffles. "I'm crying for you."

"Thanks," Maya says. "I'm not good at that."

As they continue to hold each other, Maya thinks of the hawks they saw flying along the bluffs last November. Riding the stiff north wind on their migration south, the hawks glided over the water with their wings scarcely beating. They made moving on seem so effortless; all they had to do was hold their wings open and stay airborne.

In silence, Maya and Yuko begin their trip back toward the barn. Their tires swish on the rough-surfaced path before they hit the black-top of the county highway. In a few minutes, Maya is going down the first hill, her breath making her feel as though she were flying off the bike into the blue air around her.

After Yuko drives back to town, Maya goes up to the loft. It's Monday; the store is closed. She gets out the two boxes she retrieved from Jeff's house. Digging through her sweaters and hats, she finds what she's looking for: Yuko's love charm, Dan's baseball cap, and her red wool jacket from Japan. They're crammed inside the box with photographs and old notebooks. She places the cap and the charm on the worktable and holds the jacket up by the sleeves. She was only ten when she wore it; the jacket is tiny. The purple stitches on the inside collar are still there, not faded much. Sitting down at the worktable, she traces the letters with her fingers. Then she picks up the baseball cap. The two squares she cut out on the back look like the twin lenses of binoculars.

Those early mornings they went birdwatching together, Yuko walked by her side, smiling and singing softly. Above, in the trees, chickadees and cardinals sang as if in response. For a while, Yuko thought everything was a chickadee because it was small or because it had a black spot on its throat. When flocks of orioles stopped at her hummingbird feeder one spring to drink the sugar water, she thought the females and the young, whose markings were yellow instead of orange, were grosbeaks. Maya went to see them and couldn't stop laughing. "Look at this picture in the guide," she said, opening Yuko's book. "Grosbeaks have big, conical beaks. Their beaks are chunky and yellowish. Now, look at the oriole. The beak is long and thin. They look nothing like each other." Yuko shrugged and said, "I don't have your obsession about naming everything." She flipped the book to the picture of vireos. "How come these birds look like they're tipping over and falling off the branch? Will I ever see them?"

Maya stopped asking Yuko along because she assumed Yuko was bored. She didn't know that Yuko thought of those early morning walks as a picture of their friendship. Maya imagines a painting she might have made. She and Yuko are on a narrow path surrounded by trees. Maya is looking into a thicket with her binoculars pressed to her eyes, while Yuko is looking up and laughing, letting her binoculars dangle from the strap around her neck. She's listening to the call of the cardinals and watching the blue jays overhead. The happiness that surrounds Yuko is like a bright light fanning out from a lamp. Maya is always on the edge of it even though her own eyes are fixed on the small light inside a tunnel of glass.

The two squares on Dan's cap look into nothing but the emptiness between the front and the back. Maya puts down the cap and examines the love charm. The red seed beads sewn on the navy blue fabric are almost the same color as her hooded jacket: the red of hearts and pomegranates, of apples, toy blocks, crayons, and Mother's Day carnations. Maya places the charm on the table, picks up the sewing scissors, and lets the blades touch the body of her jacket. The first snip makes her wince, the edge of the blade going through the fabric. She keeps cutting until she has a square approximately two inches on every side, the size of the white squares Eric pasted on his letter. Laying the square aside on the table, she cuts another one, then another. She takes the jacket back to the box in the closet, slips Yuko's love charm in its pocket, and puts it away.

From her sewing box, she takes out some purple embroidery floss, a similar shade to the one her father used on her jacket, and stitches her name on each of the three squares: *stone, field, true, arrow*. Dropping the third square in her kitchen drawer on top of Eric's last letter, Maya goes back to the worktable and sews the other two inside the cap, covering the holes she made all those years ago. The stitches are smaller than grains of sand; they are scarcely visible on the outside. When she is done, the cap has two red windows like those on old-fashioned Advent calendars, where each window, opened nightly, reveals an angel, a bird, a golden pear. The binoculars no longer point to an empty space. She will give the cap to Yuko and ask her, again, for forgiveness. She will tell her the stories her father had once told, about a goddess who was so wise that she had eyes in the back of her head, about a woodcutter whose magic cap helped him understand the language of the birds in the air, the insects in the grass, all the animals who walked the earth. Yuko is the goddess of perfect vision and hearing. In the midst of all the noise on the stage and in the audience, she can hear the steady beat and keep the bass line going. For years, she has interpreted Maya's silence and punctuated it with her own music.

Returning to the kitchen drawer, Maya scoops up everything in it and takes it back to the worktable. The map she tore out of the phone book is clipped to the list of birds she saw that morning. Sitting down again at the table, Maya remembers the way Eric kissed her closed eyelids after they made love; she pictures his hands with their solid knuckles and square fingernails. She wants to go back to that countryside again, to find out if the cranes are still there in the fields or were just passing through, if the marshes in late summer will be visited by snipes and sandpipers, greater and lesser yellowlegs. The ritual of giving up will have to be enacted bit by bit, not all at once. If she has to make five trips back to the place of his childhood, she will see all the birds that come through the countryside. She will keep records of each trip, a series of migration maps to chart her progress. By the time the summer birds are gone and the warblers have returned—their fall plumage duller, harder to distinguish—her loneliness may feel just as muted.

Taking a piece of the opaque paper she uses for making patterns, Maya lays it over the map. With a pen, she traces the highways, side roads, and creeks, copying their names in ink. She marks the copied map with a red X for each location where she stopped and writes down the names of the birds from her list. Comparing the list and the map, putting in more X's, she is learning her way through the countryside. The list she made is thorough, including landmarks she noted along the way: an old schoolhouse with a bell tower, a stand of maples, a drive-in diner in the middle of cornfields, a school bus stop. She draws these on the map with coloring pencils, adding Eric's mother's trailer and brown car, the farm down the road with the ravine, three children—stick figures—holding sparklers. With an orange pencil, she makes tiny patterns of fire spreading out from the black wands in their hands. Then she draws each bird next to its name and location. When she is done, the map is a cross between children's drawings of the things they love the most—a house, friends holding hands, the sun in the sky—and an old trail map showing where a treasure is buried.

Maya picks up Eric's third letter, delivered Saturday. It's a piece of cardboard covered in strips of red fabric except for one phrase, *I dream of us*, written backward in gold, like the words flying out of the angel's mouth in medieval paintings of the Annunciation. She has written three letters to him, ripped them up, and placed the fragments in the drawer. All the pieces are still there. In one letter, she told him she did not have the courage to call him for their good-bye and has decided, instead, to write it. In another, she described the dream she had in which he appeared wearing a black shirt covered with tiny words she could not read. In the third, she said she loved him and could not forget him. Anyone looking at the letters, ripped up as they are, can see the simple truth: it will take something more than birdwatching in the countryside and burning scraps of paper to give her peace.

Near the top of the pile is a one-page letter from Mr. Kubo, found among the pieces of mail Jeff had packed along with her sweaters. When she read it, the morning after she saw Jeff, she didn't think of it as more than a minor letdown. She had ceased to care about the news while she was waiting. She only put the letter in the drawer as an afterthought.

Reading it again now, she knows why she saved it to burn in her ritual, instead of crumpling it and tossing it into the trash. Like the other letter, it begins with a reference to the weather and other polite formalities, which occupy two-thirds of the page. In the last paragraph, Mr. Kubo explains why her father had said nothing, but it's no explanation at all.

By the time your father's cancer was discovered, it was too far gone for effective treatment. His doctor and I agreed that nothing should be said to your father about his condition because the knowledge would only upset him and spoil the time he had left to live. Perhaps your father sensed what was happening, but he did not say anything himself. Undoubtedly, he preferred to spend his last days in peace rather than in unpleasant and morbid discussions about death. He did not leave parting remarks for my wife or me— or you—because we all believed it was better not to dwell on a future in which he had no part. We lived from day to day, making the best of what we had. Your father had a quiet peaceful life, and his death was also peaceful. You must believe that and pray for his spirit in the next life.

The drawing her father made for her in the last year of his life is on her table. Maya has no doubt that he knew the truth of his condition even if no one told him. Kay had been right all along when she said that Japan was the loneliest place on earth. Even as he was suffering from pain and the fear of dying, Maya's father had to pretend he did not suspect the truth and was completely at peace with his fate. He could not talk about his fears or regrets and hope to be consoled. Mr. Kubo and his wife might have sincerely believed they were doing him a favor by pretending that he wasn't dying and there was no need to say anything. For them—as for her father for most of his life—words must have seemed like a burden; silence was better than speaking the painful truth. A dying person has nothing to lose by being honest. At the end of a lonely, silent life, her father could have found comfort in words for once. Love isn't always about respecting the other person's unspoken wish. Sometimes, people have to be nudged into doing something they are afraid to do. There should have been someone who could encourage her father to talk as he neared his death—someone to help him let go of his life with understanding and clarity instead of false peace. Being honest with him would have been a painful act of love. A true friend would have grieved with him instead of remaining silent.

A small part of that act is still possible. It may be the only thing left for Maya to do: to grieve for her father though she will never know all the details of his dying. For everyone else, his death is a neatly finished business with no loose ends. Mr. Kubo and his wife are satisfied that the end was calm and peaceful. Kay, too, must have found a kind of completion that allows her, now, to reclaim a part of her past. The last time they talked on the phone, she was irritated because her doctor had advised her to postpone her trip to Japan till November. "No one lives forever," she said. "I don't want to be on my deathbed someday, thinking I should have gone there at least once. I wouldn't mind seeing the places where I grew up. Nate thinks he and I should stand in front of that house in Osaka where I was so unhappy. If I stood there with him, I'd know for sure that everything in the past happened to bring us together in the end. We're still going because it's a trip we need to make." She cleared her throat and waited for Maya to say something.

"That's good," Maya responded. "I'm glad you'll be able to do that." She wasn't sure how sincerely she meant her own words. She hated the idea of Nate and Kay standing in front of her childhood house. But she had a sudden thought: if she can forget for a moment what it was that she really wanted to say, she can open her mouth and have all the right words come out—words Kay wants to hear. It gave Maya the feeling of being a psychic medium or an apostle possessed by the Holy Spirit. What she was speaking wasn't, but might as well have been, the truth. Saying something was better than saying nothing and letting her silence express her resentment.

For her father, Maya can offer no words. Still, she can acknowledge the loneliness of his life. Yuko said that being forgotten was the most painful injury. If that's true, Maya has much to be forgiven for. On the day she left Osaka, she let her father convince her to forget him. The silence he sank into was as deep as the sea that glittered under her plane. Maybe she was too young then to do anything else, but she has had all the years since then to undo his silence, to insist on words of love.

Maya closes her eyes and thinks of Eric's painting in the studio. He would have turned her father's face into a landscape full of sorrow, but with feathered brush strokes of hope left along the edges, or a thread unraveling but holding on, saved in the state of coming apart. Maya pictures Eric's face as she leaned up to kiss him in his mother's trailer. His eyes squeezed shut, he was trying to fend off the regret he felt about leaving his mother alone in that trailer. He looked like someone waiting to be hit with something hard; he wasn't sure if he could take the pain. Right now, he is hundreds of miles away from home, thinking of his mother and his childhood and wishing Maya had chosen to go with him.

Maya puts her migration map over Mr. Kubo's letter. Under the birds and the landmarks she drew in color, the words are still visible. She turns the letter upside down, transforming the words into abstract designs: curlicues and dots and slanted lines. Underneath the landscape of Eric's childhood, she is seeing the blurred shapes of her own past. Like the song of a bird she recognizes before dawn or when the bird is hidden in thick summer foliage, the combined images announce the presence of something she cannot see or fully understand. Familiar and yet mysterious, the shapes from their separate pasts intertwine like the braided hair the women threw into the solstice fire.

Years ago in Osaka, Maya cut out random patterns from the wrapping paper in which her parents received year-end gifts from the neighbors and pasted them onto her father's sketching paper. He mixed glue for her by stirring cooked rice with water and mashing it with the back of a spoon. The semitransparent paste had a sweet smell.

Maya shoos Casper away from the stove top, where he's been napping, and cooks some rice. While it's cooling, she tears open a brown bag from the shop, turns it inside out, and cuts it to the size of a manila folder. Carefully, she brushes the rice paste on the back of Mr. Kubo's letter. The paper curls immediately from the moisture. She places the letter upside down on the square made from the brown bag, centering it carefully so an inch or two of brown is left to frame it on all sides. When the glue sets behind the letter, she brushes more on the surface. The words, written in ink, dissolve and bleed. She spreads the map she made and smooths it out over the letter. The words are even less legible than when she simply laid the two pieces together. They are like trees receding in fog.

On the top with a pen, Maya writes, *Migration Map One, July 1997.* The red square she cut out of the old jacket belongs with the map. She glues it on the lower left corner, where it looks like a seal. It is a red window into her past, a doorway into the heart. She picks up the pen again and writes, next to the title, *2 Eric.* He will remember her father's drawing of the tunnel. Underneath the red square, she writes her own name and draws an arrow. Then, in the space left on the side, she adds, *I can't forget you. I love you.* There is room left for more words. She hesitates a long time before writing, *I don't think I can call to say good-bye.*

She tries to think of something more, but all her words feel like dried-up paint or broken crayons. Nothing is going to protect her from regret. No matter what she chooses, some part of her will always long for the things she chose against. Nate was right about one thing. There is no guarantee of freedom unless people can forgive and forget everything. Five years from now, living with Eric, Maya might wake up every morning wishing she had kept her own promise and stayed away. Unable to forgive herself for coming to him, she might stop loving him; she might cause him to stop loving her. Instead, she could be living alone in this loft—a simple, pure life. Looking at the blurred shapes behind the map she has made, Maya is no longer sure about purity. At best, it's an empty, flimsy consolation to be so pure. Her life alone would be like the landscapes her father showed her—a solid geometry of colors and shapes—but without the patch of sunlight or the wispy blue trees in the corner that elude the orderliness of the composition. The trick in drawing and painting is first to get the foundations right—all the major horizontal and vertical lines of the overall composition—but that is not an end in itself. Laying out the foundation allows the painter the freedom to move, to capture the shifting light that flickers across the strict gridwork of the world. Even in her weaving, Maya hasn't forsaken that principle. She couldn't help putting those few strands of mohair into her mother's afghans. Without their rough sheen, the afghans would have been pitiful things, bland, without surprise. That's what her life alone might be like. If she does not send the collage to Eric, she will go on living here in solitude, calling her mother now and then, never forgiving her for the past but going on as though she did. Year after year, she will be with Yuko, with Peg; her love for them will force her to shield them from the truth about her pain and loneliness. All her words will be as inoffensive and false as the lusterless afghans she might have woven for Kay, had she cared less about beauty.

Maya gets a large envelope from downstairs, writes Eric's address on it, and places the collage inside. There is a lot of room left in the envelope. Going through the stack on her table, she sets aside the three letters he sent her, Mr. Kubo's first letter, and her father's drawing and photograph. She gathers all the rest into the envelope—the torn pieces of her unfinished letters, the two drawings she made on the backs of envelopes, the stolen map and the notes she took. They are the pieces that did not fit into the collage.

Maya tapes the envelope across the back and walks out of the barn into her car. Down the dirt road, she drives to where it joins the main paved road. Here, she can turn left and head for the highway to town or proceed right toward the lake. It's possible, still, to stand on the bluff where she cycled with Yuko this morning and pitch the envelope into the water. With no traffic behind her, she hesitates. Her foot on the brake pedal feels heavy.

Pitching the letter into the lake is no better than everything she has done since she left her father in Osaka, trying but failing to become an artist, weaving garments and selling clothes and thinking she was honoring his memory without really having to remember him—always choosing a pure gesture over the uncertainty of what she imagined might be worse. All that time, her father was slowly dying, his own cells turned against him like the words he could not say. Sending a short, cryptic message to Eric may be a kind of failure; she should give a clearer explanation. All the same, what is inside the envelope is the only picture she can offer. She can't pitch it into the water and fool herself that she has made an important statement. Maya takes her foot off the brake, turns the wheel to the left, and proceeds toward the freeway.

At the post office on the north side of Milwaukee, Maya hands the letter to the clerk. "Two or three days by priority mail," he says.

Maya pushes her money across the counter and watches him stamp the envelope. He drops it in the box of outgoing mail as she turns to go. It's too late to change her mind. She opens the heavy glass door and walks out of the building.

Her letter may reach him too late. Yesterday, the day before yesterday, or earlier today, he may have made a resolution to forget her. It is easy to harden your heart against something you cannot have, pretending you had never wanted it. Resignation is as simple as reaching over and touching a light switch; a single action of the mind can change everything. Her letter may be too late.

If it isn't, he will call her, but his call will only be the beginning of a long, uncertain time. She has never lived more than two miles away from Yuko since she was ten. Even if Yuko forgives her for going away, their friendship will never be the same. They will only see each other a few times every year. Most of their conversations, for the rest of their lives, will take place over the telephone. Maya pictures the phone lines stretching over the flat plains of Illinois, Indiana, Ohio. Their voices will meet somewhere over in the air, like spirits. She imagines Peg alone in the barn, sitting next to Wilbur. Since leaving Jeff, Maya's future had seemed more settled than when she was married. As soon as she moved into the loft, she had envisioned herself living there till she was an old woman, running Peg's store and eventually buying it from her when she retired. It would have been a good, peaceful life. Only, whenever she thought about that future, she wished Eric would come back someday to disturb her peace, to talk her out of the simple, modest happiness she had allowed herself. Perhaps that was what her father had hoped from her. He might have had a vision of her appearing at his door someday, demanding that he choose her over the quiet life he had resigned himself to. If she had gone to see him, he would have embraced her and wept; he would never have sent her away again.

Getting into her car and driving out onto the busy street, Maya almost wishes she had burned everything in her folder. Unable to drive on, she turns into the parking lot of a grocery store across the street. Absently, she gets out of the car and starts walking toward the door. If she went back to the post office in twenty minutes and the mail hadn't gone out yet, she could ask to have the letter back. I made a mistake, she would say. I put the wrong letter in the wrong envelope.

In the first row of parked cars, a woman is opening the hatchback of her tan station wagon to load her groceries. On the shopping cart behind her, her daughter sits among the bags, her legs in white tights. Twenty yards from them, Maya freezes, thinking of Nancy and Brittany. But of course it isn't them. The woman's hair is brown instead of red. She's tall like Nancy but not as thin, dressed in an old T-shirt and baggy jeans Nancy would never wear. Her daughter's hair is pale yellow. Loading the last bag into the trunk, the mother closes the hatchback, lifts her daughter out of the cart, and buckles her into the child safety seat. Then, without looking, she gets in behind the wheel and backs out, leaving the empty cart in the lot. The rear bumper of her car almost hits the cart before she floors the gas pedal and drives out.

Maya watches the station wagon merge into the traffic. She remembers sitting behind Nate and Kay's car at the hospital with a vision of them driving away to their next life without her. Everyone is traveling on to some future, whether it's the next life or the rest of this one. Whoever that woman is, she belongs to a family moving on with a cargo of provisions and children. Maya pictures the station wagon lifting up into the sky. That's how she would paint that woman if she were still a painter. She is airlifted into the next century through her daughter, who, in the mid-twenty-first century, will stand in another parking lot in another car with her own children or grandchildren. That is how most people move on through to the future, generation after generation.

Maya looks back at her own car, with its empty bike rack, the doors rusting, the back fender bent from someone hitting it a few years ago when she wasn't even there. "Your car's not going to make it all the way to Vermont," Eric said on the morning he left. It isn't much of a vehicle to carry her anywhere. All the same, she thinks of an invisible bicycle lifting off from the rack and tilting uphill into the sky, its silver spokes spinning like prayer wheels. She will never be able to carry her father's spirit out of this century into the next by having her own children. In thirty, forty years, her life will stop, leaving no trace of her parents or the long line of men and women who came before them. All she can do for her father is grieve for him and set him free—to let him disappear into the nothingness that is as big as the sky, full of air.

Freedom is freedom no matter how you arrive at it. If her father had known he was dying, the moment of his death in the hospital or in that dark house in Osaka might still have brought him something better than the panic or fear she has been imagining. Maya pictures him walking up to the sky at night and disappearing among the stars whose stories he told her. Night after night, the stars come back in the same formations, though their light is already hundreds of years gone. Even in the universe, nothing remains the same: old stars burn out and die, some of them sending out sparks that people for centuries believed were divine heralds, harbingers of a new order. It isn't so terrible to be nothing, finally, to climb up to the sky alone to be part of the elements.